RED RIVER

RED RIVER

Peter Tonkin

This first world edition published 2010
in Great Britain and in 2011 in the USA by
SEVERN HOUSE PUBLISHERS LTD of
9–15 High Street, Sutton, Surrey, England, SM1 1DF.
Trade paperback edition first published
in Great Britain and the USA 2011 by
SEVERN HOUSE PUBLISHERS LTD.

British Library Cataloguing in Publication Data

Tonkin, Peter.
  Red river. – (Mariners series)
  1. Mariner, Richard (Fictitious character) – Fiction.
  2. Earthquake damage – Fiction. 3. Yangtze River Gorges
  (China) – Fiction. 4. Sea stories.
  I. Title II. Series
  823.9'14-dc22

ISBN-13: 978-0-7278-6968-5   (cased)
ISBN-13: 978-1-84751-297-0   (trade paper)

All Severn House titles are printed on acid-free paper.

Severn House Publishers support The Forest Stewardship Council [FSC],
the leading international forest certification organisation. All our titles that
are printed on Greenpeace-approved FSC-certified paper carry the FSC logo.

Mixed Sources
Product group from well-managed
forests and other controlled sources
www.fsc.org Cert no. SA-COC-1565
© 1996 Forest Stewardship Council

Typeset by Palimpsest Book Production Ltd.,
Falkirk, Stirlingshire.
Printed and bound in Great Britain by the
MPG Books Group, Bodmin, Cornwall.

PART ONE
THE WEIGHT OF WATER

ONE
Cha

R obin Mariner stood amid the wreckage of *Poseidon*'s command bridge during the uncounted, almost dreamlike, moments of unearthly calm that followed the cataclysm. In the strange stillness, it seemed utterly impossible that *Poseidon* had been in the grip of a full-blooded earthquake so recently.

To Robin, the specially adapted corvette was *Poseidon*. To her Chinese crew she was *Yu-quiang*. And given how deep she was in Chinese waters, Robin allowed mentally, the crew probably had a point. *Poseidon* was, after all, more than fifty miles upriver in the mouth of the mighty Yangtze – *Chang Jiang* as the locals called the massive waterway – somewhere between Shanghai and Nanjing. During the last couple of days, the plucky vessel had used her deep-sea robot to rescue a trapped submarine, had discovered treasure on the deep sea bed and brought it back, and had consequently got far too closely acquainted with a range of undesirable people. Triads. They had a range of Chinese names and titles, but Robin didn't want to think about them. Triads. *Sanhehui*. That was about as far as Robin was willing to go with the Chinese vocabulary, though. Her husband Richard was comfortable enough with both Mandarin and Cantonese, but Robin preferred English, in her thoughts especially. Particularly when the going got tough and she needed to think quickly. And, despite the stasis now, they really would need to think quickly, for less than five minutes ago, at the moment when the heaving of the earth had stopped, news had come through that the Three Gorges Dam upriver had burst and all that unimaginable mass of water was on its way down the Yangtze towards them.

A wind eased itself in through *Poseidon*'s shattered clearview window, bringing the river-smell on to the bridge strongly enough to make Robin's nose twitch. The strange compound of mud and effluent, sweat and industry that burned in her adenoids was overlain by another, less timeless stink. Most signally of burning. The stench of blazing wood and oil, strangely out of place at the heart of a wide waterway. An unnaturally ferocious heat also came with the wind, caressing her back and shoulders like the fiercest desert sun.

Behind the tall, willowy, blonde woman's left shoulder, the shattered shards of the adapted corvette's clearview lay scattered across her command console and over the hands of her helmsman, whose name translated as Steadyhand. He stood, keeping the slim vessel's head facing downriver, almost due east, watching out through slitted eyes over the bright yellow bulk of the remote deep-sea exploration vessel cradled on the corvette's foredeck. His face turned into an inhuman golden mask by the battle-sweat and simple perspiration reflecting the flames' brightness. For an unsettling moment he reminded Robin of the golden statue of Genghis Khan they had in *Poseidon*'s hold – worth twelve million US dollars. A statue the remote deep-water exploration vehicle *Neptune* had lifted from the deeps of the Yellow Sea less than seventy-two hours earlier. And the cause of much of what they had all just gone through, she suspected.

Beside Robin Mariner's left foot, the shattered glass crystals glittered like diamonds on the bridge deck until their flame-yellow, tiger-eye brightness was turned to ruby by the blood on the non-slip surface.

Had Robin turned her head, her steady grey gaze could have swept over the figures of *Poseidon*'s captain and her pilot. Both called Chang, they were in fact parent and child. The daughter in her red-smeared captain's outfit was kneeling solicitously over the prostrate figure of her father, whose blood had helped to turn the shattered glass to ruby red and marked the perfection of his own river pilot's uniform.

Had Robin twisted her slim body sufficiently, she could have seen the kneeling figure of Daniel Huuk, senior official in the Chinese government and secret head of a powerful Triad. He was naked to the waist, specked with disinfectant and spattered with blood from a bullet-wound in his shoulder. Lieutenant Commander Tan, deck-officer of the *Luyang* war ship out in the Yellow Sea nearby and, like Captain Chang, a member of Huuk's secret organization, was kneeling at his side trying to staunch the flow of blood. But it was to Robin that the wounded man was looking, his eyes ablaze with more than reflected flames and shock.

Had Robin turned right round, to glance behind her, through the shattered clearview itself, she would have seen the broad reach of the River Yangtze, heaving below a writhing shroud of mist, luridly ablaze. A red river, indeed. Littered with wreckage from a fallen motorway bridge, a huge pirate junk, all but destroyed by the deluge of steel and masonry, and the vehicles the bridge had been carrying when the earthquake had struck.

Under normal circumstances, a ship like *Poseidon*, crewed and commanded as she was, would have been hard at work already, pulling survivors out of the water. Tending to the wounded and cataloguing the dead. But it was the men in the water who, up until the earth started to quake and the bridge to come apart, had been shooting at them. Preparing to come aboard to slaughter them all; their prize for the piracy was the priceless golden artefact, studded with a further fortune in jewels, that lay in *Poseidon*'s hold. But their actual motives were far darker and much more complex than simple piratical greed. For, if Daniel Huuk was indeed dragon head of one secret Triad gang, there seemed little doubt that the men who had filled the blazing junk had been the foot soldiers of a rival one.

And that in itself seemed to present yet another problem peculiar to the adapted Chinese corvette. For Captain Chang, *Poseidon*'s commander, was a member of Daniel Huuk's Invisible Power organization. While River Pilot Chang, her father, belonged to the rival Green Gang. So the pair of them, like Daniel Huuk, and the golden statue of Genghis Khan stored below, would bear further watching – at least until their strange situation was resolved.

But instead of looking at any of the maritime, industrial, physical or emotional wreckage around her, Robin was looking back into the aft of the command bridge. Her husband Richard was standing there, framed against the aft wall, made almost super-real, like an image in the cinema, by the brightness of the flames that surrounded him. The aft bridge wall was long and narrow – letter box in ratio; wide screen, with its little shelf of tea-things miraculously preserved. His broad-shouldered, slim-hipped six-foot five-inch frame seemingly carved out of the brightness and fathomless shadows, with the long shape of the Simonov sniper rifle standing so casually at his side. The shoulder-piece of its stock rested on the deck and the mouth of its barrel was wedged beneath the narrow shelf. Long though the Russian weapon was, it barely reached his hip. For Richard was tall enough to make his blue-black hair seemingly brush the deck-head above. In the weird light, his face looked like a gargoyle mask. The square jaw was grey with stubble. The beak of a nose cast strange shadows. The bruise on his cheekbone, with the long wound at its centre, seemed to pull his countenance awry, especially when he smiled. A metal fastening had sprung loose from *Neptune* in a typhoon and lashed back hard enough to do the damage. He dismissed it airily, but she knew it still gave him considerable discomfort. She was getting used to the lopsidedness of his new grin, but it would take time. Unless, as she hoped and prayed, the scar healed to a straight white line like the duelling scar of a Hapsburg aristocrat.

It never ceased to amaze Robin that in the tightest grip of the most terrible crises, Richard could remain so calm. That, even though this was not his bridge to master – even though he was the vessel's owner – he should be so surely in command. That he should fill the whole command area – the whole command, indeed – with the simple force of his personality. That even when his powerful frame – tall enough to have earned him the nickname *Giant* amongst the Chinese crew – was utterly still, it nevertheless demanded absolute focus, unwavering respect. That, even in the face of an earthquake and all the destruction it had caused, he should choose to be doing something as apparently pointlessly domestic as brewing a cup of tea. Or, as everyone else aboard would probably call it, thought Robin wryly, *cha*.

That, while the world – quite literally it seemed – was falling to pieces around him, he should be standing there with a boiling kettle steaming in one steady hand, looking down into the throat of a coffee mug where a tea bag was wedged, apparently immovable just below the lip.

The fist holding the kettle tilted infinitesimally, as though the huge hand and the mighty forearm controlling it were part of some robotic machine. The tiniest imaginable drop of water fell steaming through the silent air. It landed in the centre of the little tea-filled pillow which seemed to be sitting so securely at the rim. And it smashed the tea bag into the bottom of the mug. Richard froze for a moment, looking down with fearsome concentration. Then the hand holding the kettle tilted decisively and the boiling water filled the mug to the brim.

'The simple weight of it is bound to be almost unimaginable,' Richard rumbled, his voice like an echo of the earthquake itself. He glanced across at Robin, the wild blue dazzle of his gaze locking with the steady grey of her own. 'If Captain Chang is right and the whole of the Three Gorges Dam failed when the earthquake struck, then the simple weight of the water coming down towards us will be almost unimaginable.'

'What did you say the Three Gorges reservoir was supposed to hold?' asked Robin, her cool voice as steady as her level gaze. 'Forty cubic kilometres? Forty cubic *kilometres* of water?'

Richard shrugged, putting the kettle down thoughtfully. 'I've heard estimates as high as seventy-five,' he said. 'But that seems simply inconceivable, I must admit. Though of course, forty times forty times forty gives us sixty-four thousand. Which is actually closer to the seventy-five cubic kilometre estimate and seems to make more sense to me. But it still leaves us with the old—'

'Don't you *dare* make any wisecracks about sixty-four thousand dollar questions!' warned Robin.

'OK,' he agreed amiably. 'Though I was tempted I must admit. No. The estimate I like best is fifty-five trillion gallons. *That* I can get my head round. That I can work with. A gallon of water weighs ten pounds, give or take. So that's five hundred and fifty trillion pounds of water. Divide it by two thousand, two hundred and forty-four for the rough tonnage.'

Robin was good at math. She divided the enormous figures in her head, not one bit worried by the thirteen noughts involved. 'That's two and a half million tons, give or take.'

'Is it?' Richard asked, as he scooped the tea bag out of the mug and reached for the milk jug an indulgent galley kept for them. 'Bloody hell. That's heavy.'

Irresistibly reminded of her student son and some of his favourite phrases – amongst which '*Heavy!*' had featured for a while – Robin frowned.

But Richard hadn't finished. 'I mean, if you translate the weight into potential and power, then I suppose it might have a destructive force measurable in megatons.'

'Like nuclear bombs?'

'Two and a half megatons. That's like two hundred Hiroshima bombs.'

'But only if a ton of water could have the same destructive force as a ton of TNT, surely,' temporized Robin. 'That's not very likely, is it?'

'I dunno. Move it fast enough, push it hard enough. Force it down a river valley, say. With a couple of cities standing in the way. You wouldn't be able to tell the difference between Honghu and Hiroshima. Or Nanjing and Nagasaki.'

TWO
Epicentre

R ichard's mug weighted the corner of the chart as the oblong of brightly coloured paper lay spread across *Poseidon*'s chart-table. It was not the same mug that Richard had brewed his tea in the moments after the earthquake, thought Robin wryly. A good deal of *cha* had been consumed during the time that had passed since he swallowed that one, fished out Admiralty Chart 1642 (Dagangto Nanjing), and its Chinese equivalent, and really got down to business.

Not that he had been alone in doing so, she allowed mentally. Captain Chang and her father the river pilot had both been patched up and were in communication with various authorities. Robin and the Captain had made an excellent medical team – and Robin had continued working alone when the Captain went up to the radio room with her father. They had announced that both Shanghai and Pudong were still standing, and that the authorities were in some kind of control.

Lieutenant Commander Tan had been in touch with his captain aboard the *Luyang* class warship out in the river approaches. Daniel Huuk had spent a little longer with Robin in the ship's sickbay but he too had been bandaged, cleaned and dressed. He had got in contact with Shanghai and Pudong, and even with Beijing, where the physical effects of the earthquake had been felt, and where the social and political effects were now being calculated.

In all of the places they had contacted, there were plans being drawn up. Plans which were far too grand to involve *Poseidon*, of course. So those aboard the little vessel were busy drawing up some plans of their own.

Poseidon's chart room was crowded to put it mildly, thought Robin. Richard was massively wedged into a corner beside her, then Daniel Huuk was crushed against her other side, his shirt unusually casual, neck wide to reveal the bandages she had taped across his chest. Its usually pristine whiteness was splattered with blood and antiseptic – especially at the back where she had treated the speckles of shrapnel wounds that resulted from an explosion in Shanghai the previous day. An explosion designed to kill him – that had only narrowly failed to do so.

Tan was wedged against Daniel's other side and the river pilot stood by the Captain beside the door, his hand swathed in a boxing glove of bandages, necessitated by the fact that the bullet that had penetrated Daniel's shoulder had taken off the smallest finger of the Pilot's right hand. The navigating officer, who Robin simply knew as Straightline, hovered out on the bridge, straining to see in. Only half able to hear because of the bustle as the cleaning and repair crews worked all around him. Not to mention the more distant – but still strident – sounds of the police, emergency, fire, search and rescue vessels hard at work on the river outside. The distractions causing poor old Straightline to shake his anxious head, thought Robin sympathetically, must be made even worse by the fact that the animated conversation he was trying to follow was being conducted in a disorientating combination of Hong Kong Cantonese, Mandarin and English.

'So,' Richard was summing up in the brutal Cantonese in which his Hong Kong years had made him almost fluent, 'the authorities are pretty certain that the epicentre was here in Jiujiang. That's the better part of five hundred miles upriver from us and the same distance down-river from the Three Gorges Dam itself. A quake strong enough to do terrible damage at both ends.' Much to Robin's relief he moved into English as his Cantonese began to fail under the weight of the increasingly technical vocabulary he needed. 'It may be the better part of a thousand miles away, but that's still a huge weight of water heading down towards us.'

'It may be more complicated than that, Richard,' added Huuk, also in English, as befitted an ex-Hong Kong naval coastguard. Albeit one who had spent most of the time Robin was dressing his wounds, speaking fluent Mandarin on a combination of radios and mobile phones with the police headquarters in Shanghai and Beijing. For the moment, at least, he was the People's Republic's senior crisis manager on this particular spot. And it looked as though the crisis was going to get a good deal worse as two and a half megatons of raging water was set to hit the megacity that contained tens of millions between Shanghai, Nanjing and Beijing itself.

Huuk leaned forward, his shoulder brushing forcefully across Robin's upper arm, static electricity between them raising goosebumps as it went. 'Look,' he growled, still speaking English for her benefit. 'Just south of Jiujiang is the Poyang Lu. It is the biggest lake in China. One of the largest in the world. Sizeable enough to have been the site of the most massive naval engagement in history. Big enough to have its own Bermuda Triangle of unexplained shipping disappearances. Twenty-five cubic kilometres trapped behind a narrow gorge which is the only thing that keeps the lake from flooding into the Yangtze River. There is very little information coming out of Jiujiang as you would expect, but we have apparently got reports not only of a massive earthquake but also of all-consuming floods.'

'Already?' asked Robin, distracted by the friction between Daniel and herself, not really following his reasoning. 'Surely it's too far for the flood water from the Three Gorges to have got there yet. Flood water moves at fifty miles per hour or so, even at full-spate. At that speed it would take a day not an hour . . .'

'So you think the quake might have been strong enough to bring the Poyang Lu flooding into the Yangtze basin as well?' inserted Richard. 'Is that what you're saying, Daniel? Because if you're right, we could have two floods to deal with and the first one will be in Nanjing soon after dawn. Down here by noon.'

'I'm just saying it's a possibility we should be aware of until we get more solid information,' said Daniel. 'There were garbled reports of serious structural damage to the mountains of Lu Shan and Nan Shan – these are the mountains that contain the lake. But, as with everything else, apparently, the early communications have all fallen silent now. There is no phone system – land-based or mobile. No radio or TV communication. Nothing. Just a thousand miles – as you observe – of darkness and silence. As though the entire heart of Eastern China has stopped beating.'

'Has there been any estimate of the quake's magnitude yet?' asked Richard, frowning fiercely down at the maps on the chart-table.

'Beijing University says it may have registered at magnitude nine on the Richter scale,' answered Daniel baldly.

'My God!' whispered Robin. 'The Haiti quake registered at seven. The Chile registered at eight point eight.'

'And moved the whole city of Sao Paulo ten feet west,' said Richard shortly. 'Nine is truly Biblical, Daniel. Are they sure?'

'Apparently so,' said Daniel. 'There was one in the region in 1927 – calculating by the western calendar. That killed a quarter of a million. It was recorded at eight point three, so I understand. The people at Beijing University say this one was of a far greater magnitude than that. And of course the area was much more sparsely populated all those years ago . . .' He too fell silent, staring down at the chart-table as intensely as Richard, suddenly seemingly overwhelmed by the enormity of what was taking place in the heart of the area the charts represented.

And well might Daniel feel overwhelmed, thought Robin sympathetically. He had been sent here a couple of days earlier to discover why the Internet had gone down. He had discovered an attempt to destroy the main cable that carried the signals that kept the Internet going, but before he could do much about it, he had become involved with a Triad war almost immediately. A Triad war and an attempt to pirate millions of dollars worth of gold out of Poseidon's holds. Now, with the Internet still out of commission, suddenly all sorts of other communication systems were breaking down as well. Just when the need for communications were of paramount importance. While the Triad war and the piracy had been reduced to irritating distractions in the face of the enormity of a magnitude nine earthquake and a flood – maybe two – of truly Biblical proportions. And a terrifying silence from the heart of the affected area.

But, distractions or not, it had been the Triad war that had got Daniel aboard *Poseidon*. Richard, Robin and Lieutenant Commander Tan had piled his unconscious body aboard the Ferrari-red Cigarette power-boat, which Richard had christened *Marilyn*, immediately after the attempt to blow him up at Ang's boatyard that fronted the Huangpu River in downtown Shanghai. And, in that amazingly powerful vessel, they had powered down the Yangtze River at the better part of eighty knots, heading for the safe haven of *Poseidon*, pursued by Green Gang assassins.

He was still here because of his wounds, she thought. Wounds that had been inflicted by the original explosion, then compounded in the brief firefight as the pirates tried to come aboard and complete the Green Gang's work before they stole away the priceless gold statue in *Poseidon*'s hold. A firefight that had only been terminated by the onset of the earthquake and the collapse of the motorway bridge on to the pirate's massive black junk. How long he would remain on board was open to question now. He really needed to be at the heart of the action if he was going to be a truly effective crisis manager. And that meant Shanghai – to begin with at least. And Beijing as soon as possible after that.

Robin's thoughts were interrupted by a stir outside on the command bridge. She looked up to see Straightline turn away from the door to join the distant work teams. Straining to look forward, she was just able to see the powerful little foredeck gantry, designed to lift and lower the deep-sea exploration vessel *Neptune*, was being used to winch *Marilyn* back aboard. She was a head-turner all right, thought Robin. Twelve metres of lean, sleek power, Ferrari-red from the tip of her cutwater to the massive black bulks of her twin Mercury outboards. No wonder Richard had fallen in love with her at first glance. Robin glanced across at her husband and saw that he was staring out at the foredeck with the expression of a moonstruck teenager. She glanced over towards Daniel and caught a similar expression on his face. But Daniel had been secretly staring at Robin herself.

Straightline was rudely shouldered out of the way by the radio operator. 'Deputy General Commissioner, I have urgent news,' he called in breathless Mandarin.

Daniel's gaze snapped forward, his expression instantly masked. 'Yes?'

'There is news from Anquing. It was reported some time ago but has only just been passed to us. There has only been silence since. Apparently the river is rising more powerfully than anyone has ever seen before . . .'

Robin's eye flashed down to the chart but Richard's finger was already there, resting on the dot that represented the city. It was the next settlement down from the earthquake's epicentre. 'It's a wonder anyone there had the equipment or the ability to send out even a brief report if things are as bad as you say,' he said. 'Looks like Lake Poyang – or part of it – has flooded through past Nan Shan after all. How big was the lake's capacity? Twenty-five cubic kilometres?' He glanced across at Robin. Bright blue gaze locking with thoughtful grey. 'Heading this way at fifty mph or so. But what we really need is news from Zhicheng.' His finger moved the equivalent of five hundred miles upriver towards the Three Gorges. 'Whatever is coming down on Anquing, at least three times more will be coming down on there.'

'Where?' Robin hadn't really followed his finger or his reasoning. 'Why?'

'Zhicheng,' answered Daniel. 'It's the next city downriver from the dam.'

'Fifty miles downriver,' emphasized Richard. 'It's due to be hit about one hour after the dam burst. He looked at the battered old steel-cased Rolex Robin had given him before their marriage. 'That would have been about fifteen minutes ago.'

Richard's grim observation was followed immediately by the shrilling of a cellphone. Which was followed by an exclamation of pain as river pilot Chang automatically reached into his pocket with his wounded hand. The phone fell on to the deck. The pilot's solicitous daughter, the captain, picked it up, switched it on and handed it over. The little pantomime was enough to focus everyone's attention on the pair. And even had it not been, the pilot's exclamations of incredulity, shock and mounting horror would have been more than enough to rivet all their eyes upon his face.

'What is it, father?' demanded Captain Chang as he lowered the phone, frowning deeply.

'It is your mother,' he answered numbly.

'She's a leading architect, built a good deal of Pudong. Expert on securing structures against earthquakes; that kind of thing,' explained Robin to both Richard and Daniel.

'She's probably been called up to help sort this lot out then,' breathed Richard.

'If she hasn't then she soon will be,' added Daniel, with all the certainty of the man who planned to take charge.

'What about Mother?' asked the Captain breathlessly.

'That was her office. She went inland two days ago. She left messages for us on email and answerphone. But I haven't checked with my service recently. And apparently there's something wrong with the Internet.'

'Messages about what, Pappi?' asked the Captain gently.

'She's been called away. Went two days ago, as I said. Apparently someone was worried and wanted her to join the team having a closer look at the cracks in the structure of the dam. You know lots of people have been worried about the cracks in the dam.'

'What cracks? What dam? Pappi, where is Mammi?'

'Cracks in the dam. The Gezhou dam. She's somewhere up there now; has been since yesterday.' The pilot turned and looked upriver as though he could see through the silent darkness for the better part of a thousand miles. 'She's up there. She's at the Three Gorges Dam.'

THREE
Yichang

Leading Architect Chang had passed almost none of her physical attributes to her daughter, the captain of *Poseidon*. Probably, whispered her Chinese upbringing, because the child had been born in a dog year, the result of careless passion rather than careful planning, even under the one-child policy. In her more western moments, the architect was happy to have passed to the young captain her powerful intellect and indomitable character and to have left the physical legacy to her solid, square, broad-shouldered ship-loving river pilot husband. It was a pity that the result hid the considerable inner beauty behind an unarguably unprepossessing exterior. Not to say an undeniably ugly one.

Leading Architect Chang, on the other hand, was a strikingly attractive woman, as befitted a creature born in the year of the monkey. Her good looks were by no means diminishing now that she was passing through her fifties. Nor were her charm, energy and physical fitness – all of which remained the envy of many of her more youthful colleagues. Her body was reed-slim, deep-bosomed and tall for one of Han ancestry. Her black-haired head was beautifully proportioned and her features exquisite; all bone and line, carried on a long neck like that of a Manchu empress.

Chang Mei-Feng noticed little of this, dwelt on less of it and worked at none of it. She had turned heads since girlhood and her horoscope assured her that this was because she had been born in a monkey year under the sign of fire. So she was far more concerned to do full justice to the fierce intelligence that burned behind her long almond eyes. She was far more interested in what her perfectly sculpted lips could say rather than the way they seemed to cause dimples when she smiled. She was far more interested in what her ears could hear and her mind understand rather than the fact that her ears – like her eyes, lips and neck – had all been the subjects of the most passionate poetry. None of which had been written by her husband the river pilot.

By the same token, it was the way in which the long fingers of her graceful hands could generate intricate designs for solid, long-lasting structures that she cared about. Perhaps that was why she had turned aside from all the dazzling, glamorous suitors of her youth in Nanjing and settled for a good, solid, unromantic seafaring man. A seafaring man who, as it happened, had been born in a dragon year and so was the perfect partner for her according to the horoscopes. And of course her own father, Shiphandler Seng, had been a sailor out of the Nanjing Docks along the mighty Chang Jiang Yangtze River too.

Mei-Feng had passed out at the top of her class in the world-renowned Urban Planning and Design course at Nanjing University's famous School of Architecture. She had joined the Nanjing City People's Architects office in the year Comrade Deng assumed leadership and the only – slight – pauses in her meteoric rise had been her marriage and the arrival of her child. Her mother – the author of many of the horoscopes by which she still understood certain aspects of her life – had warned her that women born in monkey years had weaknesses as well as strengths. Unfaithfulness in matters of the pillow, for example. And if Mei-Feng preferred to draw a discrete veil over the manner in which such weaknesses had – very occasionally – helped her rise so swiftly and efficiently, then that too was part of her complex personality. And if the river pilot, with all the wisdom and insight of a dragon man, suspected that she strayed occasionally, he too knew it was in her nature and was content that she always returned to him.

Chang Mei-Feng was also a reluctant member of a Triad society. Like her husband, she was the victim of necessity and of her burning ambition – and the knowledge that in certain crucial situations the only way forward lay in the tiny tattoo on the smallest finger of her right hand, all the more powerful for being so unusual in a woman. A tattoo in the character that signified green and marked her as a member of the Green Gang. Perhaps because of the tattoo, as well as because of all her other formidable powers, she was also the chair of several influential committees, including the Architectural Sustainability Committee. Even in the unregenerately male-orientated society in which she lived, this was a post she held both in Pudong and Shanghai – where the Green Gang had its historic headquarters – and on a visiting basis in her native Nanjing.

It was as chair of this particular body that she had been invited to Yichang to inspect the fabric of the huge Three Gorges Dam. Fabric that seemed to be cracking. There had been stories of inadequate planning from the outset, of design faults in the basic structure, of hurried workmanship, shoddy materials, graft and corruption. But, alas, that was par for the course – whether well-founded or simply media hype.

The stories had been worrying enough as the reservoir behind the dam had filled to half-capacity, and then three-quarters. But now the reservoir was at full capacity, and someone somewhere was apparently getting worried. Someone extremely important.

A little less than five minutes before the earthquake struck, the elegant figure of Chang Mei-Feng stepped out on to the roof of the Three Gorges Xiba hotel, which towered high above Jianshe Road in the Xiba district of Yichang, and walked purposefully towards the front of the building as the junior manager obsequiously closed the door behind himself, awaiting her further pleasure as he covertly admired the way her bottom moved beneath the tight shot silk of her business suit.

She had chosen to use this hotel as her base not only because of its reputation and the facilities but because it was the nearest hotel to the dam itself. And it was convenient to the open area at the cul-de-sac end of Jianshe Road where the helicopter employed to squire her around had been able to drop her as it brought her in from the airport. It also, now she thought of it, had a reassuringly pyramidal shape – its lower floors were a good deal wider than its upper reaches.

The Three Gorges Xiba hotel was popular and this was the tourist season. Only a subtle combination of pressures – at committee, government and Triad level – had secured a top-flight five star suite for her. Not to mention a seat on the flight from Pudong International to Yichang, or the neat little executive chopper that was at her command.

Which, she suspected, was why the management allowed her up on to the roof in the first place and lent her the hot-eyed little junior manager, whose gaze was currently burning a hole in the seat of her best business suit. But the chopper pilot had been equally as attentive – just as hot-eyed. It took a deep breath and a pause in her purposeful stride to clear Mei-Feng's mind of the sudden irrelevancies as she approached the front to the building and the face of the dam she was here to inspect.

Leading Architect Chang's intention was simply to perform a quick visual survey at this stage, and then to plan what she and her colleagues would need to examine in more detail. The professional in her took over as she crossed the final section of the open area thirty-five stories above street level – and yet was forced to crane her neck as she looked up towards the top of the dam towering far above her head. At nearly two kilometres long, the whole thing was as wide as the famous Golden Gate Bridge across San Francisco Bay, but at 185 metres it was nearly twice as high. The hotel was only a few hundred feet away from the massive structure, seemingly so close that the binoculars hanging round her neck appeared to be utterly unnecessary. And yet, as she pushed her hips against the safety rail that bounded the edge of the roof at this point, she found herself raising them to her eyes as though entranced by some almost invisibly remote object.

She swept the letter box of enhanced vision up across the bustle of tourists thronging the parks and gardens, streets and hillsides nearby. She could hear their voices on the occasional breaths of evening wind, like the shrill calls of birds, above the steady grumble of traffic that thronged both roadways and waterways nearby. She noted in passing the discrete lock system and the ship lift on the near side of the dam. The outflow thundering like a little Niagara into the Yangtze at the foot of the sheer, curved wall nearest her – and its twin a kilometre and a half across the river. The apparently warlike battlements that topped the massive edifice and the observation platform at its crest. And the sudden flock of waterfowl exploding in raucous flight against the hard blue sky above it all.

At least the concrete edifice that sprang into eventual close-up appeared reassuringly solid at first glance. Taking her time, she swept the clear close-up from the near side to the far side where it met the southern riverbank. It was easy to see why it had been christened The Great Wall of the Yangtze – in some American publications if nowhere else. It appeared to possess that unshakeable solidity she sought to bring to her own buildings. *Look at me,* it seemed to say, *I will stand longer than Dynasties. After this city is dust and rubble I will still be unchanging here.* And to be fair, she thought, it really needed to exude that confidence.

If ever a dam needed to flaunt its indestructibility for all to see, she thought, then this one did. For immediately behind it there stood a wall of water two kilometres wide, 200 metres high. And, behind that, a reservoir called Emerald Drop Lake that reached back, through the three gorges themselves, nearly 800 kilometres to the city of Chonquing. An *emerald drop* massive enough to have drowned more than 150 towns and cities of various sizes as it grew. To have flooded a quarter of a million acres of farmland into the bargain. To have caused the removal of nobody knew how many people out of its enhanced catchment area – but which needed thirteen sizeable cities to rehouse the ones who had been permitted to remain in the province itself. The edifice containing something of that magnitude had better be as near eternal as the slopes of the valley it spanned, she thought.

Abruptly, the whole dam seemed to spring out of focus.

Staggering a little, Mei-Feng lowered the binoculars and looked down to check the focus. She noted at some deep, subconscious level that everything around her had gone quiet. That all of a sudden she seemed to be at the heart of an enormous silence. Of an almost infinite stillness.

FOUR
Damburst

I t was the enormity of the silence that warned Mei-Feng what was happening. And it was a measure of her spirit that she reacted to it as she did. To begin with, it never occurred to her that she might not find a way of surviving whatever cataclysm was approaching. She had an excess of that confidence that her mother would have told her comes with Monkey-woman spirit. At the very least, it was the confidence that comes to a beautiful woman who has never failed in any relationship, ambition, endeavour or undertaking. And, given that, it seemed clearly to be her duty to observe and report on the matter she had been sent here to look into.

The intrepid chairperson of the Architectural Sustainability Committee spread her legs, until they were pinioned by the hem of her skirt, and leaned more firmly against the safety rail until her body assumed the strong pyramid structure of the building she was standing on top of.

Still thinking with almost superhuman speed and clarity, Mei-Feng reached into the jacket pocket of her business suit and pulled out her state-of-the-art mobile phone. With practised fingers she opened its video-camera function and secured it to the side of the binoculars, certain that whatever she observed during the next few minutes the camera would record. Then she focussed on the dam again and waited, trying to control her breathing and trembling, all too well aware that things would probably get shaken up as soon as the breathless stillness all around her came to its inevitable end.

No sooner had Mei-Feng settled herself into position than the full force of the first tremor struck. The apparently solid, rock-rooted ground on which the city had been built heaved in a series of ripples, like the thinnest of carpets lifting off the floor on the back of a stiff draught.

A thousand miles coastwards, the shaking of the river's banks was severe enough to bring down badly constructed motorway bridges; to put older and less well-constructed buildings fatally at risk. But the ground beneath Shanghai was more settled and solid; the effects far less forceful. The old city and the new city of Pudong remained largely unscathed, thanks at least in part to the work of the woman riding the bucking bronco of the hotel rooftop. For here in Yichang the ground was faulted and quake-cracked already, and the relentless river had eaten into gorges, making the earth's very mantle thinner. And the effects of the earthquake immeasurably more catastrophic.

For Mei-Feng, the experience after the tell-tale silence began with a sound as though a great wind were rushing up behind her. She could hear it roaring nearer over the city at her back. No. More than a wind, she thought. It sounded as though a huge, old steam locomotive were coming rushing at her out of a tunnel as big as the sky, its boiler blowing and its whistle screaming. She heard it coming and yet it was somehow a shocking surprise when it arrived – and arrived so swiftly.

The building beneath her heaved. Rolled like the deck of a ship in a storm. It was oddly shocking that it should do so – though she had known in her bones that it would. Trusting the architect and the strength of his design, she paid as little attention as possible to the way the hotel was pitching – and focussed instead on keeping her binoculars and videophone unwaveringly on the dam. But it was all but impossible to do so. The picture before her eyes jerked up and down – disorientatingly out of synch with the way the roof she was standing on was doing so. The eyepieces of the binoculars jumped away from her face – slammed back against her eyebrows with stunning force. Just in time to show her the ripple of movement spread across Jianshe Road like the blast-wall of some huge explosion, past the roundabout of the cul-de-sac and on, tearing through the last sections of Xiba district up to the dam itself.

Mei-Feng saw nearby buildings shatter, split apart and tumble as though they had been glass. Saw roadways rise and tear themselves wide open, saw vehicles and people upon them tossed around like skittles and broken to pieces like toys. Saw trees and pylons topple as though this were the greatest of typhoons. Saw the nearside hill slopes jump and shake as though they had been scenery painted on thin cloth in a stormbound theatre. Saw the full force of the tremor hit the dam itself.

If the hillsides shook like scenery in a theatre, the dam seemed to flap like a banner in the wind. The architect in Mei-Feng refused to admit what she was seeing. She had designed buildings which, like the hotel she was standing on, were designed to soak up ground movement like shock-absorbers in a speeding car. She had worked with computer simulations, scale models and even real buildings under the stresses of earth tremors up towards the top of magnitude eight. Had spent hours watching video footage like the footage she was shooting now. But this was something different. It was greater; more destructive. Real. The movement generated by the continuing heaving of the earth travelled across the near side of the dam and its outer workings – the locks and the ship lift – making them jump out of focus as they shook. Then that strange ripple, like the effect of some other-worldly weapon in a science-fiction movie, seemed to spread across the face of the dam, as though the fabric of reality was being twisted out of shape while the tremor went under the river-bed and hit the heights of the opposite bank.

The surface of the river at the dam's foot burst into foam seemingly suddenly superheated. Ten-thousand-ton river-barges waiting to use the ship lift were abruptly overwhelmed, tossed about like the bath-toys of an impatient child. The two-hundred metre cliff above them was suddenly dusted with grey smoke. No. Not smoke, thought Mei-Feng, the masonry was simply exploding into dust. Then, amid the dust, there were grains, like sand on a sheer grey beach. And, behind the grains, pebbles. Then, above the pebbles, stones, rocks, chunks. The heaving letter box of the binoculars' vision showed a spider's web of cracks, as though the dam were the windscreen of a car shattering in a collision.

But the dust was suddenly thick enough to obscure the whole facade like a cold grey sea-fog blown across the face of a coastal crag. Mei-Feng swept the binoculars from side to side, shouting in frustration, unaware just how completely the frail and puny sound she was making was subsumed by the roaring tumult of the earthquake itself – just as she was really unaware of how wildly the building beneath her was beginning to move.

The door behind the under-manager was wrenched inwards as though by an unseen hand and he was simply pitched backwards into the void where the stairwell and the lift shaft had been. He hit the wreckage of what was left of them two stories down and was knocked unconscious at once. The inner structure began to fail – and his insensible body joined the hundreds below, the thousands in Xiba district and the millions in the city, as each floor collapsed on to the ones below.

Under Mei-Feng's incredulous gaze, the centre of the tortured dam seemed to sag. For a horrified moment, it seemed to the architect that the whole structure was going to burst like an overblown balloon. But no. A sudden waterfall up on the left top of her letter box vision tore her whole lithe body round. She shouted with shock and horror. The far side of the structure was yielding, tearing away from the opposite bank as though desperate to ease the pressure on its sagging belly. 'Run!' she yelled to the long-vanished under-manager. 'The dam is giving way. We must warn—'

But she stopped, struck almost at once by how futile it would be to send out one single message when anyone who could see anything – hear anything, feel anything – must surely know the truth. The little gap in the dam's far upper corner was widening as though the whole structure was being slowly ripped apart. The main body of the concrete wall was beginning to give way as well, falling slowly back and tumbling in chunks the size of houses.

Mei-Feng suddenly realized that the industrial real estate on the bank below the dam's farside foot was under water. That hungry waves more than fifty feet high were roaring like terrible storm-surf over the green parks and observation areas. And, with a lurch that nearly loosened her bowels, she saw that the same thing was beginning to happen on this bank too. That she was utterly alone, like some peasant marooned in the legend of Yu the Great, flood-conqueror.

She looked straight down just in time to see the first fifty-foot wall of water exploding into the air above the square wall of the hotel's annexe, which was just one street closer to the dam. The sturdy building stood against the onslaught like an intrepid barrage until the hull of a 10,000-ton river barge exploded against it and simply smashed the building down. The massive hull was just the first, she realized, of the queue of barges that had been waiting to use the ship lift. All of which were now being swept this way.

The Three Gorges Xiba took the first impact of the water then, seeming to lurch back a metre or more; apparently held erect solely by its strongly pyramidal shape. Mei-Feng knew now that her earlier confidence had been severely – perhaps fatally – misplaced. The door to the distant stairwell gaped vacantly. The hot-eyed young under-manager had clearly abandoned her long since. Though a glance down at her videophone showed how time had been twisted as strangely as the fabric of the dam. The little clock in the corner showed that she had been recording for less than five minutes. She pocketed the phone and ran for the doorway, some vague plan forming in her mind that she would follow the under-manager down to the relative safety of street-level. But she had only taken two steps before she was thrown to her knees. The whole building shook as though it had taken a direct hit from some kind of guided missile. She dropped the binoculars to dangle round her neck and reached for her phone with some vague idea of calling for help at last. She pulled herself back on to her feet, but the roof lurched beneath her once more. Far beyond any real chance of controlling herself, she span in a kind of pirouette, dictated by the destruction of the hotel, of the district, of the city – of the province – beneath her.

Mei-Feng found herself facing the dam once again, looking at its near end as it towered above her. Like a tourist in Tibet looking up at a vertiginous mountainside. The vast grey slope was sliding majestically down into the heaving welter of wreckage, rubble and wild white foam. While pure, clear water, in a liquid wall two hundred metres high, was pouring over the opening lip. Like a new level of reality arriving. A new universe being born.

FIVE
Flood

Leading Architect Chang Mei-Feng knew then that she was dead. The simple sound of what was happening around her threatened to stamp her to oblivion like the foot of an elephant crushing an ant. The vibrations of the dam's destruction seemed to be tearing the air itself apart. Breath thudded in her lungs and throat as though the oxygen were suddenly liquid and boiling. The whole of her chest throbbed like a drum being beaten at a military tattoo. For some reason the gargantuan scale of the construction figures popped into her head then, perhaps as a way of controlling the sudden pain. Figures she had read in the chopper as she clattered in from the airport.

Even if you didn't count the weight of the water, there were eleven million tons of cement, two million tons of steel and nearly two million tons of timber in the construction that was just about to fall on top of her. The totality of the obliteration that would be visited upon her when that mountain of water, timber, steel and masonry hit her would be as complete as the devastation of the city around her.

Even those buildings like the Three Gorges Hotel, which had been able to withstand the earthquake, would yield in the face of such a wilderness of water, whose naked power seemed so far beyond accurate computation – even to a mind such as hers. And those few structures capable of withstanding the megatons of liquid hurling down on them would simply be annihilated by the fifteen million tons of building material, the fleet of 10,000-ton barges, and everything else being whirled around in the heart of the maelstrom. Like morsels of *mai* in the mouth of a starving man, crushed by his relentlessly chewing molars and washed down his salivating throat.

Mei-Feng felt her heart beginning to break. She sagged, finding it hard to breathe, let alone stand. Her head felt as though it was about to burst. There were shooting pains in her ears. Her eyes were streaming with tears. Possibly because the whole of her being – and everything around it now – was shaking so rapidly that it was impossible for her to focus, and she felt that she must be going blind on top of everything else, as her eyeballs threatened to shake loose in their sockets. Her chattering teeth had caught her tongue or cheek, for her mouth was full of blood.

The thunderous roaring of the waterfall seemed to attain a kind of throbbing power that pulsed into a battering downdraught of wind which simply knocked her back on to her protesting knees, even as she felt the roof beneath her beginning to yield at last, and the certainty of death loomed like a shadow hovering immediately over her. And just as it did so, something whacked her brutally across the back.

Then it hit her shoulders.

Then the back of her head.

At the third assault she was outraged enough to look up, and there in front of her was just the very thing that a monkey-woman would wish to see in the moment of her last extremity.

Something to climb.

What Mei-Feng saw first was the bottom rung of a ladder. And that was enough to start with. She hurled herself up at it, losing her shoes in the process, but keeping tight hold of her phone. One step was enough for her to shove it back into her jacket pocket. Then the rung that had hit her on the back, shoulders and head, thumped into her chest and she was glad of the pain. It proved beyond a doubt that she was still alive. That this was not some kind of hope-enhanced dream. She reached up and grasped the fourth rung high above her head. Wound herself into the solid fabric of the thing. Found out the hard way that the binoculars she thought she had dropped were still round her neck. But, as her bare feet found purchase on the lowest rung and thrust her up without further thought, the strap broke and they fell free.

Tricked into looking down after the binoculars, Mai-Feng was horrified to see that in the instant it had taken for her to get this far, the hotel had all but vanished beneath that overwhelming torrent. The field glasses simply tumbled away into a yawning vacancy floored by a welter of foam. The wild river heaved like a storm-surf over a sunken reef. Abruptly, the massive hull of a river barge heaved out of the water where the hotel had been, showing its keel like a rusty sandbank far below. And she realized that just as the hotel's roof had been falling away, so she and the ladder she was clinging to had been rising into the sky at breakneck speed.

Mei-Feng looked up at last, and there, surprisingly close above her, was the underside of the neat little helicopter that had been sent to squire her around. Clearly the hot-eyed, young pilot was made of sterner stuff than the absent under-manager, she thought grimly as she began to pull herself upwards.

SIX
Red

As befitted a vehicle sent to assist an architect in her study of the interface between a dam and the water it was designed to contain, the helicopter was fitted with floats as well as wheels. Mei-Feng pulled herself over the plump out-thrust of a water-ski and then used it as a foothold to push herself safely aboard. As calmly as circumstances would allow, she pulled the ladder aboard and slammed the door shut. Then she literally crawled the couple of metres along the centre of the fuselage, between the bucket seats designed to accommodate passengers and on up to the co-pilot's seat, which she had occupied on the flight down from the airport.

Her natural desire to thank the pilot for saving her was stymied by a combination of factors. First, his absolute concentration on the job in hand. Secondly, her realization, as she dumped herself into the seat and started searching for the straps, that she had lost a good deal more than her shoes in the ordeal. The forceful departure of the binoculars had done untold damage to her upper clothing, while the climb up the ladder and the clamber across the float had left her skirt in almost equal disarray. She now resembled a decadent western model advertising lingerie rather than a respectable Han professional woman, wife and mother.

But, thirdly and overwhelmingly, the scene that they were overflying simply robbed her of the ability to speak. To do anything, indeed, other than to gape in unbelieving horror. And, with the last shred of her professional pride, to reach for her videophone and to continue recording, praying to the sky that neither the memory's capacity nor the battery's charge would let her down.

The water of the Emerald Drop so close below them seemed to be writhing as though it was a nest of wrestling water dragons. The forces released below the surface by the sudden collapsing of the barrier downstream made the water writhe and twist in a feral desire to be free.

Huge longitudinal waves ran upstream from the white wilderness spreading outwards from the breach. The low evening sun threw the strange green slopes of water into sharp relief, like the gargantuan ropes of giant Yangtze trackers striving to pull some immense invisible Yangtze barge upstream. They looked so solid, so permanent, that it was all too easy to imagine that they were stable and substantial features. Like the valley slopes they mimicked so accurately. But the comfortable illusion of steadiness was shattered immediately as a six-decked river cruiser swept by, utterly out of control, a plaything of the mighty forces, like a feather in a mill race. Terrified passengers were hurling themselves overboard; individuals with arms waving wildly and couples holding hands. Families in pathetic lines with a precious child between two solicitous parents. Foreign tourist families made all too obvious by the fact that the parents strove to protect more than one child.

Even those few wearing life jackets stood no chance. Their heads simply vanished as the ravening waters sucked them down. But at least they lasted longer than the cruiser itself, which was obliterated by a barge that seemed to appear from nowhere and was simply swept down on top of her. The pair of them rolled over and under. And the helpless passengers and crew followed them. Under the surface. Then out through the gaping dam-wall to be spewed over the devastated city below.

Further upstream, other vessels, cruisers, boats and barges, began to feel the irresistible pull of those huge watery ropes. One by one, facing upstream or down, they began to slide, as helpless as motes of dust in the outflow of an emptying bath.

The chopper tilted as the pilot swung her on to a new heading. He glanced across at Mei-Feng and she realized, red-faced, that she had done nothing about the state of her clothing. 'I'm trying to find somewhere we can put down and get to civilization,' he shouted. 'Civilization and maybe more gas. We'll try the airport first.'

Mei-Feng nodded to show that she understood and approved, then set about rearranging her clothing. The helicopter skipped over hillsides marked with landslides that still seemed to be tumbling down the lower slopes and swooped towards the airport on the city's northern outskirts. At least the water wouldn't have reached this far, she thought, using her wide experience of urban development, combined with a sharp eye for the lie of the land. But then she saw that this was almost a matter of regret. For the ground in front of the chopper was suddenly obscured not by white water but by black smoke. The whole place was ablaze.

A gust of wind swept the oil-thick clouds back for an instant to reveal airport buildings in ruins; runways, taxi-areas and hardstandings shattered and littered with the broken remains of jets, most of them burning fiercely. Tiny dots ran wildly hither and thither.

The pilot pulled his headset off. 'The tower's stopped broadcasting,' he said. 'Power's out.'

'Of course it is,' said Mei-Feng. 'The power for the whole district was supplied by the hydroelectric systems on the dam. The whole of the national power system is going to notice that eighteen million kilowatts has suddenly gone off-line. Where shall we try next, Mr . . . I'm sorry, I can't remember your name.'

'Quing,' he introduced himself with a strange little bow. 'Quing Sun-Yat. They call me Chopper Quing.'

'Hello, Chopper,' she said. 'Thank you for saving my life. What do you think we should do next?'

'I'll try and get some kind of signal on my radio. Do you think the power will be out over a wide area?'

'Everywhere between Chonquing and Jingzhou, I'd guess. That's just with the loss of power from the hydro from the dam. From the look of the earthquake damage before the floods hit, most of the grid will have been knocked out for the foreseeable future. There's no way of estimating where the epicentre of the quake that did this was located. Or what the magnitude of the thing was. But wherever the epicentre is, the situation there will be even worse than this. So even the back-up power stations will be down. Communications crippled. Roads out. Cities destroyed. Airfields like the airport down there.'

'Can you get any signal on your cellphone?' asked Chopper.

She switched off the video function and tried. The signal was dead. 'No,' she said regretfully.

'Right. Well, most of the big towns nearby are downstream. We'd never make Chongquing in any case. We can try for Jingzhou, I guess. But like you say, it'll be a hell of a mess if that quake was anything to go by. With worse to come when the floodwater hits. We'll be lucky to find what we need, but at least we'll be able to warn them that they're about to get their feet wet.'

'If it's our best bet, Chopper, then I think we should go for it.'

'OK,' said Chopper, clearly glad to be sharing some of the responsibility here. 'Downstream it is. And fast enough to get ahead of the flood.'

'Pausing only to warn anyone we see on the way,' added Mei-Feng feelingly.

The chopper swung back towards the Yangtze and dropped its nose purposefully, beginning to pick up speed. The sun was almost set now and its rays were affecting the spectrum of light that governed the whole scene.

Below and dead ahead lay the ruins of Yichang. A city that had been home to more than four million people – independently of the hundreds of thousands of tourists flocking there at the height of the season. The devastation brought by the earthquake must have simply crushed millions of them and now the water was washing through the wreckage, adding to the devastation. As though seeing the whole thing in slow-motion, she observed the way the wall of water that had so recently been caged by the dam was running riot through the city, contained for the time being by the slopes of the valley to either side. Block after block, district after district was swept under the wild water.

Mei-Feng's little videophone could never hope to record the enormity of the sight, and it suddenly seemed politic to preserve its battery in the hope she might be able to use it for its primary function and actually make contact with someone. But she still felt she should be a witness to the horror. As her mother's mother had been a witness to the Rape of Nanjing by the Japanese. But the thought of Nanjing planted the seed of an idea in her mind.

'How far can this thing go on a full tank?' she asked, her voice suddenly throaty and ragged.

'Two hundred and fifty miles,' he answered readily enough. 'But I have some auxiliaries on this which will give us another hundred on top of that if we need it. I filled up all tanks at the airport just before I came to look for you at the Three Gorges Hotel.'

'I haven't thanked you properly for that,' she said feelingly. 'It was a brave act to pull me off the roof like that.'

'Lucky I saw you as I came in,' he said dismissively. 'But besides . . .'

'Besides what?'

'It would have been a simple sin to let a woman such as yourself go to waste. If I may say so. Under the circumstances.'

Mei-Feng allowed a little silence to linger between them. At the very least it allowed her to collect herself after the horror of what she had witnessed. Then, 'Three hundred and fifty miles,' she said, closing her eyes and bringing to mind the river charts that had filled her childhood, and, latterly, her marriage and motherhood. 'Three hundred and fifty miles would get us to Jiujiang.'

'It would,' he agreed a little doubtfully, 'if we flew straight rather than following the river. But why there? Why Jiujiang?'

'It's halfway to Nanjing,' she answered. 'If we can make Jiujiang and pick up some fuel there, then we can get to Nanjing. Then it's just a hop and a skip down the river to Shanghai.'

'Right,' said Chopper, as though he understood what in all the Middle Kingdom she was talking about.

SEVEN
River

'**N**o power. No communications. No news!' raged Deputy General Commissioner Daniel Huuk of the Institute of Public Security.

Daniel was in full fighting fettle now and very much in command of his extensive official responsibilities, thought Richard as he watched his old friend pacing, quite literally, like a caged tiger. So he thought better of adding that there was no Internet, no email and precious little else involving computers either. Particularly as he had never before seen Daniel so completely remove his accustomed mask of inscrutability and oriental calm. It was, frankly, unnerving. Especially as Richard had come to understand within the last twenty-four hours just how terrifyingly powerful the Deputy General Commissioner could be. Let alone the Son of the Dragon, head of the Invisible Power Triad. It was like having Genghis Khan and Julius Caesar all rolled into one. No wonder his feeling so helpless in the face of such an enormous disaster was almost literally sending him over the edge.

Daniel's mood had been darkening relentlessly during the night watch as his energy returned and his aches and pains no doubt got worse. Made worse by the fact that it was he who had insisted on dealing with the petty – if well meaning and punctilious – officialdom with which they had been briefly overrun. As the only undamaged vessel in the immediate vicinity, it was to *Poseidon* that the Civil Defence, Accident and Emergency, Fire, Police and Militia attending the tragic aftermath of the earthquake had come. Captain Chang had wisely written up the logs herself at the earliest opportunity, carefully editing *Poseidon*'s innocent involvement in the events immediately before and during the incident. Richard, Robin and Lieutenant Commander Tan had added some details. But matters such as *Poseidon*'s brief grounding and the impact of the earthquake on the men who were fighting to come aboard, slaughter them all, assassinate the Dragon Head and pirate away the golden statue in the hold had been most carefully glossed over. And by the time the first importunate, self-important little *tai-pan* had heaved himself aboard, the damage to the ship could as easily have come from the destruction of the motorway bridge so close above them, as from the gun-battle with the Green Gang pirates.

But the more Daniel had become involved in the immediate, smaller-scale, requirements of the situation between here and Shanghai, the more it became clear that there was a far larger scale situation upriver. A situation that was almost certainly getting exponentially worse minute by minute. And there was a burning need for someone to take control of it. Especially as Daniel, via the full range of radio equipment aboard, using a series of passwords familiar to only half a dozen members of the Politburo Standing Committee – who took all the most important decisions in the country – was able to make contact with the President himself. The Standing Committee was being summoned, Daniel was informed. There would be no hasty rush to action until the wise heads of the elders had met and due discussions had taken place. If and when Daniel's own input was required, he would be informed. In the meantime, he might best involve himself with supporting the local authorities, which would at the very least ease the tensions that existed between Beijing and the Special Economic Zone of the Shanghai/Pudong complex.

At the quiet insistence of her intrepid captain, *Poseidon*'s normal watch routines had been reinstated and her complement readied for instant departure. Captain Chang was seated in the pilot's chair now, Richard observed, listening silently to the fuming of her all-too-powerful and unwanted guest.

Robin had gone below, announcing pointedly that someone had better be rested enough to get on top of things tomorrow when the going was likely to get tough. But Richard hadn't taken the hint. He knew he could work for forty-eight hours straight without losing much energy if he had to. Seventy-two if push came to shove. He had never tried for ninety-six. And quite frankly he would be surprised if Robin was actually asleep in any case.

'At least you're in communication with both Shanghai and Beijing,' Richard argued soothingly now, gesturing at the door to the radio room and avoiding the Captain's eye. 'That's one area where *Poseidon* is your perfect operations base. I don't think even Commander Tan's big *Luyang* destroyer is better equipped.'

'Though she is much better armed and very much more secure, of course,' added Captain Chang.

In fact, the *Luyang* was on its way here now, picking its way upriver with all possible speed through the ship-management channels in the face of the freighters which were almost all outbound, frightened by the possibility that the river was going to flood. A rumour had spread like wildfire in spite of the lack of information solid enough to satisfy either Richard or the raging Daniel Huuk. At both Tan and Chang's suggestion, Daniel was planning to transfer aboard her and then to sail up the Huangpu into Shanghai. Even if there were still Green Gang rival Triad members ready to kill him there, they would hardly be able to reach him on the command bridge of his own destroyer. And the recently refitted warship certainly had communications systems equal to *Poseidon*'s – and superior to anything likely to be available in Shanghai itself. And it was the perfect command centre if the rivers did, in fact, flood badly enough to swamp the cities on the riverbanks.

Richard had suggested – with the support of both the Captain and the pilot – that as soon as Daniel's transfer was complete, *Poseidon* would be best employed running upriver to report in detail what the situation was in Nanjing, the nearest of the great riverine ports to have fallen so sinisterly silent. Like the *Luyang*, they would at the very least meet a great deal of traffic outbound, as they – and they alone in all probability – went upriver instead of down. They should get their first reports – be they rumour or eyewitness – from the men aboard the fleeing ships. And he could pass the news back to Daniel aboard the *Luyang*.

'Then, if you can get the people in Shanghai to pass your orders down both military and civilian command chains, you won't be so badly briefed and powerless,' Richard persisted, as things began to settle down after twelve thirty.

'True,' answered Daniel more thoughtfully. 'But no-one in either Shanghai or Beijing seems to know any more than I do. And if the President is waiting for the Standing Committee before he takes action . . .' He broke off and crossed to stand beside the helmsman looking downriver as though he hoped to see the incoming *Luyang*. Richard crossed to stand at his shoulder. The flames on the river were almost all quenched now. The rescue vessels were still searching for survivors, their searchlight beams reflecting off the oily water and illuminating the underside of the bridge-span that ended so abruptly ten metres out from the cliff of the bank above them. The last of the vehicle headlights that had shone so eerily from the river-bed was dark now. There was enough darkness, in fact, for Daniel's frustrated expression to be reflected in the clearview. His strange dark eyes met Richard's. 'The whole heart of the People's Republic has gone dark and silent,' he said quietly. 'And, as likely as not, *dead*! Have you any idea how many millions of people must be involved? Might be at risk? Could already be dead and dying as we speak?'

The question seemed rhetorical to Richard so he didn't hazard an answer. But it made him think. Certainly, starting with Nanjing and reaching right up to Yichang and the Three Gorges Dam itself, there seemed to be a great void the better part of a thousand miles across. What little they knew from both Nanjing and Yichang at either extremity consisted of sketchy, soon-silenced reports of earthquake damage, rising casualty figures and water-levels. Then nothing more. There was some doubt in Richard's mind – and clearly in Daniel's too – as to whether anyone in authority out there was actually on top of things.

Especially, Daniel observed bitterly, as even Beijing had no reports of any sign of life between Nanjing and Yichang either. They had yet to receive absolute confirmation that any of the wild rumours was actually true. No one had actually established, for instance, that the Three Gorges Dam was actually down, as the earliest reports had suggested it was. All they had to go on was one hysterical, soon-silenced report and the fact that a couple of million kilowatts seemed to have vanished off the national electricity grid. There seemed to be neither power nor communication with significant portions of Hubei Province, Jiangxi, Anhi and even Jiangsu. Had the great lake of Puyang actually flooded? What was the situation in the epicentre, Jiujiang? The night was dark and the overcast impenetrable. Satellites were blind. Google Earth was out of the question – and out of date for the current crisis in any case. Getting *Poseidon* upriver and into that mysterious void seemed like the best and swiftest way of establishing a few solid facts. Especially if it could carry the full weight of Daniel's authority with it. And, with the greatest of all river pilots aboard and one of the most knowledgeable captains, the vessel was ready to go. As soon as Daniel and Commander Tan could be transferred.

'In the meantime,' persisted Richard after a few more moments of silent thought, 'why not use the eyes you do have in the sky? Just to get some sort of a first impression?'

'What do you mean,' demanded Daniel, turning away from the clearview to meet his old friend's gaze directly.

'There must be some planes still in the sky above the cloud cover who could go down and give you some kind of eyewitness report. Under the circumstances, I bet you can order any airlines still overflying the area to go down for a closer look. Those that you can contact, anyway. Even those that aren't part of your own domestic and international services are using your airspace, surely . . .'

And so the first part of the Deputy General Commissioner's plan sprang into being. Was suggested to the President and the Committee; was agreed. As, for the time being, they gave Daniel carte blanche to take youthfully decisive action, while the wiser, elder heads thought through the longer-term implications and priorities.

As Richard had observed, the diversion of the airliners passing through Chinese airspace had become a matter of some urgency, in any case. But their usefulness as observers had to be balanced against the fact that those still in the air over the stricken area also had to be re-routed to safe destinations. A few intrepid captains took their planes below the cloud cover as they turned towards safety, and they reported darkness sometimes speckled with distant fires and – when they tried to contact nearby airfields – silence. All local radio stations were offline. They gave permission for passengers to try their cellphones and contact any local numbers. They told anyone with flight-safe computers to try and raise local TV broadcasts. With no success. One or two planes reported near-misses of one sort or another, for the weather was terrible and there were electrical storms powerful enough to interfere with the most sophisticated instruments.

Within an hour, by the time the *Luyang* destroyer came out of the black night to slide alongside *Poseidon*, all the airborne information had dried up.

EIGHT
Command

Even as the lines between the destroyer and the little corvette were being secured, and Daniel was distracted by the need to choose between a scaling ladder, a breeches buoy or a short hop in a chopper to get from one command to the other, so the next stage of his plan was being put in place via the acquiescent elders in Beijing. Jian-10 fighter planes were scrambled into the midnight darkness from the net of air force bases south and west of Beijing. But all they could see – even flying dangerously low through the misty, drizzling lower air with their enhanced equipment on full-power – was gloom and confusion. Gloom so impenetrable that even the People's Liberation Army Air Force's strongest computers, to which the signals were beamed back at once, could make little or no sense of the signals. Even when these were forwarded to the Beijing University's School of Electronic Engineering and Computer Science, not far from the Geography Department, which had first confirmed the quake as measuring nine on the Richter scale, things got no clearer at all. All in all, the Jian-10s' information was little better – or longer lived – than that of the airliners.

'What we need,' Daniel decided, as he and Tan prepared to board the *Luyang*'s chopper parked on *Poseidon*'s little helideck, 'is boots on the ground, as the Americans have it.'

'It's the next logical step,' agreed Richard, standing at the foot of the boarding ladder beside them, trying not to pay too much attention to the fact that Robin was standing on the after section of the bridge's upper deck, looking down at the departing men. 'That, and sending vessels upriver and down.'

'Don't worry,' said Daniel. 'You'll be able to get under way soon. But, before I go across, I'll just go back to the radio room and get things under way. And, now I think of it, if I'm sending you upriver, then I'd better offer you a little more in the way of support.'

As Richard pondered the precise meaning of Daniel's promise, all the nearest units of the People's Liberation Army were mobilized. They were on the move even before the last of the Jian-10s were back at base. They left in their fastest vehicles from the camps nearest the edges of the dark and silent area. But almost immediately they began to report that the roads had been rendered impassable by a combination of damage and landslides. Off-road areas were scarcely any better and there seemed to be extensive flooding. Swift elite cavalry units were forced to slow down and wait for engineers. Only their helicopter squadrons made any progress – but even they found it hard to find landing places and were constricted to increasingly hopeless overflights. The army's information took several hours to come in with any detail – in sharp contrast to the air force's. But it quickly became clear that the soldiers were not going to make appreciable inroads into the area. Especially as the sound of the helicopters had stirred the first great waves of survivors, so that, all too soon, the army found itself inundated with refugees. There were hundreds of thousands of individual stories that varied from the harrowing to the miraculous, but very little sense of what was happening on the larger, city-wide and provincial scale. And still no idea at all of what was happening nearer the epicentre.

Though, it was at this point that the city authorities in Chonquing confirmed that the Yangtze was falling rapidly. That the Emerald Drop reservoir was clearly draining away.

'That's it,' Daniel fumed as he, Richard and Tan hurried back towards the helideck, leaving Captain Chang frozen in her formal salute of farewell. 'We have to assume the Three Gorges Dam is at least partially breached. And what the implications of that fact are, only the Sky and the Gods above it know.'

The three of them strode out into the security lighting surrounding the chopper. Richard automatically glanced up again but Robin was no longer standing on the out-thrust of the upper deck, like a maiden in a romance bidding farewell to her knights errant. Instead, the metal wall of the *Luyang*'s side heaved in a dark grey cliff of smoothly riveted metal.

Daniel swung back, his hand outthrust. 'I'll need to get the Committee and the Generals organized pretty bloody quickly, whatever,' he said decisively. 'You know what *Poseidon* needs to be doing.'

'Captain Chang does. She's in command . . .'

'Of course she is,' said Daniel with a kind of grim cheeriness.

Their hands met. They exchanged a brief handshake, for all the world, thought Richard, like a pair of army officers heading over the top, out of the trenches at the Somme. 'Tell her to wait for the helicopter to return before she gets under way,' advised Daniel.

The chopper clattered up in to the black night sky. Richard turned back, his mind full of what *Poseidon* was commanded to do. And with just a tiny corner of it speculating as to what Daniel was going to be doing, too. In the greater scheme of things.

The senior generals of the Central Committee of the People's Liberation Army had arrived at the offices of the Politburo Standing Committee by now – or, like Daniel after he had settled aboard the *Luyang*, were available via radio or slow old-fashioned broadcast video-link. They represented the air and naval arms of the Central Defence Services, as well as the army. And although each one had his own bailiwick to defend, his own axe to grind – particularly as each of them had seen their arm of the service called into action without their immediate agreement – they were as well aware as the Committee of the need to get moving as fast as possible. There was an enormous amount of *face* to be lost here – as well as a colossal number of lives.

By this time, the *Luyang*'s helicopter had returned and deposited a command of a dozen fully-armed marines aboard the corvette. Their commander introduced himself as Lieutenant Ping and Steady named him 'Paradeground' on the spot. Captain Chang ordered him to put his men's arms in the armoury and detailed Straightline to find them bunks. Ping himself lingered, however, catching Richard's eye.

'The Deputy General Commissioner told me to give you this,' said the marine commander, handing over a slim booklet. 'You must give it to the Mayor of Nanjing. It will be vital when he gets his communications back up and running.'

'What is it?' asked Richard intrigued. It was printed in Chinese characters that were utterly impenetrable to him.

'You must guard it carefully,' said Ping in all seriousness. 'With your life. It is the call log from the *Luyang*. It contains the wavelength, call sign and security code for every military and major civilian contact that can be accessed by radio.'

And on that note, the dapper little marine was gone after his men and Richard returned to the bridge – via his cabin. One more secret, he thought to himself. One more near-impossible mission. Deliver this to the Mayor of Nanjing – if they could get to him.

Then Richard, Robin and the river pilot joined Captain Chang on *Poseidon*'s bridge as the sleek corvette moved carefully through the *Luyang*'s widening wake. *Poseidon* swung in a 180-degree turn, made more complicated and lengthy by the fact that the bustle of the outward bound shipping was so severe, the panic so great, that the intricate laning system had broken down altogether.

'We'll just have to pick our way through them and keep our eyes peeled,' said Chang to her fuming father. 'Father, keep a close eye on the radar until the navigator returns. We've been aground once already tonight and I have no intention of repeating the adventure, even under these circumstances! Radio operator, I want a broadband signal warning all outward bound ships of our intentions – and of the fact that we intend to follow the laning restrictions that they are so flagrantly disregarding. Say I will fire on any vessel that gets too close on a reciprocal course.'

'Can she do that?' asked Robin, sotto voce, leaning up towards Richard.

'She can do anything I say she can,' answered Richard. He opened his right hand. There, passed during the final handshake before Daniel followed Tan up into the *Luyang*'s helicopter, was the personal chop of the Deputy Director of the Institute of Public Security. All Richard had to do was to show it to anyone in authority and he would get almost anything he demanded, almost the instant he asked for it. 'Though when she says she will *fire*, she means she will fire with the small arms from the gun-locker and with whatever Ping's men have brought aboard.'

Robin frowned and shivered. For the identification authority was partially wrapped in something else she recognized. A piece of rice paper so thin that it was only preserved by the fact that Richard's steady palm was utterly dry. The paper also held a mark. But this one was like the Black Spot passed by Blind Pew to the doomed captain Billy Bones in *Treasure Island*. This was the seal of the Dragon Head of the Invisible Power Triad. With those two passes in his possession, Richard could get anything Daniel could get from anyone he might meet in the entire Middle Kingdom.

Including getting himself killed, she thought grimly, thinking back through less than twelve hours to the bomb and the gunfight which had both been designed to assassinate their friend.

'Right,' said Captain Chang, as Robin gave another superstitious shiver and a huffing Straightline clattered back on to the bridge. 'One hundred and eighty degree turn completed. Navigator, lay in a course for Nanjing. Engineer, bring the engines up to three quarter power. Let's not hang about here!'

And the river pilot looked down at his decisive daughter with a smile of quiet pride, even though it should have been he who issued the orders. There was no doubt who was in command here – for the time being at least.

NINE
Steady

In marked contrast to all the big-scale planning that Richard, Robin, Daniel Huuk and Lieutenant Commander Tan had been involved in, the concerns of the helmsman were of an intensely personal magnitude.

The helmsman's name was Xin and all the crew knew him as Steadyhand – Steady for short. The name was an apt one in several regards. Steady was physically square and possessed an air of rock-like solidity. Even his skull seemed square – though that was an illusion fostered by a wide jaw, jug-handle ears and a flat-topped crew cut. And the fact that his high forehead led down past overhanging brows to almost Mongol cheekbones and a nose crushed flat in numberless youthful fights. Between brows and cheekbones, between nose and chin there were slits of mouth and eyes that hardly disturbed the flat, square aspect of his face. Except when he smiled. Steady possessed an unexpectedly cheery and contagious grin that had a habit of deepening into a chuckle that shook the whole of his massive frame.

If you needed someone to support a team, physically or emotionally, Steady was your man. He took pride in being unflappable and utterly reliable. The crew brought him their problems – and so did a wider circle of friends and family, certain of the steady good sense of his advice and help. His hands were steady. No matter how stressful the situation or how dangerous the task, Steady's grip was dry, powerful yet gentle, and it never betrayed a tremor. As well as doing duty as *Poseidon*'s most reliable helmsman, Steady was crewman of choice to share control of the deep-sea remote exploration vessel *Neptune* when she was winched off the foredeck and sent down to plumb the depths.

But the actual and metaphorical breadth of Steady's shoulders came at an unexpected price. Less than a week ago, before *Poseidon* set sail into the outer reaches of the Yellow Sea, Steady's younger brother had asked for his help. Younger Brother was in debt to a gambler backed by the Green Gang. And the Green Gang collected unpaid debts an inch at a time. With a cleaver. An inch of a finger the first day. An inch of a finger the second day. An inch of a hand after the first three weeks, when there were no fingers left . . .

Steady had sent all the money he could spare, enough to keep Younger Brother's fingers safe in the short-term. And then, little more than seventy hours earlier, it seemed, he had tried to ease the family's terrible dilemma by alerting the Green Gang to the existence of a treasure that would more than cancel every debt they owed.

For there was, in *Poseidon*'s most secure hold, a priceless statue of Genghis Khan. *Neptune* had discovered it in a wreck on the floor of an abyssal trench and brought it aboard at the direction of the gweilo giant and his golden-haired demon wife. The statue, which Steady had helped carry to its current resting place, stood the better part of a metre high. It was made of solid gold and was encrusted with precious jewels. It was clearly worth millions of dollars in meltdown value alone. Its worth in yen or the currency of the People's Republic, RBM, could hardly be calculated. Any more than the danger it posed to the ship and everyone aboard her, because of Steady, his foolish brother and the ruthless greed of the Green Gang.

As the helmsman stood solidly, guiding *Poseidon* up the increasingly empty waterway through the intense darkness, he was able to survey the men and women he felt he had condemned. For their reflections in the recently fixed clearview ahead of him were as clear as though he had been looking into a mirror.

The Giant – the other crewmen called him the Good Luck Giant, though Steady was by no means so sure – certainly stood tall. He was a ship's captain and this vessel's owner. And he had stood against the Green Gang as solidly as he had stood against the typhoon, keeping them all alive for the time being. He was a man Steady would have admired, had the helmsman not been so consumed with guilt.

Steady merely glanced at the golden-haired demon wife the giant had brought aboard with him. Her attributes might have attracted a western man, or a man like Dragon Head Huuk who had been seduced by western ways, but Steady saw little to admire in her. Except that she seemed to share some of her husband's spirit. For she, too, had stood against both the typhoon and the pirates in a manner that would have won the admiration of anyone. Anyone except the man who had called the pirates down on them.

The demon woman actually shared some characteristics with *Poseidon*'s captain. The men called Captain Chang 'Mongol' behind her back. This was not because of the soldier-like shortness of her hairstyle – a military pageboy bob – nor because of the squareness of her bearing. Nor even because of the pristine perfection of her uniform, worthy of a parade at the academy, even in the midst of battle.

Nor did Captain Mongol Chang have that particular nickname

because of the fact that her face was a twin of the golden statue's –
except in the matter of moustache and beard. It was a reference to the
intrepidity of her leadership. She was, it was generally agreed, potentially the finest captain in the people's Liberation Army Navy; even
though she had by sheer bad luck got herself mixed up with the giant
and his demon wife, who were trying to buy *Poseidon* and take her
away from the Mongol. Had the statue of Genghis in the hold below
sprung suddenly to life, he would not have been ashamed to acknowledge Captain Chang as his kinswoman.

And then there was the man who did acknowledge Captain Chang
as his kinswoman – his daughter, in fact – and in so doing simply
added to her *face* by being a man of legendary standing, not only along
the river, but up and down the coast from Hong Kong to Dalian. One
look at River Pilot Chang and it was easy to see where she had got
her legendary ugliness from. Stand them in a row, and except for the
matter of moustache and beard, it would be hard to distinguish father
or daughter from the statue in the hold.

The statue in the hold . . . Steady Xin's thoughts went dark, and
darker still – as befitted the inky scene in front of him.

'Steady!' the abrupt voice of the bridge's last occupant jerked the
helmsman back to the present. Navigating Officer 'Straightline' Jiang
loomed in the clearview's reflection, his youthful face folded in a glow-
ering frown. As his nickname suggested, the navigator was happiest
with deep-sea work. His idea of bliss was to follow some great circle
route, marked as a straight line from one landfall to another on his
wide blue fathomless deep-water chart. The constant shifting, continuous checking, minute variations and eternal vigilance required in river
navigation was sending him simply insane. Especially since the reduc-
tion in power on the electricity grids nearby had all but wiped out the
shore-based guidance systems, while the wild rush downriver had
played havoc with the floating channel markers. Added to which, the
low wattage made radio reception and broadcast from the ports and
authorities along the shorelines north and south of them patchy to say
the least of it. But most worryingly, he was performing his exacting
duties under the eyes of the river pilot.

Pilot Chang crossed from the pilot's chair, roused by the lieutenant's
word. He looked out past Steady's reflection into the darkness, then he
glanced down at the radar display that Straightline was hovering over.
'Look there,' he ordered quietly. Both helmsman and navigator obeyed.
'You can just make out the marks that show where the deep-water
channel is. The old marks – none of your new-fangled illuminated buoys
that have been torn away from their anchorages. These are the marks

the junk and barge captains used in the time of the Ming emperors when Nanjing was the capital of the whole Middle Kingdom. We haven't seen any traffic in a while, so we will disregard the laning. Stick to those marks, helm. Follow the deep course, navigator and remain at thirty-five knots. We will be in Nanjing by sunrise.'

'I hesitate to disagree, father,' came the Captain's quiet voice. 'But the bunkerage is low. We are running fast and the river is rising against us. To maintain thirty-five knots along the shore we must run at more than forty against the current. Where can we stop for more fuel?'

'Jiangyin is the nearest river port,' answered the Pilot, as Straightline was feverishly consulting his charts. 'We should be there within the hour. Even in this . . .', his broad hand gestured at the darkness beyond the clearview, '. . . we should be able to see the Jiangyin Bridge. But we may be able to get in contact with the Port Authority on the radio. Let's try that first.'

The radio operator was in contact with Jiangyin just before the pallid, partially illuminated arch of the bridge soared from shore to shore above their heads. The pilot and the Captain stood shoulder to shoulder as the Captain did the talking.

'This is vessel *Poseidon*. We are under the direct commission of the Deputy Director of the Committee for Public security. We require bunkerage . . .'

'I am sorry, vessel *Poseidon*.' The harbourmaster's voice was faint. Power was low. Range restricted. Volume almost non-existent. But his words were clear enough. 'You could be under the direct orders of the President himself, and I would be unable to help you. If you have been coming upriver you must have been aware of the amount of shipping bound downriver against you. There has been nothing short of panic here. I have never experienced anything like it. Vessels of all sizes have been in filling their bunkerage. Jiangyin is dry. Until I get a chance to refill my bunkerage tanks you will get no fuel here. I am almost alone in the harbour in any case. The crews of the departing vessels have been talking of a terrible flood coming downstream behind them. All of my people here – and half the city besides – have run for the high ground. And to be frank, I feel that it would be wise for me to join them. My tanks are empty, my power is almost gone and my batteries all but dead. It is out of my hands. I am sorry . . .'

'If it was panic buying,' growled Richard from the door, 'then maybe there will be some bunkerage upstream, somewhere that requires more thought and planning to get at it.'

'An excellent thought,' the Captain's father said. 'Wait! Harbourmaster, just one last thing. This is River Pilot Chang. Where is there bunkerage upstream that might be harder to come by? Somewhere too difficult or complicated for frightened men to deal with? I have in mind somewhere back from the river itself. Accessible via a canal or channel, perhaps. Ah! I can see it in my memory but I cannot bring the name to mind . . .'

'Zhenjiang,' said the Jiangyin harbourmaster faintly, his voice little more than a thread of sound as his radio battery died. 'You have just described Zhenjiang.'

TEN
Gang

'Easy,' said Pilot Chang quietly. 'Stay on one twenty at slow ahead, we should be fine.'

'The depth is now reading three and a half metres,' warned Straightline. 'And its shelving.'

Richard looked across at the navigating officer. His face was set in a frown that showed the strain he was feeling as he read the array of radar screens in front of him; his focus mainly on the equipment's estimate of how much clearance they had under the keel. He had run them aground once already tonight and had no intention of repeating the experience. But at least they were finally sailing in a straight line, thought Richard wryly. That had to be a plus at least.

The problem was that the straight line was up a shallow, narrow access channel leading at 120 degrees south-east in from the Yangtze's Jiaoushan Shuidao channel into the port of Zhenjiang. The corvette's searchlights were scanning the darkness of the flats on either side and the port city itself was little more than a dull glow dead ahead. There seemed hardly enough power to bring much light to the city itself. Certainly there had only just been enough to allow the harbourmaster to confirm that he could supply their fuel wants – via a radio signal that was so faint and crackly that it seemed to have been bounced off a distant galaxy.

But the fact that the vessel had turned back on its course – even partially, and was running south-east now instead of generally west along the main course of the Yangtze, had an unexpected side effect. On the right-hand side of the clearview, the city of Zhenjiang glimmered dully. On the left, and out through the left-hand windows of the bridge itself, there was a gathering brightness, low in the distant east that had remained unobserved until now because it had been so solidly astern of them. It seemed that dawn was threatening.

Richard looked up at the clock on the bulkhead above the clearview between the blank CCTV screens. It was half past five, local time. Richard frowned, trying to remember the conversation he had had with Daniel about the timings of the flood if that lake – whatever it was called – really had flooded out by the mountain called Nan Shan. Dawn

had featured in that conversation, if he could just remember how . . .
But he was distracted at once by the tension on the bridge, for this
was an extremely narrow channel which was likely to be leading them
into a difficult – not to say dangerous – situation.

It was this channel – usually the exit from the port – and the mudflats
and fish-traps guarding its more normal downriver-facing entrance that
had kept the port safe from the panic, thought Richard, crossing to the
left of the bridge and disregarding the distant glimmer as he looked
straight down on to the nearby flats. No matter how you entered or
exited Zhenjiang, it took time, care, patience, forethought and planning. All qualities in short supply among a motley fleet running away
from the rumour of a flood.

River Pilot Chang was intimately familiar with the Yangtze up as
far as Nanjing, but even he was silent and unsettled. The absence of
river traffic, the dimness – or absence – of the navigational features
he was used to relying on, the increasingly disturbing contacts with
increasingly desperate harbourmasters – many of whom he had known
for years – was unsettling him. And things it seemed were simply
going from bad to worse – even before the threatened floods arrived.
There had been desperate fights over the last of the oil in Dangang,
and the harbourmaster in Jianbi had been left for dead when he had
tried to stop a frightened mob from forcing its way aboard the last
vessel let out of the port with a full load of fuel.

Richard shrewdly suspected there would be more problems like that
one when the panic aboard the fleeing vessels began to spread into
the low-lying riverside cities in the path of the threatened flood. To
make matters worse, the military and the militia were being moved
away from the river itself and up into the launch-areas for the rescue
missions into the dark area beyond Nanjing. Leaving room for a certain
amount of lawlessness behind, and a great deal of mounting terror.
Compounding the difficulty by being granted first call on what transport, power and supplies there were available. Like fuel-oil, transport
and batteries were at a premium.

And everything likely to drain the power from the local systems needed
to be switched off unless it was vital. Which didn't make much difference for most TVs and radios because there were so few broadcasts
coming through. But it did make a difference when harbourmasters needed
help and ships' captains needed guidance. When street lighting dimmed,
releasing a deepening flood of shadows guaranteed to compound terrors
and cover lawlessness.

God alone knew what they might find when they reached Nanjing.
Steady Xin guided *Poseidon* out of the mouth of the rule-straight

channel and into the protected water of the port, twenty careful minutes after swinging on to 120 degrees at the pilot's quiet command. Straightline took a deep, shuddering breath as the radar read a depth of 4.5 metres beneath the keel. The corvette's big searchlights cut through the gloom across the little bay to the range of piers and facilities jutting out from its inner side. 'Go to the middle one,' directed the pilot, 'but use the deeper water to reverse your course and back her into position against the pier.'

A manoeuvre made possible – easy, in fact – by the array of CCTV video cameras and laser positioning equipment aboard, thought Richard. As he began to obey, Straightline flicked a series of switches and suddenly the monitors above the clearview gave a perfect view of what was happening behind the ship – with rolling figures in the lower right-hand corners detailing measurements, running through safe green to warning red.

'You should be fine going straight out on the reciprocal,' added Captain Chang quietly over the stirring bustle. 'But the harbour is shallow outside the main channel and we'd better use the added manoeuvrability that will be lost to us when we have full tanks and sit the better part of half a metre deeper in the water. Even so,' she added, unconsciously prophetic, 'watch the gang.' She gestured to the radar display. A tongue of mud stretched out into a series of shallows that seemed to reach almost to the middle of the harbour. On Straightline's charts, the feature was labelled *Zhenjiang Gang*.

'And,' whispered Richard to Robin, certain that no one could overhear him, 'if he avoids the gang and gets well in, then we're in position for a swift getaway if it's needed.'

'Why would we need a swift getaway?' whispered Robin in return.

'Independently of the adventures of the night so far you mean? Leaving aside the fact that we look like the last hope to a lot of desperate people? Forgetting entirely that we have how many million dollars' worth of gold down in our main hold? Leaving all that aside, I'd still say it'd be good insurance, simply judging by the look of things on the dock we're just about to reverse alongside. Seems like there's a *gang* there of quite another sort . . .' He gestured at the all-too-clear picture on the monitor showing the dock that now lay beneath *Poseidon*'s left side.

'Stop engines. Stay clear!' ordered Captain Chang, bringing her command to a dead stop well clear of the dockside wall.

She too had seen the video picture showing a sizeable mob on the pier thrusting dangerously up against the wire security barrier around the bunkerage area. Under the bright beam of *Poseidon*'s searchlights they looked pale-faced, wild-eyed, desperate. On the video screen, robbed of colour by the flat light, they looked like an army of zombies from one of their children's video games.

'Looks like a bit of a stand-off,' said Robin grimly. 'If we get close enough to bring any fuel aboard, we'll probably get that lot into the bargain!'

'Yup, looks like it to me too,' said Richard thoughtfully. 'But if *that lot* as you put it – or most of them anyway – are really only interested in getting away from the flood, then they've chosen the wrong ship, haven't they? Let's just see . . .' And he strode purposely over to the Changs who were standing side by side, deep in a worried conversation.

As much to ease the tension she was feeling as for any other reason, Robin crossed to stand between Straightline and Steady. The navigator's English was far better than her Mandarin; but the helmsman's understanding was far more acute than she suspected. 'What do you think?' she asked the navigating officer. 'Are they just trying to get away – or are they trying to come aboard and pirate Genghis Khan?'

'I think these are frightened people,' answered Straightline stiffly. 'It is not known how news of the golden statue leaked out of the ship but I am certain even such a rumour could never have spread this far . . .'

'It'll be common knowledge wherever there's a Green Gang foot soldier, I'd say,' observed Robin grimly.

'The Green Gang, if such an organization actually exists beyond legend and fairy-tale,' snapped Straightline at his most austere, 'was associated entirely with the history of Shanghai!'

'Modern times bring modern approaches,' observed Robin easily, unwilling to give ground. 'Daniel Huuk said it was the Green Gang who tried to kill him in Shanghai – so they've come out of the history books for a start. And I reckon it was them that tried to finish the job last night. And that they hoped to pirate away young Genghis down below. And that attack happened well outside Shanghai.'

She dropped her voice and leaned forward, glancing across the bridge as she hissed, 'Furthermore, we know River Pilot Chang was a member, though he seems to have resigned. So they're out of the history books *and* out of the city. That means, as far as I'm concerned, that they could turn up anywhere, anytime.'

Straightline huffed, and turned away, fighting to preserve *face* as the truth of her words struck home.

Steady Xin looked straight forward, feigning ignorance of the English words, thanking every god and ancestor he could call to mind that this insightful demon woman had not yet discovered his own relationship with the terrible ever-present Green Gang.

'Either way, Green Gang or not, that mob looks pretty dangerous to me,' said Robin, raising her voice once more. 'Maybe we'd better break out the ship's armaments once again . . .'

But her grim suggestion was overtaken by events. 'People of Zhenjiang,' boomed an immense voice, echoing across the harbour. It was speaking Mandarin, but Straightline obliged Robin with a whispered translation.

'People of Zhenjiang,' repeated the voice of River Pilot Chang, roaring through the ship's loudhailer at full volume. 'It is impressive to see such selfless bravery in the face of such mortal danger. I cannot guess how you learned our poor ship is bound upriver on a suicide mission to try and relieve the desperate citizens of Nanjing as the terrible floods threaten to annihilate them, but only in a brave town like Zhenjiang, only in a noble province such as Jiangsu would we find so many men and comrades willing to face death to help protect their capital city. We will have to rename the province. No longer The Land of Fish and Rice, but The Land of Fish, Rice and Brave Hearts . . .'

A lone, thin voice, which must have sounded truly Stentorian on the dock, called in utter disbelief, 'You're heading *up*river?'

'Upriver to Nanjing, to face the floods with our comrades there, if floods there are . . .' boomed the river pilot in reply. 'You have my word as Senior River Pilot. Now who will be first to come aboard with us . . .?'

But his question echoed over an abruptly empty dock. The mob had simply evaporated.

'Reverse right in, tie up and get the oil aboard as fast as you can,' ordered the pilot, lifting his broad thumb off the BROADCAST button and lowering the loudhailer microphone. 'I would suggest an armed guard on the dockside by the security fence and at either end of the gangplank. It won't be long before it occurs to someone out there that just because *we* want to go upriver, that's no reason why *they* shouldn't take the ship and sail her wherever they want to go.'

'Over my dead body,' snarled the Captain.

'I suspect they'd be happy with that bargain, child. Take the greatest possible care,' said her father fondly.

Of course, he was wasting his words.

Captain Chang led from the front with no apparent sense of the danger she might be putting herself in. And her father had the wisdom – though achieved at some cost, thought Robin, to stand back and let her get on with it in her own way. The only concession she made to security – to the security of her command rather than of her person – was to make sure everyone dockside was carrying a two-way radio. And she deployed Paradeground Ping and the crack marines that Daniel had sent aboard from *Luyang*, together with the authority of the Deputy Commissioner and the power of the Dragon Head.

As Robin and the river pilot watched her, Captain Chang sent four of Ping's men down to the wire security fence, then she and Straightline, who doubled as lading officer as well as navigator, went down to talk to the harassed, frightened-looking harbourmaster. As she crossed the deck, four men followed her and her lading officer. Two armed guards took up their positions at the head of the gangplank as soon as she stepped on to it. Then, as she descended her gangplank, two more guards followed and took up their positions at the foot of it on the dockside, with all the precision of crack special forces. Paradeground Ping stood at attention on the deck, overseeing the whole operation.

In the shadows behind the bright gold beams of the ship's searchlights, Richard took up position on the after deck, just at the spot where Robin had stood watching him prepare to take his leave of Daniel Huuk. He carried, resting in the crook of his arm with apparently casual familiarity, the long lean Simonov sniper rifle that he had zeroed so carefully the previous afternoon. And used against the pirates that same evening.

Standing in the darkest spot, with his shoulder against the corner of the bridge house for steadiness, Richard brought the rifle to his shoulder, leaned his bandaged but still sensitive cheek against the cool stock and settled the icy monocle ring of the scope against his eye. He had no intention of firing – certainly not with his shoulder trapped between the stock and the corner, all too liable to be broken by the gun's considerable kick. He just wanted to survey the scene through the scope's enhanced magnification and light-enhancing sniper-system.

At first, Richard found it a little disturbing to be pointing the sniper scope at the top of Captain Chang's perfectly straight cap. Against the pale circle of it – made oval by distance and angle, made bright and greenish by the light enhancement – the markings of the scope were all too clear and the pip of the sight at the far end of the barrel seemed to linger on the target, as though regretful to be missing such an easy shot. But once he had established where the Captain was – deep in conversation with the harbourmaster beside the great pipes that would soon be attached to *Poseidon* and pumping the oil aboard, it was easy to move away, past the guards at the fence, to quarter the darkness where the angry mob had gathered. And it did seem to Richard that there was some movement there. Erratic, unpredictable, apparently random. Too vague to be defined even when the light enhancement was thumbed up to full power.

But movement nevertheless.

The bustle on the deck below intensified and Richard didn't need to look away from the scope to know that the Chief Engineer and his oilers had been called to bring the pipes aboard and attach them to the fuel inlets. Abruptly, Straightline marched across his field of vision, returning aboard to take charge of the lading process. Not long now. Maybe three-quarters of an hour. It depended what pressure the shore-pumps could produce – 500 cubic metres per hour was pretty standard now, and *Poseidon* probably only needed 300 metric tonnes to top up her 500-tonne tanks. The Captain, he noted, stayed on the front line with the men in her command who were most at risk.

Without thinking, he lowered the Simonov, stood it against the corner and crossed to the far side of the little platform, where he could look eastwards once again. But the sky downriver was dark again. Maybe he had imagined that glow he mistook for dawn. Maybe it had been some other glimmer of brightness. Maybe there was thick cloud moving in across the sky above the South China Sea. Whatever. The promise of dawn was gone for the moment.

Without thinking, Richard took a deep breath in through his nose, perhaps hoping to scent the dawn wind. But all he could smell was a stomach-clenching amalgam of oil, effluent, rancid mudflats and rotting fish. He turned away with a gasp of disgust. Hesitated. Turned back again, holding his breath. Not against the stench, but in order to hear better. For there was a stirring in the water beside the ship.

Sufficiently furtive to arouse his suspicions at once. Close enough to *Poseidon* to appear threatening. Near enough to silence to appear sinister.

Five strides took Richard to the Simonov. Five strides took him back again with the stock hard to his shoulder and cold against his cheek as he frowned down the scope, swinging the enhanced sniper vision across the water of the anchorage. Right at the outer range of what he could see, the stern of a boat pulled away into the channel dead ahead of *Poseidon*. A boat that sat low, apparently full of men. Then there was only the oily rippling of the slimy water in the silent little vessel's wake.

ELEVEN
Barrier

I t was the better part of an hour before the corvette's tanks were full. Richard spent the whole time patrolling the upper outer reaches of *Poseidon*'s bridge house, as lean, focussed and disturbingly out of the general run of things as a hunting wolf. He carried the Simonov sometimes in the crook of his arm, sometimes slung over his shoulder, occasionally at 'slope arms' across his chest. It depended on where he was and what he was planning. One or two unfortunates disturbed him when he was fully on watch with the sniper scope pressed to his eye. They were greeted by an unexpectedly threatening sight as he swung the whole rifle round towards them, glaring down the scope.

Robin was among the first of these as she went to find out where he was and what he was up to. Inured by years of marriage, she simply shook her head, tutted, and went her way, muttering about boys' toys and James Bond fixations. But Richard stayed doggedly on guard, some atavistic part of him sensing impending danger. However, the channel remained quiet, and the east – like the more immediate vicinity – remained dark and vaguely threatening.

The mob from Zhenjiang returned just as the fuel lines were being disengaged, as though summoned by some secret signal. They did not appear to be armed. Even through the sniper scope, Richard only saw the occasional flash of teeth and eyes – nothing obvious that might signal guns, knives or choppers. The guards at the foot of the gangway doubled over to join their colleagues at the barrier and Captain Chang broke away from the harbourmaster to join her men at once. Seven well-armed marines seemed enough to give the mob some second thoughts for the time being, thought Richard grimly. Though what would happen when the little shore patrol tried to get back aboard, heaven knew. He flipped the safety off the Simonov and wished it had an automatic fire function instead of the sniper's single shot.

But even as Richard made his mental wish, he heard Paradeground Ping giving quiet orders from the deck below, and when he looked down he saw that there was a considerable little command drawn up ready to give covering fire across the pier if need be. I hope we're well supplied with ammunition, he thought. They had used a good deal already tonight, and if that was anything to go by they might well be needing more before the day was out.

'You need to fall back to the gangplank now, in a line, remaining on guard,' River Pilot was saying into his walkie-talkie to his daughter, clearly taking orders from the marine Lieutenant at his side. 'I haven't been able to raise any authorities in Zhenjiang; no militia, nothing. But we have you covered from the deck.'

'We're on our way,' came the crackling reply through the Pilot's two-way. 'If you have to open fire, aim above their heads until I say different. Harbourmaster . . .' But what she said to the harbourmaster was cut off as she raised her thumb from the BROADCAST button.

Richard swung the Simonov up. He had heard the order, but if he opened fire, he would be doing so only if things became genuinely life-threatening; kill or be killed. And if it came to that point, he would be choosing his targets carefully. And he would not be firing above their heads.

The harbourmaster's team pulled the fuel hoses ashore as the Chief's team passed them carefully overboard. Chang and her men began to walk smoothly backwards across the flagstones that topped the facility, rifles at the ready. Chang herself held what looked like a powerful little Norinco 9mm handgun. Leant to her, no doubt, by Ping – certainly, Richard hadn't seen it before the marines came aboard. And he had seen a good deal of the ship's weaponry in one way or another. And, by the look of things, the handgun matched the semi-automatics Ping's men held. The Captain and her men handled them with the confidence of practised familiarity. Whether the men beyond the wire fence realized how much firepower was ranged against them or not, the sight of the seven unwavering gun-barrels made them pause, for the moment at least.

For one moment.

Then someone at the back of the desperate crowd shouted and the whole lot of them surged forward. Those at the front – many of them cowering in expectation of getting shot – crashed into the barrier. The wire fence yielded easily – it had clearly been erected for form's sake rather than as a serious defence work. Those in front stumbled over it and many of them went sprawling. The next in line hesitated, trying to avoid trampling their friends and neighbours, but once again the loud group in the rear yelled and charged. The mob came forward once more, moving almost entirely out of the shadows into the dim security lighting. Richard was raking the rearmost ranks with the Simonov's scope. The front of the mob came under *Poseidon*'s searchlights now and hesitated for the third time as though the beams of brightness were dangerous in themselves.

Richard saw a little phalanx of a dozen or so right in the rear shouting and shoving ruthlessly. The hesitation was over. The mob stumbled forward, their momentum picking up.

Captain Chang and her men were halfway to the gangplank, falling back on a rigid line, the men with their semi-automatics at their shoulders, the Captain with her handgun steady and rigid, level with her command's weapons. 'Fire!' she ordered. The guns spat in unison, one crisp shot, causing the front row to cringe again. But the back ranks, made brave by the wall of bodies in front of them, pushed forward ruthlessly. At the second shot, they didn't even cringe.

'Fire,' commanded the Pilot.

'Aim high,' commanded Ping as an instant echo. A rather larger explosion of automatic fire rang across the anchorage as his command consisted of a dozen. Still the mob did not hesitate. As even those in the front realized that no one had actually been hit by any of the shots so far, their courage returned and they broke into a run.

Richard glanced away from the sniper scope and caught an instantaneous vision of the desperation on Captain Chang's face. She and her men were falling back at the double now. And they needed to, for that dangerous little group at the rear were screaming, pushing and shoving relentlessly. The whole mob was charging full-tilt towards the gangplank.

Richard chose one of them at random, zeroed in on a fist upraised and shaking with anger. His thumb flicked off the safety, taking his time but breathing slowly and evenly – even as he felt the thudding of the shore-party's feet on the gangplank at last. He was thinking, let's see how brave you are with a bullet through your hand . . . And, to be fair, taking very great care to ensure that he was only going to shoot the upraised fist, not the heads that kept bobbing up in front of it or behind it.

He closed his left eye. Concentrating so hard that the roaring of the mob, the pounding of the footsteps on the gangplank, the last fusillade of shots and the shouted orders faded away into the background, as his finger smoothly tightened on the cool curve of the trigger. He held his breath.

But he never took the shot.

Poseidon lurched into motion.

Richard tore the scope out of his eye hard enough to graze the underside of his eyebrow and looked down. The fuel pipes were blessedly clear. The shorelines were unravelling. The gangplank was at a crazy angle, dragging along the top of the dock. One of the guards was there at the head of it, shouting something Richard couldn't quite make out and gesturing. The shore party were all aboard. All except one.

Captain Chang was halfway along the dragging plank, holding on grimly with her left hand while her right fist held her pistol unwaveringly in the face of the first of the mob – who was also on the gangplank, a matter of inches away from her. The rest of them were streaming along the dockside shouting in anger and frustration. It was a situation that could not last long. The lashings holding the head of the gangplank on *Poseidon*'s deck were unravelling almost as swiftly as the shorelines.

The pilot arrived there and began trying to secure the writhing ropes, shouting to his daughter as he looked ahead along the vanishing dockside towards the sheer drop that would pitch the plank and the bodies on it into the waters of the anchorage. 'Shoot!' the desperate father yelled to his daughter. 'Shoot him and come aboard!'

But then there were two other figures beside the desperate father; Ping and one of his marines. Then, with an all too familiar sense of inevitability, Richard recognized Robin's bright curls as she too swung in beside Pilot Chang and helped him hold the ropes in place for those few vital seconds longer. While a square, strong, solid shape leaped past them on to the ridged plank. With no ceremony at all he slipped his right hand round his captain's trim waist. Then using her moment of rigid outrage as a firm platform, he reached in over her right shoulder with an arm a good few inches longer than hers. And where her fist held a gun, his considerably larger fist did not. It hit the importunate boarder square between the eyes, flattening the bridge of his nose and splitting his forehead open. Then he was whirling his captain back aboard, even as the man went sprawling on the last of the pier head and the gangplank fell away into the stinking black foulness of the anchorage.

'Steady!' shouted the outraged woman as he stood her up safely on the deck of her command, between the still figure of her father and the rigid outline of the marine. She caught her breath, straightened her uniform; took due account of the fact that her men were all cheering. 'Thank you,' she said breathlessly. 'Thank you, Lieutenant Ping. Thank you, Steady.' There was a tiny pause, then she shouted, 'Steady . . . Who is *steering my ship*?'

It was Straightline, as Richard discovered when he arrived on the command bridge at the same moment as everyone else. With the engines set to the top of the green and the heading reading 300 – the exact reciprocal of the 120 degrees that had brought them in here – the navigating officer was taking them directly along the straight line that would get them out.

Steady relieved him at once and Straightline was apparently relieved to return to his charts, radar and depth-sounders. And he needed to keep an eye on them, thought Richard. As the Captain had predicted, *Poseidon* with full tanks sat a good solid metre deeper in the water than she had done when she ran in here almost empty. There was still clearance, but, as with the banks thrusting in from the flats on either side, everything ahead of them needed careful watching. Particularly as they seemed to be leaving Zhenjiang at the kinds of speed he associated with his Cigarette speedboat *Marilyn*.

Captain Chang and her father fell into their accustomed positions on the bridge. Richard left the Simonov down by the door jamb, out of everyone's way, then he and Robin wandered forward to stand side by side in the clear space to Steady's left. The dim brightness in the eastern sky downriver had returned, Richard noted. It was bright enough to define the edges of what looked like a stormy overcast. But for a clear view forward along the channel, *Poseidon* was still relying on her searchlights. Straightline was fixated on his instruments and even Steady seemed to be focussed on the 300 degree compass reading. The Captain and the pilot were deep in conversation – careful father berating foolhardy daughter.

So it was Richard who first saw the danger.

'They've blocked the channel!' he snapped in English. Only Robin looked up. 'Obstruction dead ahead!' he called in Mandarin. 'Steady! Reverse all. Can you stop us in time?'

'No,' answered the Captain, running forward to Richard's shoulder. 'He can't. What is the obstruction? What damage will it do?'

'Looks like nets and boats. Fish traps maybe,' answered Richard. 'It's hard to say. The rowing boats might dent the hull. But the nets might well foul the propellers. I'd say that's what they're hoping for.'

Captain Chang hesitated. The way came off the corvette. Everyone on the bridge looked forward along the line of the searchlight beam towards the wall of boats and netting that had been thrown across the channel. A gang of men stood on the mud of the flats waiting for the opportunity to board as the vessel inevitably hesitated, either by coming to a stop or foundering after breaking through the barrier, with the propellers fouled and temporarily powerless.

This explained a lot of things, thought Richard grimly. What the almost silent stirring by the ship's side had been. It had been this lot sneaking down here to lay their trap. What had motivated that little phalanx behind the larger mob. They had been keen to keep Chang's command focussed on what lay behind – not what lay ahead. Why no one on the Zhenjiang dockside had any weapons. This lot had them all.

'We've no choice,' decided the Captain. 'Drive on. Full ahead.'

TWELVE
Wave

No sooner did Captain Chang rap out her order than the bridge filled with the deafening sound of an alarm.

'Captain,' called Straightline. 'The collision alarm . . .' and it began to sound even more stridently even as he spoke, echoing through the entire vessel with its urgent warning.

'Override it,' snapped the Captain.

'Yes, Captain. But I can only switch it off temporarily. It will sound again immediately before collision. There is nothing I can do—'

'Do what you can!'

The sound died. The relative silence simply emphasized the pounding of the engines as *Poseidon* did her best to emulate a racehorse at the 'off'.

As soon as the men on the flats saw the corvette beginning to gather way again, they played their final ace. The makeshift barrier burst into flames.

'Full ahead!' snapped Captain Chang again. 'Stay on three hundred! *Steady!*'

Richard turned and ran to the door. He grabbed the Simonov which he had left standing there earlier. Ten strides took him back to the bridge-wing door. 'Richard!' gasped Robin. 'What on earth . . .'

But he was out on the starboard bridge-wing, the fetid stench of the night like a soiled shadowy shroud around him, the scope to his eye, zeroing in on the suddenly brightly illuminated group. He looked straight ahead along the sleek length of *Marilyn* as she lay on the fore-deck beside *Neptune*. There were more men than he could easily count – certainly more than twenty. Almost all of them had guns but they were waving the weapons in the air. No one seemed to be getting ready to shoot. Leaving the safety on, therefore, he swung the scope to his left, leaning forward with the safety rail snugly across his hips. For an instant the fire was a greenish dazzle in the light-enhancing scope. Then he was looking past the bulk of the deep-sea exploration vessel at the other side of the little creek. There were more men here, but these seemed to be a slightly different kettle of fish. They were organized. They had boats pulled up on to the muddy flat in front of them.

They were, if anything, better armed than their companions on the other side of the creek. Their weapons were pointing purposefully towards *Poseidon*. Richard flicked the safety off.

Robin arrived beside him. 'Richard,' she repeated. 'What—'

The first bullet ricocheted off *Neptune*'s yellow carapace immediately in front of them and screamed away into the night.

'Bloody—' swore Robin. There was probably another word as well, possibly more than one, but she stepped smartly back into the bridge house and closed the door, so Richard didn't hear anything else she said.

'Here we go again,' whispered Richard to himself, drawing a bead on the muzzle flash.

But once again he did not take the shot. Instead, something on the broad, shadowy riverscape behind the target caught his attention. He lifted the scope, refocussing on whatever had suddenly caught his eye upriver. It looked for all the world like a wide line of paleness, something like a fogbank surprisingly close behind the attackers. Close and getting closer by the nanosecond. 'Hell's teeth,' he swore.

He ground the end of the scope into his eye socket as he tried to get his head round what he was seeing. But it was so different from anything he had experienced – so unlike anything he had expected or even envisioned, that he found it almost impossible to comprehend.

For that one vital second at any rate.

Another shot ricocheted off *Neptune* and screamed away, its fading whine emphasizing the growing rumble that was just beginning to separate itself from the gusty roaring of the fire dead ahead. As though an avalanche were approaching from a great distance.

'Hell's teeth,' he said again. Then he jerked the Simonov up and whirled on to the bridge. 'Chang!' he spat, happy that the one word grabbed the attention of both captain and pilot. 'Look upriver. Can you see that?'

The two Changs did as he suggested, and gasped with shock. But their horror at what Richard was showing them had to take its place in the order of crises they were facing. A fusillade of bullets rattled against the metal of the bridge house and only a near-miracle preserved the glass of the side windows, doors and clearviews. Straightline's collision alarm began shrieking, beyond his ability to override it.

'BRACE! BRACE!' boomed the pilot's voice over the loudhailer, though the collision alarm seemed to be sounding right throughout the vessel – so everyone had some sort of a warning in any case, thought Richard. He slipped an arm round Robin and braced the pair of them against the port-side bridge-wing door. Everyone else was looking ahead, focussed on the burning barrier they were just about to ram. Richard was looking upriver, two steps and more ahead, trying to calculate what they would do when they broke through into the main channel and faced the monster wave rushing wildly down it.

Timing would be crucial, of course, Richard calculated grimly. They would have to turn upstream – or down – and meet it with either bow or stern. If it hit them side-on it would simply roll them over by the look of things. But its speed, its height and the steepness of its leading edge were impossible to calculate with any accuracy. Its simple width beggared belief, despite the fact that he could only see the southward sweep of it washing over the mudbanks on the nearside of the main stream.

Richard wished he could risk using the sniper scope in here – or had thought to grab the binoculars. But in the absence of enhanced vision, he simply shut his eyes.

In his mind, Richard's photographic memory presented him with an almost perfect reproduction of the chart for this stretch of the river. He visualized in the second before the impact, the Admiralty's diagrams of the river – translating them into best-guess estimates of what they would face. Both banks of the Yangtze were low and flat here. The river upstream divided into two channels, flowing round an island that was little more than a mudbank. Then they met again a little way upstream from the opening to the channel *Poseidon* was trying to break out of. The main flow followed the lower channel in a meander south of the island. This was the Yizheng Reach. To the north of the island, there was a shorter, straighter channel, the Yizhengjie Reach. And that meant . . .

Poseidon hit the barrier then. 'Stop all!' ordered Captain Chang as the bows bit into the blazing wall of boats and nets. As Richard had advised, she was protecting her propellers from any tangles of cordage that might wrap around the spinning shafts. But she had two advantages that the pirates were probably unaware of. The propellers themselves did not have conventional blades like a fan or a turboprop aircraft. *Poseidon*'s propulsion units ended in conical corkscrews with continuous blades. And those blades, so much more efficient than old-fashioned configurations, were protected by cages of steel.

Poseidon rode up over the blazing barricade, pushed forward at the better part of thirty knots by her simple momentum. Everyone aboard staggered as the impact slowed her forward motion and made her seesaw up and down as her head jumped out of the water and then crashed back again as though she were riding over a big sea. The barrier broke apart, swamped and smothered by the waves the corvette's long hull caused with all this violent motion.

Then she was through.

'Full ahead!' ordered the Captain, her voice hoarse. 'Take your time, Steady! It looks as though we have a moment of breathing space before the wave in the main channel comes down on us.'

'Captain!' called Richard. 'You have no time! Come left. You must turn upriver at once!'

All eyes on the bridge turned on to him at once and it was perhaps just as well that only Robin could see that his own eyes were still tightly closed. But like some blind prophet in legend, he could see more than all the rest of them.

And he was right.

For the wave – or the part of it that they could see most clearly – was coming at them down the main channel, round the lengthy southward meander. On the far side of the low island, a mudbank just high enough to hide it from them, the leading edge of the wall of water was coming much more swiftly down the canal-straight to the north.

And, even as *Poseidon* swung a little wildly into the main channel, powering up to full speed and swinging due west once more, the wave exploded out of the northern channel and was down on them at once.

Nothing more than simple chance dictated that *Poseidon* was in the ideal position to face the unexpected onslaught. She had not completed her turn, was still facing roughly north-west. The rogue wave exploded out of the northern channel and spread south across the still calm river as it rushed on eastwards, racing its slower sibling towards the distant dawn. *Poseidon* buried her nose in it, but her original designers had fashioned her to be a deep-sea fighting vessel before she had been adapted to carry a deep-sea exploration vessel. Her foredeck had a low steel wall a couple of metres back from her needle-pointed forecastle head. It was as sharp as her cutwater and was designed to shrug off just such seas as the river was now trying to imitate. Up she came, therefore, shrugging off tons of filthy, foaming surf. *Neptune* sat steadily in her cradle, as though secure in the knowledge that this was not quite as powerful as the typhoon that had so nearly destroyed her only a few days earlier. And even *Marilyn*, having slipped overboard once already, seemed content to stay with them.

The power of that first onslaught knocked *Poseidon*'s head left, bringing her round on to the course that Captain Chang had been calling for. Just in time to meet the second, slower, section of the wave. Once again the sturdy vessel dug in her nose then heaved herself up, shook herself off and settled to work, pushing herself back upstream towards distant Nanjing. But the combination of the waves had pushed her back downstream for the better part of half a mile into the heart of the Jiaoushan reach.

Richard at last opened his eyes to look out of the port side windows, through the filth of the streaming foam. The little channel they had followed up to Zhenjiang was gone. The mudflats it had cut through were gone. The whole out-thrust of shoreline with its channels, fish-traps, its barrier and its desperate pirates was gone. From the look of things, the piers and dockside of Zhenjiang harbour were gone. The island that had cut the wave in two was little more than a hump some-where to starboard. No longer anything more than an islet on the huge expanse of the flooded river, which seemed to stretch from horizon to horizon ahead of them.

As if to emphasize the desolation, the sun broke through the eastern clouds into a full dawn-brightness. Great beams of golden light sped past the heaving corvette and pierced the darkness ahead of her, revealing a restless, watery wilderness, marked with whorls and wavelets as the outward surge of the resurgent river set up new currents, eddies, rips and undertows. Revealing a devastation of flotsam, jetsam, wreckage and ruin.

As though in a daze, Richard opened the door and stepped out on to the bridge-wing. He stood there, silent, simply shocked by the speed and totality of the devastation he had just experienced – was still witnessing. There was a stirring at his shoulder. It was River Pilot Chang.

'I think we'll have to redraw the charts,' said Chang quietly.

'Not yet you won't,' said Richard.

'Why?'

'Because, if what we've been warned about is right, then that was just a taste of what is still to come. There's another wave three times the size of that one on its way downriver towards us.'

The pilot shook his head. The movement took his gaze across to the brown waves washing over the docks at Zhenjiang, seeming to be flowing relentlessly further and further into the distant city itself.

'Maybe we should go back in there,' he said, uncharacteristically uncertain. 'They'll need help in Zhenjiang now.'

But even as he spoke, a big square of hoarding was swept along *Poseidon*'s side, and swirled lazily beneath the bridge-wing where they were standing. There was a battered Chinese character written on it and part of an English word. Richard had no idea what the character signified, but the English letters said *NANJI* . . .

'We'll warn Daniel about what's happened,' he said. 'Let him take care of the damage down here where he can get things organized fast and on a large scale. We have orders. And a mission up beyond the places he can reach so easily.'

The pilot nodded, and, side by side, they went back into the bridge.

As *Poseidon* powered upriver, with the full force of the dawn striking in from astern of her, two lines that had become attached to her aft rail tightened, jerking as though great fish were caught on them. And, wearily, hand over hand, two of the pirates who had been standing by the blazing barrier began to pull themselves aboard, each of them, just as pirates should be, armed to the teeth.

PART TWO
YANGTZE

THIRTEEN
Luyang

'Why do you place such faith in this gweilo giant and his golden-haired demon of a wife?' asked Tan respectfully. In spite of the fact that he was back on the bridge of his ship, the *Luyang* destroyer, he was speaking not as the lieutenant commander but as a lowly member of the Invisible Power Triad. He was speaking in little more than a whisper to the man who was effectively Dragon Head of his secret order behind the back of his commanding officer, Commodore Shan, who was snoozing in the watchkeeper's chair. Despite his courtesy and professional conduct towards them, he did not trust the westerners himself. He certainly did not share the general feeling of the crew aboard *Poseidon* (though he thought of the ship in her original Chinese name *Yu-quiang*) that the western giant brought good luck. Nor was he in any way enamoured of the tall, slim, golden-haired woman, with her chest that was too large and her eyes which were too round. The western couple seemed shockingly out of place to him. Interlopers into the ancient military and social systems of the Middle Kingdom. Not even their attempts to speak Cantonese and Mandarin, or their clumsy attempts to behave with courtesy and preserve *face*, came anywhere near to impressing him.

Daniel Huuk turned towards Tan, his outline framed against the promise of a stormy dawn, for the destroyer was sailing along that section of the Huangpu that effectively faces east. She was bound for Shanghai, where Daniel had every intention of using the vessel's bridge as his command centre as he assumed overall charge of crisis management for the whole of the area from Shanghai to Nanjing, as far north as Huayin, as far south as Wenzhou if need be. His responsibilities, actions and precise area of command were likely to be dictated by whatever was coming down the Yangtze, as much as by decisions made in Beijing or marks on maps and charts.

Daniel frowned now, aware of Tan's concerns about the Mariners – well able to understand them – and gave some thought as to how best to meet them. For his relationship with both of them, with Robin most of all, was far too complex to be explained – even to be considered for the moment.

'As with so much in the Middle Kingdom,' he answered Tan. 'It is because of history. In this case, the history I share with Captain Mariner and his wife. One day I will tell you some part of our long and complex story. But not today.'

Huuk turned away and looked out across the Huangpu, towards the buildings of the Caozhen district on the Pudong shore and the cloudy east beyond. Shadows came and went across his face as the thick black clouds moved across the gathering promise of the rising sun. He strove to order his mental priorities. What new crisis should he prepare for next?

However, Tan's question tricked off a series of thoughts, memories and desires in Daniel Huuk's mind that were an unwelcome distraction in the face of the current situation. Robin Mariner rose in his imagination, gold hair gleaming, grey eyes beckoning. How long had he desired her? He could hardly tell any longer. Since he had first seen her back in Hong Kong. While her husband had still been in hospital, his memory wiped blank by the fact that Daniel himself had shot him in the head – albeit with an anti-personnel round. In the days when he had still been an officer in the Hong Kong Coastguard, and Richard, standing accused of a mass murder he had no memory of witnessing – let alone committing – was facing execution.

In days long past. Long before he had become a member of the Invisible Power Triad. Before he had risen to eminence in the People's Republic.

Five, maybe six mistresses ago. Mistresses whose faces, bodies, names, had faded into nothingness beside his ever-present, never satisfied, simple lust for her.

With an effort of will that cost him his good humour, if nothing else, Daniel forced himself back to the matters in hand. With the coming of dawn, the true scale of the devastation was beginning to become clear to the old men in Beijing and, via them, to everyone else. But dawn was coming out of the Eastern Sea and over Shanghai first. For a little while yet, the sun would shine on Daniel, and Daniel alone of the Politburo Standing Committee. What should he do with those extra moments he had in hand before the great orb swung up out of Bo Hai Bay and lit up Tiannenman Square?

The Special Forces units in their helicopters had been particularly effective in penetrating the heart of silence and darkness a thousand miles west, which had persisted for the better part of twelve hours now. Their reports told of colossal devastation – and yet none of them had got nearer than a couple of hundred miles from the epicentre. An epicentre that had certainly been the subject not only of the worst earthquake in recorded history, but one of the greatest floods ever to be visited on the vast Yangtze valley.

Daniel knew that for certain, because one of the Flying Dragon helicopters had reached Yichang and confirmed that the Three Gorges Dam was down and the entire city was underwater. Lost beneath a flood that was still, twelve hours after the breach, as near as they could calculate, pouring out over the dam. Though admittedly with less force now. And, with matters becoming clearer, the committee in Beijing also had a clearer idea of what they needed to do.

Daniel turned once again and froze. Just for a fleeting instant he thought he caught sight of Robin Mariner's reflection as though she were standing like a ghost just behind him. The first sunbeam of dawn was striking in through the great warship's clearview and reflecting off the gold braid that decorated the snoozing Commodore Shan's uniform. But the combination of sparkling gold, light and shadow brought her back to him, as he had seen her once, naked and restlessly asleep, covered by the merest wisp of silken sheet.

'Commodore Shan,' he spat, his voice unaccustomedly rough and hoarse. 'How far can we get upriver before the bridges block the *Luyang*'s passage?'

Commodore Shan woke up with a start, looked around in momentary confusion, then rose and drew himself up to full height. He was not used to being addressed in such tones, even by a passenger of such elevated status as this.

Tan stepped smoothly back into his Lieutenant Commander role. The junior Triad member took a back seat to the senior navigating officer. 'If I may answer, Commodore. It is my belief, Deputy General Commissioner, that we should be able to reach the Shanghai Shipyard at Gaoxiong Road. That is very near the heart of the city. As you are aware, we have come beneath several bridges with extremely high spans, and I believe that both the Neihuan elevated roadway and the bridge joining the Westin Bund Centre to the Super Brand Mall on Pudong will also allow us to pass quite easily, as will the two-tier road and rail bridge between Shanghai Tan gardens and Yangjaiwan.

'I am not so certain that the Lupu bridge above or the Dapu road tunnel below will allow sufficient clearance to proceed further upriver than that.'

'Very well,' decided Daniel. 'We will go as far upriver as the shipyard. If that is acceptable to Commodore Shan?'

'I am at your service along with my command, Deputy General Commissioner. It is at times such as these—' The Commodore's attempt to save face was interrupted by the communications officer, who came out of the radio room clearly big with news and spoke without taking due notice of what was going on.

'Message for the Deputy General Commissioner, sir,' he said. '*Poseidon* is on the ship-to-ship. It's important, they say.'

Daniel would have come at once without the added information. Only people actually on the ground, or as close to it as they could get, were communicating via the radio.

Daniel took the speaker and headphones from the radio officer. He was too much of a politician not to be extremely careful about letting information leak out before he had planned how he was going to deal with it. 'Deputy Commissioner Huuk . . .' he began, expecting to be communicating with Captain Chang or her radio operator.

But no: 'Daniel?' came the voice he least expected and found most distracting.

'Yes, Robin?'

'We're just past Zhenjiang, sailing up the Yizhengjie Shuidao . . .'

Daniel pressed the mute button on the microphone stalk. 'Chart,' he bellowed, his voice harsh and ragged once again. 'I want to look at the Yizhengjie Shuidao.'

'But we've just been hit by an extremely serious wave. We estimate that it was at least three metres high – perhaps four – and moving in excess of fifty kph. The water level behind it has been raised by at least a metre, maybe two, and is also running at full spate. A couple of metres may not sound too much, but the valley behind the wave is really badly flooded. Zhenjiang city is in some trouble. The settlements downstream will be hit one after the other.

'Richard estimates it will be at the mouth of the Huangpu in less than two hours' time and with you pretty quickly after that. Everything at the mouth of the Yangtze will be at risk of course. But we simply cannot estimate what will happen at Shanghai or Pudong. And of course, if our calculations are correct, then there will be another wave maybe three times as high twelve hours behind this one.'

'I see,' said Daniel breathlessly. 'Thank you for the warning. You are proceeding upriver?'

'It's more like a lake than a river now, but yes.'

'Take care.'

'I think Captain Chang and her father are taking the greatest possible care. We seem to be sailing through the wreckage of a good deal of Nanjing. With more of the city washing down on us.'

'No . . .' Daniel hesitated. He had meant his advice more personally. He wanted Robin herself to take care.

But before he could articulate his feelings – or even begin to calculate how he could do so without losing his *face* as well as his heart, events overtook him.

Overtook them all.

'Hands up,' bellowed a raucous voice in heavily-accented Mandarin at the far end of the line on *Poseidon*'s bridge. 'We control the ship now. You make one move and we shoot you dead.'

And, as if to emphasize the reality of the threat, the whip crack of a gunshot rang out.

There was the faintest gasp from Robin, a thump, then the hissing of a broken connection.

FOURTEEN
Wuhan

I t was the big bridge at Wuhan that saved them. The bridge, Wuchang railway station and Nanhu Airport a couple of kilometres south of it. But most of all, perhaps, it was the thunderstorm.

As Leading Architect Chang Mei-Feng finally rearranged her clothing, adjusted her straps and settled in for the long haul, Chopper Quing dropped his helicopter's nose and plunged the game little bird due east along the raging river-course into the great ocean of the night.

Chopper was by no means certain of his route, so he was content to settle lower and lower, doing his best to keep the Yangtze in view. After a quarter of an hour, they overtook the leading edge of the flood from the dam, and the river ahead of the broad red crescent of wild destruction became strangely still, flowing apparently sleepily between the earthquake damaged banks.

The calm, as Mei-Feng observed, moving a western cliché into an eastern consideration of Fate, after the storm – but before the holocaust.

Chopper slowed and settled closer to the ground, grunting as he assessed the terrible accuracy of her assessment. But he had other concerns, of course. Not least the fact that the clouds ahead were thickening. Darkening with more than the onset of night.

'There's stormy weather ahead, no matter how you look at it,' he said, giving Mei-Feng a totally inaccurate opinion of his wit, insight and enjoyment of wordplay.

'The two greatest dangers I can see,' he explained after a little silence, as much for something to say as for any other reason, 'are getting lost and running out of fuel in some remote and desolated spot where getting down safely would be near-impossible and getting back up again out of the question.'

'Not to mention,' added Mei-Feng prophetically, looking down at the devastation below, 'the chance of getting swamped by crowds of panicking people desperate to get away . . .'

They went over Yidu, therefore at less than a hundred feet, flying at little more than a hundred kph. Even in the deepening darkness, it was possible to get a clear impression of the damage. The neat squares of the city blocks were toppled, spread in rubble across the dark, deserted streets. There was no municipal lighting or power that the architect could see. The only brightness came from the fires that seemed to be quite liberally dotted around the place, persisting in the face of a gathering downpour. The only activity, seemingly, the weary efforts of those few still trying to fight them.

'They're wasting their time,' observed Chopper grimly as he brought the helicopter over the largest of these and hovered, looking down. On the ground below, maybe twenty men were trying to contain the blaze using buckets of water. But the fire was so big – the sound of it so loud – that they didn't even realize there was a helicopter fifty feet above their heads. They just toiled on doggedly and helplessly in the face of the almost inconceivable scale of what was happening to them. Unaware that this was only the beginning.

'Those fires are going to get put out in a quarter of an hour or so in any case,' observed Chopper grimly. 'They should just leave them and head for higher ground! Should we warn them?'

'We daren't land, surely!' answered Mei-Feng. 'Have we got any kind of loudhailer?'

'No.'

'It's hopeless then. Even if we went right down and shouted to them they'd never hear us over the sound of the rotors . . .' Mei-Feng's voice was heavy with frustration and the beginnings of survivor guilt. It was all too obvious that they wouldn't actually be able to do anything to help the people they were overflying. All they could do was to land and surrender themselves in some kind of heroic self-sacrifice. Which Mei-Feng would do for her family in Nanjing or Pudong without a second thought, but not for strangers. Not here. Not now.

'There's nothing we can do, Chopper,' she said. 'Let's go.'

But even as the helicopter lifted away and swooped back towards the dull gleam of the Yangtze, which led like Ariadne's thread through the ruined maze of Hubei Province, the red wall of water came roaring into the western outskirts of the city. Mei-Feng turned away and looked east into the darkness, trying to blot out of her mind the vision of that wilderness of fires being snuffed out one after the other by the quick, broad reach of the devastating flood.

During the next hour or so, Mei-Feng dozed fitfully, deep in the grasp of clinical shock. The helicopter settled lower and lower through the intensifying sheets of rain, following the river as it became a highway of inky darkness leading sinuously through the fires that continued to mark the major settlements of Yidu and Zhijang, as they spread in one long urban sprawl into the city of Jingzhou.

Chopper hesitated once again at the heart of Jingzhou, dropping low over the massive bridge that spanned the river here. Unlike most of the buildings on either bank below them, the bridge still seemed to be standing. It was even illuminated – if faintly. The tops of its suspension towers glimmered with warning-lights; one or two of the spans seemed to be lit up too – but then Mei-Feng saw that the brightness came from the headlights of cars that had been abandoned on the roadway there. Their beams given a kind of form by the driving rain, like the blades of light-sabres in *Star Wars*.

'Why would people abandon their cars? Surely . . .' she began. But then Chopper brought their helicopter low enough for her to see the gaping cracks in the shattered road-surface, their raised edges given a glassy sheen by the wetness of the broken roadway. There were people on the bridge, sheltering from the downpour as best they could, waiting to be rescued. They were far enough away from the pandemonium in the city to hear the helicopter and they looked up, waving and shouting, their calls reduced to the pantomime of a silent movie by the thudding of the rotors and the rumble of the engine.

'Is there nothing we can do?' asked Mei-Feng once again, talking more to herself than to the taciturn pilot. 'I mean if they're still there when the flood hits . . .'

But even as she spoke, events overtook them all once more.

The first aftershock arrived. The river itself seemed to heave. There was just enough light for Mei-Feng to see great waves suddenly appearing as the river bed twisted and shook. The bridge took up the wild motion of the restless water, more cracks appearing in the bright headlight beams, chunks of masonry beginning to tumble into the foaming wilderness below.

Chopper shouted and the architect felt the seat beneath her rising like a fairground ride. She looked across at her companion, shocked. But then she saw, beyond his straining face, the lines of the suspension bridge whipping and twisting like a nest of angry snakes. She hurled herself against the window at her shoulder, looking down.

Just in time to see the weakened structure of the great bridge yielding to this new onslaught. Slowly, almost elegantly, the twisting spans tore free of their whipping suspension lines and tumbled into the river, shrugging off the cars, lorries and buses as they fell. The tall suspension towers slowly toppled until even here the river was nothing more than a broad thoroughfare of featureless darkness, leading through the brightness of the burning heartland. The helicopter settled, swung level.

Mei-Feng, still looking down in utter horror, found that she was gasping gutturally as though she had sprinted for a mile or more. That her eyes were flooding with tears.

'Oh!' she said. 'Oh . . .' but she simply could not form the words to express the magnitude of what she felt.

'The river runs south from here,' said Chopper matter-of-factly. 'That was why I stopped at the bridge. Good signpost so to speak. But we want to go east. I reckon if we fly directly east by the instruments at exactly one hundred kph then we'll reach the big bridge at Wuhan in one hundred minutes from now. And even if we miss the bridge itself, or if it's . . .' He paused. 'Even if we miss the bridge itself, we will be bound to hit the river again because it runs north again there, right across our course.'

'Even in the dark?'

'It's not dark,' he said.

'There's low overcast, thick clouds and pouring rain,' she persisted.

'And about a million fires on the ground. When we hit the next big band of blackness in the middle of all this lot, then we'll know we're back over the Yangtze and we'll follow it east. Except . . .'

'Except?' she asked.

'Except that we'll need to stop off somewhere for some gas.'

'Lets cross that bridge when we get to it,' she suggested bracingly.

'Let's hope the big bridge is there to cross in any case,' he muttered underneath his breath, and swung on to a heading that read eighty-five degrees. Due east, allowing for the five-degree local magnetic variation.

Leading Architect Chang slipped off a cliff of exhaustion and tumbled into a deep and dreamless sleep, as black as the depths of the river they were hoping to find in one hundred minutes' time.

Mei-Feng was awoken by the sound of the helicopter's low fuel alarm. She had no idea what it was, but it sounded urgent, not to say threatening. She opened her eyes to find that the cockpit was filled with pulsing redness from a flashing warning light. 'What's the matter?' she asked at once. She was the sort of person who sprang from deep sleep into full wakefulness in an instant. And even had she not been, the alarm released a flood of adrenaline into her system that would have sobered a drunkard.

'What?' yelled Chopper, and Mei-Feng realized that there was a huge amount of ambient noise all around them. Not just the screaming of the alarm. The thunder of rain on the canopy above them. Even, she thought, some distant thunder. But the racket nearby made it hard to tell. Just as the flashing of the red alarm light made it difficult to be certain whether there really was sheet lightning flickering in the cloud canopy above them.

'What's the matter?' she repeated, straining her throat.

'We're almost out of fuel,' shouted Chopper in reply. 'The spare tank wasn't as full as I thought, I guess.'

'Where are we?' Mei-Feng strained to see out of the window. There was a sea of fire shockingly close below. It seemed at once that she could feel the heat of it through the window, and even through the fuselage with her cheeks and the soles of her feet.

'Not sure,' grated Chopper. 'Wuhan with any luck. It's been one hundred minutes now . . .'

'Wuhan *with any luck* . . .'

'Can't be a hundred per cent certain. We're over a wide band of darkness. I was going down to see if it's the Yangtze. It's in the right place and seems to be on the correct heading. North–south . . .' He hesitated for an instant. 'But I can't see enough to be certain . . .'

And that was where the thunderstorm lent a hand. A bolt of lightning leaped out of the clouds ahead of them. It was a bolt of pure energy that seemed to persist for an unnatural length of time, and even when it died it left its image etched on their retinas. Its image and a picture of everything it revealed in the dazzling instant of its existence. The fork of lightning leaped vertically out of the sky perhaps half a mile ahead. Its top vanished into the upper reaches of the thunderhead that gave it birth. Its lower end seemed to leap from one upright of the Great Bridge of Wuhan to the next, and back again. The aura of brightness that the lightning bolt ignited showed the whole of the bridge itself, and a certain amount of the city at either end of it.

Then it was gone.

'I know where we are!' bellowed Chopper. 'I know where we are!'

But Mei-Feng did not hear him. Blinded already, she was deafened at once by the artillery-barrage of the thunder, the sound of it so immediately overwhelming that it seemed to knock the helicopter back through the air.

But in fact Chopper was pulling back on the control column and swinging hard right. The helicopter fell towards the riverbank and skimmed over the tops of the first shore-side buildings. Chopper angled the nose down, his half-blind eyes feverishly searching for the next landmark like a pilot from generations earlier. At last, he was able to use the one thing he had been saving for just this moment. The helicopter's landing light. Its beam – a little more powerful than a car's headlight – focussed down on the ground immediately below them. And there it was! The railway line leading towards the big Wuchang railway station. Once he had sight of that, he followed it until he was sure of his position, then he turned again, heading right on his new course until the glimmers of burning buildings simply stopped. Gingerly, he settled lower looking along the headlight beams at an unfocussed buddle of brightness that seemed to mean nothing, fighting to see through the downpour, praying for more lightning to give him that last vital clue. Fighting to keep his concentration going and his confidence – like his helicopter – up for just a little longer.

Another bolt of lightning pounced to earth somewhere behind them – perhaps to the top of the big bridge again. It gave just enough light to reveal the big picture, and for him to orientate himself once again.

The helicopter hopped over the security fence closest to the handling areas of Nanhu Airport, the beams momentarily illuminating the DANGER KEEP OUT sign, and settled on to the streaming apron beside a huge fuel lorry immediately outside the nearest hangar.

When Chopper turned off the engines, the alarm stopped and silence returned to the cabin. Relative silence at any rate – for the motors were still winding down and the blades still whistling through the air. And the rain was still pounding on the canopy like a waterfall. Mei-Feng sat back in her seat and took a breath so deep that it hurt her ribs. 'That was close,' she said.

Chopper did not answer. He simply leaned back in his seat and closed his eyes, exhausted.

So it was Mei-Feng who first saw the huge man with the gun, as he walked into the brightness of the helicopter's landing light.

FIFTEEN
Wu

I t took Mei-Feng an instant to understand that the gigantic vision was real, then she reached across and shook Chopper by the arm.

'Wake up, Chopper,' she said, fighting to keep her voice calm, 'we may have trouble here'.

Chopper's eyes opened fractionally. He took in the gun. It was some kind of a rifle, but that was all he could see. It was being carried in the crook of the man's arm. He took in the simple size of the man coming towards them. The slow, deliberate movements. The yellow wet-weather cape, whose wide folds seemed to add to the massive bulk. The uniform cap. He swore quietly. 'Airport security,' he said. 'Still on duty in the middle of all this mayhem! Who'd have believed it?'

The armed man stopped at the side of the helicopter. Reached up; but didn't have to reach up all that far. Rapped on the pilot's door.

Chopper pulled himself up wearily in his seat, reached across and swung the door open just wide enough to allow conversation.

'Do you have permission to land here?' asked the stranger, shouting over the rumble of the downpour. His voice was surprisingly light and high to be coming from such a massive body. He would pass as a Japanese Sumo wrestler, thought Mei-Feng. It was not just the size – it was the physical power he exuded.

'No,' answered Chopper, keeping his weary voice level and reasonable. 'It was an emergency landing. I was running out of fuel. Couldn't raise the control tower on the radio.'

'I don't think there's anyone in the control tower,' said the stranger, glancing across into the distant darkness. 'It was mostly destroyed in the quake. Like most of the terminal buildings. Then the power went out anyway. And that was even before the aftershocks started. Papers?'

Chopper handed over the helicopter's log book and papers.

'These are all for Yichang. You don't have permission to be in Wuhan airspace at all . . .'

'We were up there when the dam went. Yichang and Zhijiang are gone. Underwater. Jingzhou too, by now . . .'

'The *dam*? The *Three Gorges* Dam? It's burst?'

'Burst wide open. We've been coming along the river warning people that there's bad floods coming. Trying to convince them to get to high ground if they can. But we ran out of fuel. Ask Leading Architect Chang if you don't believe me. Her papers are in there with the Yichang flight plan. She's the chair of more committees than you've had rice dinners.'

The big man lowered his gun. Stood on tiptoe, which must have made him top six foot six. Looked across at Mei-Feng. 'Is this true?' he asked.

Mei-Feng took a gamble then. In more ways than one. She reached across Chopper and casually leaned her weight on one hand as she talked to the stranger. The way she put her hand on the control fascia showed her fingers quite clearly in the cockpit lights. Especially her little finger with its tiny tattoo that identified her as a member of the Green Gang Triad of Shanghai.

She looked down into the stranger's eye. Saw them flicker as he noticed her finger and understood the significance of the tattoo.

She smiled sweetly and continued Chopper's lies. 'It's just as Pilot Quing has said,' she purred. 'And you'd better start moving yourself. The flood will be here in a couple of hours at the most. And unless you have some kind of transport you'll be lucky to escape. I mean, you're less than a kilometre from the river here in an area so low it's full of lakes. After the flood comes this will all be one *big* lake. With what's left of Wuhan at the bottom of it.'

The stranger looked around, his expression suddenly wary. 'A couple of hours,' he said. 'That's not much time.'

'It's all you've got,' said Mei-Feng matter-of-factly.

'On the other hand,' temporized Chopper quickly, 'we need fuel if we're going to get safely out of here ourselves. If you could help us get it, then maybe we could help you too. Maybe give you a lift out of the danger zone . . .'

The security man frowned. 'Wait here,' he said. 'I'll be back.'

'Be quick!' called Mei-Feng, feeling her confidence beginning to rise. 'We haven't much time!'

A huge hand was raised. The gigantic figure disappeared.

Mei-Feng and Chopper both sagged back into their seats, simply exhausted. 'Is that what you reckon,' asked Chopper. 'A couple of hours?'

'It was a guess. Give me the chart and I'll work it out more accurately. But I can rough it out, I suppose. We've been in the air for two and a half hours moving at a hundred kph. The flood is moving at say fifty. And it's coming round the longer way, but it's coming. So we may have two hours. Two and a half. Maybe three. Who knows?'

Chopper nodded. 'I hope you're right,' he said. 'Because without power we'll have to pump the fuel aboard by hand. That won't be easy or quick. And I'm all in. If I'm going to fly this thing much further, then I need at least an hour's sleep.'

The giant loomed out of the shadows then. There was a tiny figure at his side, apparently his daughter. But no.

'My name is Wu,' he said as Chopper opened the door fractionally again. 'Most people call me Big Wu. This is my wife Lilac Blossom.'

'Most people just call me Blossom,' inserted the tiny figure forcefully.' Mei-Feng could just see the top of her head. She was wearing a CAAC cap.

'Blossom is an airline receptionist,' explained Big Wu. 'I'm a security guard. Since the earthquake Blossom's been trying to help out at the terminal. I've been doing my patrol. This is about the only building left standing on the whole airfield, so it's the one I felt I ought to guard. Also, there's that bowser full of avgas. That has to be worth something. Especially when things start getting back to normal. Most of the others ran for their lives when the quake struck and I moved a couple who were hurt up nearer the terminal. That's how I found out Blossom was still OK . . .'

'It's been terrible,' said Blossom. 'So many people needing so much help, and so few of us still uninjured and able to lend a hand. And they're getting more and more desperate by the hour. You were lucky the thunderstorm covered the sound of your motor or you'd have had everyone able to walk out here begging for a lift. We had to be really careful how we slipped away. But I wasn't with the main body of the hurt and wounded any more, in any case. You see, I had to give up in the end and come away. I couldn't help myself. You see, I'm . . .'

'Blossom is due to have our child in three months' time,' explained Big Wu, his voice shaking with pride. 'If I help you get the fuel you need, could you take Blossom and our baby . . .'

Mei-Feng leaned over even further, stretching her straps to the maximum. At last she was able to look down into the flower-like face that had prompted her parents to name her so accurately, if originally. Except that 'Lilac' symbolized modesty in Chinese lore. Blossom didn't seem all that modest to Mei-Feng. But then, to be fair, modesty was the last virtue they needed at the moment. She smiled. Looked up from Lilac Blossom's almond eyes to Big Wu's anxious face. 'We'd be happy to take all three of you,' she promised.

Big Wu knew where the keys to the fuel bowser were kept, and he was able to start it up and reverse it into position quite easily.

Chopper made sure they understood how to connect the hoses correctly and how to use the handles that would pump the fuel aboard, then he collapsed into his seat and fell into a deep sleep.

Big Wu did most of the work, of course, though Mei-Feng felt honour bound to help him every now and then. Blossom vanished into the shadows once again, returning after a while with a range of supplies that suggested very strongly that she had found some way of breaking into several vending machines. Eyeing the cans of Coca-Cola and packets of chips and chocolate, and remembering some of her more outrageous demands when she had been carrying little Jiang Quing, Mei-Feng found herself wishing for tea and rice. But then her stomach growled and she realized she was well past being picky. Pregnant or not, chips and Coke would be fine.

By the time Chopper stirred ninety minutes later, the helicopter's main tank was full. While he too had something to eat, he oversaw the filling of the spare tanks. They all relieved themselves in the little toilet that occupied the far corner of the hangar. Blossom brought the soap from the tiny handbasin there and Big Wu tore the towel dispenser off the wall. Then, their ablutions taken care of – now and for the immediate future – the pair of them strapped themselves into the passenger seats by the rear door where the ladder lay rolled, and they were all off.

The rain had eased by this time and the clouds were breaking up, allowing a full bright moon to gleam through occasionally. By the less than reliable light, Chopper guided them back across the dark ground to the railway line, then, with the nose low and the lights on, he followed the line back up past Wuchang railway station, along the viaduct over Shahu Lake and back to the Yangtze. The unreliable moonlight showed them the river now, for they were halfway between the two bridges – the big bridge and the new. The downpour seemed to have extinguished most of the fires in the city, so the moonlight was a blessing, allowing Chopper to set a course eastwards along the river.

And they were only just in time.

For, in the moments between their arrival over the river and Chopper's selection of course, height and speed, the flood finally caught them up.

Blossom saw it first, but as she had not seen it before and had no clear idea of its true scale or limitless force, she simply could not quite understand what she was seeing. The wall of water seemed to reach from horizon to horizon. It gleamed under the uncertain moonlight like a distant range of snow-clad Himalayan peaks. As she was sitting, confused, genuinely wondering where these mountains could possibly have come from – whether it was some trick of perception played by the fact that she was up in a helicopter – she realized that they were moving.

'Look!' she whispered. And there was something about the whisper that made it carry to the others. They all looked. In the time that it took them to turn their heads, the foaming mountain range had leaped nearer still. 'It must reach from Xintao to Puqui,' she whispered. 'A hundred kilometres. More . . .'

Even as she made this awestruck calculation, the water reached Wuhan. Chopper opened the throttled and took them away north, out of the path of the monster, swinging west almost at once to follow the silvery, shadowy river under the inconstant moon. So that the last thing Blossom, Mei-Feng and Big Wu saw was the big bridge of Wuhan being smashed to pieces, as the water tore past it to drown the mighty city whose halves it had once joined together.

SIXTEEN
Shi

D aniel Huuk looked at the radio in simple horror. Some impulse made him press the BROADCAST button so that the hiss of disconnection whispered eerily round the bridge.

'What is it?' asked Tan, shocked. 'D . . .' he paused. He had been on the point of saying Dragon Head. 'Deputy Commissioner,' he corrected himself. 'What is the matter?'

'She's been taken,' said Huuk, as though anyone else would know what he was talking about. 'Taken by pirates.'

'*Yu-quiang*?' asked Tan. '*Poseidon*?'

The use of the vessel's western name seemed to waken Huuk. '*Poseidon*,' he confirmed. But he had not meant *Poseidon* at all. He had meant Robin. 'Yes. *Poseidon* seems to have been taken by river pirates somewhere in the Yizheng Shuidao river reach. They were just reporting a wave three, perhaps four metres high with a flood behind it at least two metres deep. It seems to have inundated much of the valley there . . .'

In Daniel's mind, nightmare visions interpreted and reinterpreted the last few sounds he had heard. The gunshot. The gasp. The gentle thump. His imagination saw Robin struck by the bullet, blood exploding across the pristine whiteness of her shirt-breast.

'A couple of metres,' rasped Commodore Shan. 'That's not so much.'

'But, with respect, sir, a four-metre wave is. It would do a great deal of damage sweeping unchecked through a city. Especially one already part-ruined by an earthquake. And for anyone trapped at ground level – or below it, even a metre of water means death, does it not?'

'And she . . .' Daniel paused, pulling himself together. '*They* suggested, of course that if we are correct, then an eight or ten metre wave will be following in twelve hours' time.' Daniel paused again, and they all supposed him to be calculating the effect of the next disaster he was describing. All, perhaps, except Tan.

But he was thinking what if she wasn't dead? What if she was wounded? Helpless? In the hands of rapacious criminals.

'And that would be on top of what is already there, of course,' said Tan thoughtfully at last, seeing that his leader remained distracted.

'What do you mean?' demanded Shan.

'If the river upstream really has settled at two metres above its usual level, then the next flood will arrive on top of that will it not? So the next wave will effectively be an extra two metres higher – an eight metre wave will crest at ten metres, perhaps thirty feet, above the old water level. A ten metre wave would crest at twelve metres, nearly forty feet. And if it settles back to four added metres behind it, then the Yangtze will have risen six metres – say twenty feet – in twenty-four hours. Six metres that will stay in place until the reservoir behind the Three Gorges Dam has drained entirely away and things return to normal.'

He crossed to the bridge window and gestured out at the shoreline. The river running along the Pudong shore was high, near the top of the bank. 'Another two metres will take it over into Pudong,' he said grimly. Four more metres on top of that and it's goodbye Shanghai Shi. Until the river sinks back to its usual level, the seashore will effectively be somewhere over there,' he gestured to the Shanghai shore. 'Hell, if Lake Tai goes, then Shanghai could become an island and the shoreline could be as far inland as Ningguo.'

Everyone on the bridge looked at the young navigating officer with varying degrees of horror.

'But Ningguo is more than two hundred kilometres inland,' breathed Commodore Shan. Part of the horror he was expressing arose from the fact that he himself owned a considerable property on the Shanghai-side shore of the lake. It was where his wife, children and parents lived. If Tan was right, then his family and his property were likely to get swept away before the day was out.

Then, collecting himself, he gave a derisory laugh, dismissing the fool-ishness of Tan's suggestion. He looked around at the other faces nearby, seeking support. The only answering grin came from Political Officer Leung, a young man that Shan neither liked nor trusted. Not only was Leung a law unto himself, but he used the license of his position to widen his uniform requirements in disturbingly anti-establishment directions. In the matter of designer sunglasses, watches and rings. Non-regulation shirts that bore such names as Armani, Burberry and Boss. Shan suspected that a certain amount of Leung's freedom and confidence originated not only from his political position, but also from membership of some secret Triad society. Which made him like and trust him even less. But he nodded once and gave an almost conspiratorial wink, thinking *any port in a storm.*

'But we have more immediate concerns,' grated Daniel, taking control of himself and of the situation. 'First, we now have a clear estimate of what is coming downriver and when it will arrive with us. Second, putting aside speculation as to what may happen later, we now know what we are likely to be facing in the areas we are directly responsible for, both here and upriver. And it is therefore time for more decisive action.

'I will remain here and coordinate preparations and outcomes with the Shanghai authorities while staying in contact with Beijing. Commodore Shan, I would be grateful of an estimate as to when we will be able to berth at the shipyards and set up our floating head-quarters there. In the meantime, with your permission, I would like to delegate my authority to Lieutenant Commander Tan and send him upriver to Zhenjiang with a command of your best marines – or as many as we can fit into the largest helicopter we can commandeer.'

'Of course, Deputy Director! As you know, we have a helicopter aboard—'

'You are very kind, Commodore, but your helicopter is too small for Commander Tan and his contingent – and in any case I will be requiring that myself as I wish to survey Shanghai, Pudong and the Shanghai Shi, including the shipping lanes and inner approaches, to try and estimate what will be the effect of each of the waves and the floods when they arrive.'

'I will call for it to be fuelled and readied,' said the Commodore accommodatingly. 'In the meantime, Lieutenant Commander Tan, you are still navigating officer aboard my vessel. And officer of the watch, come to that. So, if you could oversee our anchoring at the shipyards before you prepare to select your men and go aboard whatever helicopter the Deputy Director can get hold of for you.'

What Daniel got hold of was the 15th Airborne Division, who still maintained a small command just outside Shanghai. Their big SA321 troop carriers had just returned from an abortive explorative sortie up-country. The Deputy General Commissioner – via the military council in Beijing – was able to commandeer one of these with two pilots and fifteen crack marines – all battlefield medical trained – to supplement the fifteen Tan was planning to take off *Luyang*.

By the time arrangements were finalized, Tan had brought the big *Luyang* destroyer alongside the Shanghai shipyards and anchored her out in the main stream, just beyond the vacant berth number one, facing back the way she had come so that she would meet the wave when it arrived with her high bow and strong, sharp cutwater. It had only been possible to manoeuvre the destroyer's 150 metre length in the river because the

Huangpu was almost as bereft of traffic as the yard was apparently lacking in business. As with the vessels on the Yangtze itself, anyone who could get out to sea had gone out to sea. The only ships left in the yard were those who, for one reason or another, could not move.

Like Tan, Daniel was eager to be up in his helicopter as quickly as possible, so that he could get some kind of an idea what the first wave was going to hit when it arrived – he checked the ship's chronometer and double-checked against his slim Patek Phillipe wristwatch – in little more than an hour's time. He was also aware that only vigorous and all-consuming action would keep his mind clear of increasingly garish visions of what might be happening to Robin Mariner aboard *Poseidon* under the pirates' control. Now, when his long-held dream of her naked under the silken wisp of a sheet popped into his head, she was no longer alone. No longer asleep.

Daniel bustled down to the deck where Tan was assembling his little command, ready to go ashore. The men were lined up along a passageway that opened into a bulkhead door in the side of the ship, which lead out on to a suspended gangplank sloping down to a little platform where the ship's cutter waited to ferry them ashore.

In the near distance, a big grey helicopter was settling on to a clear area on the dockside.

'Send the men down first,' said Daniel, and then as they doubled into the cutter at Tan's command, he took the Lieutenant Commander aside. 'Of course Zhenjiang is your highest priority,' he said quietly. 'Just as Shanghai and Pudong are mine. But I am relying on *Poseidon* to get to Nanjing and report to me from there. I am very concerned by their last report, and the fact that we haven't heard anything more since it came through. If you get the chance, check up on her would you? She shouldn't be hard to spot. She'll be the only vessel bound upriver. Maybe the only vessel on the water at all . . .'

Tan nodded, his eyes wise and understanding. At the very least he saw promotion up the Triad ranks, if not up the naval ones, if any of them got out of this alive. 'Of course, Deputy Commissioner,' he said, coming to attention and saluting smartly. Then, with just a little more emphasis, when he was sure they were alone, 'You may rely on me, Dragon Head.'

Tan turned and went clattering down the gangplank after the last of his men. Daniel stepped back, swung round and walked rapidly towards the companionway that would take him back up to the command bridge. It was time to get aboard the *Luyang*'s helicopter and wing his way over the Shanghai Shi.

*   *   *

Daniel was just climbing aboard the helicopter waiting on the helideck aft of the main bridge house when Political Officer Leung came hurrying out after him, carrying what looked like a bulky briefcase. 'Excuse me, Deputy General Commissioner,' he said, climbing aboard after him, 'but I have here messages and contacts for the Mayor of Shanghai, the Bureau of Public Security and the Bureau of Justice as well as Finance, Civil Affairs and Transport who are all coordinating the recovery from the earthquake and aftershocks, as well as preparing for whatever might be expected to happen next. I know you will want to be briefed up to speed so that you can deal with them most efficiently, as time seems to be so short.'

Daniel opened his mouth to protest that he had these contacts, but the political officer pushed smoothly on. Settling into the seat beside him, putting the briefcase on his knees and reaching for the seat belt.

'I also have contacts for the District Governor's Office in Pudong as well as contacts for the relevant Deputy Governors responsible for that side of the river, not to mention the Provincial Governor's office for Shanghai Shi and wider sub-Shanghai area. Finally, I have made contact with an operative named Bing at the Port Authority Office. Bing is in contact with all the Port Authority pilots currently aboard vessels on the river or in the approaches. Except for Senior River Pilot Chang aboard *Poseidon*, of course.'

He opened the top of the briefcase to reveal an old-fashioned looking wireless communications centre, with a telephone handset and a small screen sitting on top of a keyboard that seemed mostly to consist of numbers. 'As the Internet is still down, this old portable communications centre seemed the best way forward. May I tell the pilot to lift off while I contact the Mayor's office for you?'

As the helicopter flew over Shanghai itself, Daniel discussed with the Mayor what damage had been done by the earthquake, what would be done by a surge four or five metres high and a flood at two deep – not to mention a surge that might be a further eight metres high and a flood four metres deeper behind it.

Looking down, Daniel was able to see how well matters were being coordinated here. Not for nothing had the mayorship of Shanghai long been seen as a lift-off point for higher office in Beijing. There were rescue and recovery teams hard at work looking for survivors under damaged buildings and in littered streets. Restoration teams clearing thoroughfares and fighting to restore transport and communications systems. And, it seemed, even as Daniel and the Mayor discussed what was likely to happen during the next two hours – then the next fourteen hours – a third set of teams appeared with sandbags. And as the helicopter turned towards Pudong, Huangpu Park was piled with sand-bags as a makeshift embankment was being erected all the way down the Bund. And the Mayor made it his highest priority to try and get the power back to the Shanghai Shi's massive Flood Control system.

Daniel found himself staring down at the relatively unscathed streets of Pudong and wondering. Wondering not at the excellence of the architecture that had kept the buildings safe against the earthquake, but at how far up their exquisite sides the first – and then the second flood would rise. He numbly began to tick off in his mind the structures most at risk. Starting with the dazzling new building that had been erected for the 2010 Expo.

Things got no better when the helicopter soared into the lower sky above the Shanghai Shi, heading across the low-lying coastal flats towards the mouth of the Yangtze itself. Daniel could see all too clearly how accurately Tan's prediction was likely to come true. It seemed to the exhausted, deflated and deeply worried man that much of this would vanish beneath the first flood – let alone the second. The certainty was compounded by the growing realization that what had been lightly populated mudflats on his last visit was now largely reclaimed. He could see towns, roads, schools, sports facilities, golf courses.

Then there was the expressway going along its low sweep of causeway out to the islands, south of the river's mouth itself. Mile after mile, like the causeway that joined the Florida Keys in America.

'Doomed,' he whispered to himself. 'All doomed.'

SEVENTEEN
Pirated

The pirate's wildly fired bullet zipped past Robin's cheek, smashed open the side of the radio operator's head, inundating Robin and the radio with a mixture of blood and brain-matter as it buried itself in the heart of the dying equipment. Robin had never fainted in her life, but simple shock laid her out on the floor of the radio room as effectively as a mugger's cosh.

All Richard could see through the cloud of acrid, steamy smoke that filled the bridge immediately after the shot, was Robin's blood-soaked body on the floor, while the radio operator was slumped on the smoking ruins on his desk. Each one looked as dead as the other. With a guttural bellow of shock and outrage, he leaped forward wildly reaching for his Simonov. The second pirate, clearly unnerved by being confronted by a gweilo giant, and apparently genuinely frightened by the unexpected mayhem arising from his companion's random shot, simply lashed out with his own rifle. The barrel drove into Richard's belly with enough force to bring him to his knees, but that was by no means enough to stop him. He was pulling himself erect when the first pirate, also seemingly shocked by the fact that his waterlogged weapon had fired on a hair trigger, let alone with what he had done with the shot, slammed the stock of his smoking rifle into the raging giant's head.

Richard was smashed back on to his knees, blood pouring from a cut in his scalp, but such was his ungovernable reaction to what had apparently been done to Robin, he simply would not stop. Shaking blood out of his eyes, still snarling, he was on his way up yet again when Robin groaned, rolled over and slipped back into unconsciousness.

The fact that the blood-soaked woman was still alive stopped them all in their tracks.

Richard sank down silently. Raised one massive hand and brushed the combination of blood and matted hair back off his forehead. Through the buzzing and the flashing lights of mild concussion, he began to try and assess just how badly Robin was actually hurt. Began to calculate how best to take control of the situation. Began to think.

'That is better,' said the first pirate in harsh, thickly-accented Mandarin. 'If everyone remains calm there will be no need for further bloodshed.' He looked around the bridge, his face folding into a fierce frown. 'We are in command here now,' he continued, waving the rifle vigorously enough to spray river-water from its sopping shoulder-strap across the bridge. 'You will do as we tell you.' He shifted his feet, the thin rubber soles of his cheap trainers squealing in the considerable puddle that was accumulating beneath the turn-ups of his filthy jeans.

This was little more than a buffoon, Richard thought. But dangerous, and fatally easy to underestimate. He noted the bandoliers of ammunition slung across the filthy T-shirt moulded to his skinny chest. The handguns and heavy meat cleavers hanging from his belt. He registered that the man's companion, too, was a walking armoury. Dripping but deadly.

Richard noted most clearly of all that the hand holding the rifle, its fingers curled around the stock, kept its index finger on the trigger at all times. And the little finger two digits down from it was adorned with a tiny tattoo in the character that meant green. Perhaps the swaggering buffoonery was not without support. For there were other members of the Green Gang aboard *Poseidon* – some of which they knew about and some of whom they didn't. As yet.

Richard caught the Captain's eye, glanced pointedly at the tell-tale tattoo. She nodded infinitesimally. She had seen it too. She glanced at the second pirate. No surprise if they were members of the same Triad, as they were of the same profession – and, likely, the same crew. And that made things complicated, for the last such Triad mark Richard had seen was the Green Gang mark on River Pilot Chang's now missing little finger. It was difficult to assess where his loyalties might lie. Certainly, he was doing his best to make himself invisible now. Apparently uncertain himself – and in no mood to come up hard against the need to make a decision.

Something his daughter clearly had to take into account.

'Very well,' said Captain Chang coldly. 'Then tell us what to do.'

'Who are you?' demanded the pirate.

'I am Captain Chang. Who are you?'

'You may call me Gan,' answered the pirate after a moment. He gestured to his companion with his rife forcefully enough to make the man quail. 'That is Cai.' He thought a little longer. '*Captain* Gan,' he added, gesturing to himself. 'Captain Cai.'

'Very well, Captain Gan,' said Chang. 'What are your orders?'

'Show me the treasure,' answered Gan immediately. 'Captain Cai, you stay in control of the bridge.'

'Yes,' said Cai. He waved his gun about, spraying more water.

'Just a moment, Captain Gan,' said Chang. 'I will show you the treasure but in return you must let the gweilo look at his wife. You have hurt her. You may have killed her as you have killed my radio operator.'

Gan shrugged. 'Very well. The gweilo may look at his wife. Helmsman, where were you heading?'

Steady looked across at Chang and she nodded infinitesimally.

'For Nanjing,' he answered with the gruff lack of respect he lavished on most people. He didn't even pay the pirate captain the courtesy of assuming he would understand a heading, thought Richard.

'Good,' huffed Gan. 'You may proceed. We have friends in Nanjing.'

'They'll only still be there if they can swim,' said Steady, grimly.

'Shut up and steer,' snapped Gan. 'Now, you. Captain. Take me down and show me the treasure.'

Captain Chang shrugged in apparent defeat, exchanged a brief look with her father, and led the pirate off the bridge.

In the sudden silence after they had gone, Captain Cai stood a little uncertainly at the back of the bridge, watching the machine of the watch swing back into action. The river pilot and the navigating officer conferred briefly, then Straightline ordered, 'Steer two thirty-five degrees, Steady; we'll stay in the main channel. If that's agreeable to you, Captain Cai?'

'Yes,' answered Cai, starting as though an electric current had passed through his wiry body. 'That course. Steer that course.'

'Aye aye, *Captain*,' answered Steady. '*That course* it is . . .'

'But stay at slow ahead and watch out for the Runchang Bridge,' warned Pilot Chang more soberly. 'It should cross the river dead ahead. If it's still standing we might be trapped; with the water this high we'd be lucky to get under it.'

'Two thirty-five degrees,' echoed Steady brusquely. 'If the bridge is in the way then we could probably pick our way round it, Pilot.'

Richard only half listened to this conversation. He pulled himself up and walked towards the radio room. As he passed the pirate Captain Cai, it occurred to him that this might be the best moment to attack the nervous and disorientated man. But his concern for Robin over-rode everything else for the moment. At the very least he had to find out for certain how badly hurt she was – then get her to safety and tend to her before he took any further action.

Even as he knelt in the reeking slaughterhouse of the radio room and began to check her inert body for wounds, however, a part of Richard's mind kept pace with what was happening to the vessel through the medium of the cryptic conversation on the bridge.

As Richard assured himself that there was no wound on Robin's head, and that the congealing mess painted over the left side of her skull and face – reminding him irresistibly of lumpy blackcurrant jam – had all come from the unfortunate radio operator, *Poseidon* picked her way through the wreckage of the road bridge. As he parted the clinging red cotton mess that had once been a perfectly pressed blouse and assured himself that there were no holes on the soft warm flesh beneath, *Poseidon* passed between the tops of inundated channel markers that had once stood proud of the surface by a good two metres and more. And by the time he gently lifted her into his arms and straightened up with her like a sleeping child across his chest, Pilot Chang and Straightline were telling Steady to push the engine revolutions up and come to two eighty-five degrees, as *Poseidon* exited the Yizheng Suido and began to power on up the main channel, nudging aside more wreckage from Nanjing as she did so.

Robin woke to a strange, sensual world. She found herself lying apparently naked, on her bed, being gently sponged with warm water. It ran down her chest and tummy, tickling her everywhere from her armpit to the tops of her thighs. Tickling, trickling, cooling against her hot skin. She hadn't had a bed bath since infancy and she wondered briefly whether all her adult memories were some sort of a dream. Whether she would wake to find herself back in the great old house called Cold Fell, where she had grown up, in the grip of some childhood fever with Mother or Nanny tending to her.

When she half opened her eyes and saw Richard, it was strangely almost as though she were seeing him for the first time. Her heart skipped a beat, her breath went short, her skin clenched into goosebumps that made her nipples harden with simple sensuality. She stirred languorously. 'Now just what is it you're up to sailor?' she purred throatily.

Richard simply swept her into his arms and crushed her to him. Over his shoulder, she saw the familiar little cabin they shared aboard *Poseidon*. The curtain that replaced a door, the three-dimensional jigsaw of built-in furniture secured against rough weather. And, at the foot of the little chest of drawers, a pile of blood-soaked clothing that she recognized with a gasp of shock as belonging to her.

'The radio operator?' she asked, returning Richard's hug with interest.

'Dead,' he answered shortly. 'So's the radio. We're completely cut off. But look on the bright side. I thought Captain Gan had killed you too.'

'That's the name of the man with the gun?'

'There are two of them. Gan and Cai,' Richard explained, still hugging her to him with fierce protectiveness. 'But Gan and Cai won't be their real names. I seem to remember that there are already some famous Chinese pirates called Gan Ning and Cai Quian. They call themselves captains too, but I doubt they've skippered anything much bigger than a rowing boat. They look like junior Green Gang pirates to me. They're certainly after our treasure down below. They say they have friends in Nanjing – and that's where they hope to dispose of poor old Genghis, I suppose. If their friends in Nanjing are still in any fit condition to dispose of anything.'

He sat back. 'Now,' he said. 'Let's find some clothes and get you dressed now that you're clean.'

He stooped to lift a bowl full of bloody water from the floor. As he did so, Robin noticed the ridge of dried blood across the top of his scalp. 'What happened to you?' she asked.

'Banged my head,' he answered offhandedly, turning away.

Just as he did so, the curtain that served as a doorway was torn aside and Captain Gan peered suspiciously in from the corridor. Robin gave a gasp and her hands flew to cover her nakedness, but she was too slow. The pirate had seen everything there was to see. He lingered in the doorway for an instant, his entire being focussed on the pink flesh and golden curls that haunted Daniel Huuk's dreams. Then he turned and was gone.

Richard stood, frowning. For Captain Chang had been standing just behind the pirate. She was carrying a jewelled sword – obviously taken from the golden statue they had just been looking at. It was a small sword – but it looked heavy and would have made an effective club if nothing else. That moment in which the pirate had been completely focussed on Robin had presented her with the perfect opportunity to lay him out stone cold. And yet she had hesitated. Let the chance slip by.

Now why had she done that? he wondered.

EIGHTEEN
Minds

'I hesitate because I am in two minds about how best to proceed!' hissed Captain Chang in her strangely sibilant American-accented English. 'I will not rush in until I have thought things through.'

The pair of them were in the chart room, watching from a distance, as Gan showed Cai the jewelled sword Captain Chang had taken off the statue and carried up here at the pirate's command. Chang was here because she wanted to stay close to the centre of her command. Richard was here because he had chosen to watch Gan rather than to stay on guard with Robin. Not that she would have allowed him to do so in any case. They were whispering in English in case they should be overheard, as Richard tried to fathom what part of the captain's plans had stopped her braining Gan with the sword when she had the opportunity.

'In what way in two minds?' demanded Richard.

'I do not trust the crew,' she spat back. 'You know that! Think back! What was the first thing we did after we took the golden statue aboard?'

'We confiscated their cellphones . . .'

'Precisely! Even though we were in a communications black spot at the time. And yet what happened within hours?'

'The first gang of pirates came after us,' allowed Richard, his eyes narrow as he began to assess the implications of what she was revealing – not about what had happened so much as about the effect that it had had upon Captain Chang's own thinking. One or two things made more sense the more he thought. Although it had been a matter of mere days since they had brought the priceless statue aboard, for instance, there had been several incidents, not to mention adventures. The Captain could no longer trust her crew. Had not been able to trust them since at least one of them had called the Green Gang pirates down upon their heads.

'Even though we were still well out to sea!' Chang emphasized. 'Someone aboard somehow alerted them almost immediately. And we have never found out who that was! *Someone under my command is Green Gang!*'

Like your father, thought Richard. And that's a fact that must, at the very least, have shaken you rigid into the bargain. But he was too wise to say anything. 'Or someone aboard is helping the pirates by accident or design at least,' he temporized, trying to counter her paranoia. 'Maybe . . .'

'Maybe more than one person,' she persisted, paying no attention at all to his measured tone or his reassuring words. 'Therefore I do not know who will back me if I confront these pirates. Or who will help them. I do not wish to risk a mutiny by proceeding before I have a clearer idea. A mutiny that would inevitably lead to a lot of death or prison time. It is bad enough that we are dragging them upriver into so much danger without even consulting them. Especially with Ping and these new men pushing them out of their bunks and eating too much of their limited rations. To test them further now of all times would be madness. Or so it seems to me.'

'And you think that you'll get a clearer idea of the lie of the land by letting things stand for the moment?'

'Yes! It could be just what I need. A breathing space after all that has happened at the very least. I will allow these two legendary captains Gan and Cai – whatever their real names are – to strut around my command for a while and I will watch who seems most willing to offer them help or advice. Then I will begin to get a clearer idea of who aboard I can least trust – either because they are Green Gang or because they are tempted too strongly by the promise of great wealth . . .'

The pair of them glanced out on to the command bridge. Gan and Cai were poring over the jewelled sword like a couple of misers, apparently utterly unaware that theirs were not the only eyes fastened on the priceless artefact. Richard, irredeemably literate, was suddenly put in mind of one of Chaucer's *Canterbury Tales*, where Death simply hid a bag of gold under a tree and watched as everybody else in the story killed each other in pursuit of it.

Chang asked him a question he only half heard.

'Pardon?'

'Will you back me up in this?' she repeated.

'All right. We'll play along. For the time being. Though I advise you to act fast if you want Ping to hold fire. But I will follow your lead and keep my eyes peeled. Two heads are better than one. Four eyes. Two minds; but not in the way you mean. We have some time in hand before we get anywhere near Nanjing in any case.'

A shadow fell across them. They looked up guiltily. It was Gan. 'You have guns aboard. Take me to the armoury at once,' he demanded in his coarse Mandarin.

'Who told you we had guns aboard?' demanded Chang.

'The gweilo giant.' Gan pointed with his chin. 'He has a Russian sniper rifle for a start. Or had. We have it now. And we were neither blind nor deaf down on the dock in Zhenjiang. We saw – and heard – many guns. You are fortunate that your men did not kill any of my friends or brothers. Or there would be many more dead men aboard this vessel. Starting with you, Captain! Now move!'

Richard strolled apparently casually out on to the main bridge, then, as Gan and Captain Chang vanished down the companionway towards the armoury, he began to follow. Captain Cai glanced across at him, uncertain whether to stop him leaving or not, and clearly decided on masterly inaction. He returned to his drooling examination of the jewelled sword.

River Pilot Chang loomed at Richard's shoulder briefly as he passed. 'Keep an eye on my daughter,' he whispered.

Richard gave a curt nod. But something of Captain Chang's paranoia infected Richard's own thoughts. As he tailed the distant pair down to the armoury, he started going through the crew in his mind, trying to assess who might be a Green Gang mole. The Captain herself belonged to Daniel Huuk's Invisible Power Triad. A secret society of the brightest and the best dedicated to pushing themselves, and each other, into the highest possible ranks and offices in the country. Motivated for the common good. Like he supposed the Masons were in Europe and her old empires.

Chang's father had been Green Gang – apparently a way to get on in the circles he moved in. But it seemed to Richard that the old man had had a change of heart recently. But the question remained – how permanent was that change of heart? Indeed, her mother the architect, lost somewhere in the chaos upriver, had been Green Gang too, now he thought of it.

The rest of *Poseidon*'s officers and crew were less easy to read. The navigating officer, Straightline, seemed a simple straightforward soul. As was often the case with Chinese nicknames, the one they had given Straightline, revealed a good deal more than the navigator's preferred approach to laying in a course.

Powerhouse Wang, the engineering officer, not only powered the ship but was a restless ball of energy into the bargain. Powerhouse would not be content to remain in his present post for long. Would membership of the Green Gang be an easy ladder up for him? Or was he more likely to be an Invisible Power man? And if he was indeed Invisible Power, then why had he not been fawning over the wounded Dragon Head Daniel Huuk like Lieutenant Commander Tan, for instance, had been?

Then there was the electrical engineer simply known as Zhong. That was his rank – Zhong Wei, Junior Lieutenant. The fact that he had no further nickname also revealed that the crew thought of him as next to invisible. Nothing more than a pair of black-rimmed glasses and an earnest frown. Like Straightline, he seemed too slight and bland a person to carry the weight of Green Gang membership – let alone the cunning to conceal it.

The radio officer Broadband had been taken out of the calculations by Captain Gan's hair trigger. That was about it for the officers, thought Richard. And, now he thought of them all as a group, it occurred to him most forcefully that he had had the opportunity to examine their hands quite closely at one time or another. And none of them had a tattoo on any of their fingers.

Ironically, it was just as his mind was turning to the non-commissioned officers aboard that things took an unexpected turn. He was just beginning to consider Lieutenant Paradeground Ping, the commander of the little band of marines who had behaved so well on the pier at Zhenjiang. And he was actually thinking of the man who was closest to a chief petty officer or boatswain that *Poseidon* boasted – Steadyhand Xin the helmsman – when his thoughts were interrupted.

There came the sounds of shouting and scuffling from the ship's little armoury. The crisp crunch of a hard blow. A gasp of pain. With his mind suddenly filling with the river pilot's fears for his daughter, Richard sprinted forward and swung into the doorway. His arrival made the two in there spring apart. No – made Gan spring back, his clenched fist still raised.

Captain Chang stood erect, defiant, fists half raised as though preparing for a boxing match. There was a bruise darkening on her cheek where the pirate had punched her. Her hat lay on the deck at her feet, revealing for the first time the bangs of her page-boy haircut. But the pirate didn't seem to notice Richard's sudden arrival.

And, looking beyond the gasping man, he could see why.

The armoury was empty. Every gun and all the ammunition was gone.

NINETEEN
Jiujiang

Mei-Feng stirred as Chopper reached across and started shaking her. She sat up abruptly, by no means happy to have her sleep rudely interrupted. 'What?'

'That,' he said, pointing forward and down.

All Mei-Feng could see was yet more dark water. The helicopter had come lower while she slept, and seemed to be hovering just above the heaving surface of a vast lake. Mei-Feng sat forward, her mind whirling. 'What?' she said again.

The helicopter rose suddenly as Chopper pulled her up and span her round. The still-bemused architect saw moonlight gleaming across a jumble of rocks that lay strewn haphazardly away upriver into a narrower channel. Rocks that vanished under the flooding outwash. Rocks that suddenly looked unnaturally ordered. Almost man-made. The helicopter went higher still, and the moon stayed faithful, so that Mai-Feng could see a waterfall pouring relentlessly over the slopes of the nearby mountain.

.'What is this?' she asked at last. 'Where are we?'

'Jiujiang,' he answered.

Mei-Feng simply stared. Somewhere down there, in that wilderness of rubble, and under the lake that now seemed to cover most of it, were a million and more city dwellers who normally thronged the City of Nine Rivers. In the wider area, there were perhaps four million more.

Then it hit her. She looked at her watch. It was still the small hours. 'How in the name of the sky did the flood from the Three Gorges get this far so swiftly?' she asked shakily.

'It didn't,' answered Chopper. 'This is something else.'

The helicopter was still high enough for Mei-Feng to see over the top of the massive waterfall. Her blood quite literally ran cold.

'If this is Jiujiang,' she said, 'then that is Mount Lushan, or what's left of it. And that is Lake Poyang which seems to be pouring into the watercourse.'

'Shit!' Chopper swore under his breath. 'If Lake Poyang is flowing out into the river then we may find ourselves in very serious trouble. You see, I can only navigate by following the river. And our plan was to hop from one city to another until we found that last tank full of fuel that will get us to Nanjing, where the Leading Architect has family. But from here on downstream, we may well find all the riverside cities not only damaged but pretty well flooded too – even if we stay ahead of the big wave from the Three Gorges.'

'Lake Poyang is huge,' emphasized Mei-Feng. 'It is what, a quarter of the size of the Three Gorges reservoir? Maybe more. There will be a lot of damage ahead of us.'

'Though nothing compared to how much damage there will be when the water behind us gets up on top of the water ahead of us,' added Big Wu, proving there was more to him than muscle.

'We were very lucky to find yourself and your husband,' continued Chopper. 'More lucky still to get fuel for the helicopter at the same time. But unless we get to be just as lucky all over again, then we'll have to ditch long before we get to Nanjing.'

'Not that there'll be all that much left of Nanjing if this flood is anything like the one that hit Yichang,' added Mei-Feng, suddenly icy with fear for her parents and family in their house on the Beijing Donglu Road, right up by the old city wall.

'Anywhere down by the river is likely to be flooded,' emphasized Chopper. 'It's just a question of how badly. And I'm flying blind here, really. If I don't follow the river, I'll get lost. What we need is somewhere near enough to the river so that I can get there and back just flying by sight. But it has to be somewhere that's high enough to be well clear of the flood. And able to supply us with safe landing and fuel. Tall order, huh?'

'Do either of you know a place like that?' asked Mei-Feng, keeping her voice level, trying hard not to patronize their passengers..

'Well,' said Big Wu, giving her question the courteous consideration owed to someone who had saved not only his life but his family. 'My brother is a mining engineer. He specializes in non-ferrous metals, but he is really more of an administrator these days. We were born before the one-child policy. He has a good brain so he went to the best schools, the best university. The College of Material Science and Engineering at the new Wuhan University, as a matter of fact. He passed out top of his class. Got a job with the Tongling Non-Ferrous Metals Group. State run of course. He has done well. My late parents were very proud of him—'

'Your brother,' Mei-Feng said courteously. 'He's a mining engineer you say . . .'

'Non-ferrous metals,' confirmed Big Wu, his voice ringing with pride.

'And how can he help us?'

'I'm not sure he can, but we could ask, I suppose. We were never what you'd call close. But I guess if I asked him he'd help us if he could, all right.'

'How could he help us?' prompted Mei-Feng.

'Well, he works in Tongling. Tongling Non-Ferrous Metals Group, as I said. That's where the copper mines are. Up in the hills over-looking the river. Just like you said. Close to the shore but a couple of hundred metres up in the foothills. It's only, what, a couple of hundred miles north east of Jiujiang, I suppose. And they're both right there on the river, so you should be able to find it all right. I mean, independently of the city itself, the mine has an area of nearly seventy thousand square metres. I'd say that'd be hard to miss if there's any kind of light at all. And since the mine had that huge extension back in 2007, it's got its own landing area for helicopters. Now I come to think of it, maybe Little Brother would let me and Blossom stay there. They have good facilities and all. And I guess they'd have fuel there all right, if they'll let us have some to keep you safely in the air.'

TWENTY
Tongling

The Tongling Non-Ferrous Metals Group's great copper mine in the mountains above Tongling City was a haven of life, light, order and calm. And after the mayhem upriver, it was a doubly welcome sight when it finally swung into being beneath the helicopter.

Chopper Quing brought them low up the river, under a pallid, setting moon. His eyes were on the broad ribbon of water as it guided him out of the heart of darkness and into the promise of safety. Mei-Feng's eyes were on it too, as the Leading Architect in her assessed the scale of the dreadful damage the first flood had done – and how further damage might be planned for – hopefully avoided – in the face of the monster that was following them.

They swept low over the wide, shallow lake that had once been the city of Guichi and the squat islands that had once broken the surface of the winding river facing it, which now disturbed the writhing surface as sunken sandbars. Now the Datong river reach was a lake that spread perhaps ten miles across low marshes of the Fengji Shan, and those on the bank opposite. Meigeng was underwater and invisible; Datong hardly any better, with the river lapping at the walls of the ancient fortress at its heart and the tributary streams full to bursting as far back as the hanging monastery.

But none of the people aboard the helicopter knew this section of Shanxi province all that well, so they really had no idea what they were looking at. Except that they were following the river, and praying that someone would recognize Tongling – if enough of the city still existed to be recognizable.

There was just enough brightness for Mei-Feng to see that the wide flood plain that had been so dangerously inundated upriver was constricted by banks that were high, narrow and backed with mountains. First Zangmu Shan and then Tongguan Shan – which Big Wu recognized, calling excitedly through into the cockpit. The flood waters did not enjoy being restrained after their miles of reckless freedom and the water looked dangerous, even in the moonlight. There were swirls large enough to count as whirlpools; skeins of foam denoting rocks and other hazards just beneath the agitated surface; currents

running fast enough to twist the glassy element as the massive outflow
had taken strange, dragon-like shapes when the Emerald Drop tore
through the heart of Yichang. What that flood, big brother to this one,
would do when it arrived was something Mei-Feng really did not want
to contemplate. She looked away, suddenly feeling tiny and helpless.
Then she looked back, hope beginning to stir again, for something
different suddenly caught her eye.

On the eastern bank, the right-hand bank as she was looking at it,
there were signs of life and order, and these seemed to increase as
they went on along the river and as the banks rose higher and higher
still on their right. There were settlements here high enough up the
foothill slopes to have avoided the floods so far; and they had apparently also survived the earthquake relatively unscathed. There was
enough brightness to define the streets of towns, the blocks of cities.
Not electric light, as far as she could see – but not the disturbing
brightness of wild fires either. Had she been forced to make her mind
up she would have thought that there were simple oil and candle
lanterns burning down there. Fireflies of light and hope that seemed
to cluster ever thicker as the helicopter eased lower and swung inland,
while Big Wu called instructions from the back – for he had visited
Little Brother Wu and he knew what Tongling looked like from the
air.

Tongling City sat nearly fifty metres above the high-water mark and
it seemed to have survived unscathed by the earthquake. Though Mei-
Feng observed that it too seemed to be relying on lanterns rather than
electric lights. And, if she looked away to the north, it was possible
to see that the lower marshy promontory of the Tongling Sha was
under silver-surfaced water now.

Chopper brought the helicopter low above the streets – though to
be fair this was an effect caused by the fact that the ground was rising
rather than that the helicopter was losing altitude.

'Nearly there,' called Big Wu exultantly. 'Not far now . . .'

Suddenly the radio sprang to life. 'This is the TNMG mine at
Tongling. Say again the TNMG mine at Tongling . . .'

'TNMG mine, this is helicopter . . .' Chopper started feeding in the
helicopter's call-sign, his voice shaking with relief and excitement.

They were guided in across the last few miles by the steady voice
on the radio, whose calm professionalism simply could not disguise
the straightforward awe generated by the fact that, amid everything
else that was going on, it should be talking to a helicopter from Yichang
that had stopped off in Wuhan to pick up the boss's big brother, his
sister-in-law and his prospective nephew.

Mei-Feng and the others were equally awed by what they saw as they came closer to the compound itself. For it seemed to have been completely untouched by the disaster that was claiming the rest of the country nearby. The compound was a blaze of electrical light – power supplied by oil-fuelled generators, they later discovered. It seemed to be working at full capacity in full production, though they found that the underground work had been halted as soon as the quake struck and the main power went down.

On top of that, the mine compound's facilities had clearly been thrown open to anyone from the immediate neighbourhood who needed safety, reassurance or tending of any sort. But the crowds that were thronging in through the open gates and moving towards what were clearly the medical facilities were quiet, well ordered and patient. Some of them looked up as Chopper brought the helicopter in low over their heads, but most did not.

The helipad was in the centre of the compound. Like everything else nearby, it was spotless and perfectly maintained, so that as Chopper eased the machine on to the ground at last, it didn't even kick up any dust. The slight figure in the perfectly pressed grey business suit, who came running out to greet them, didn't actually need the clean white handkerchief he held fastidiously over his mouth and nose.

As the rotors idled and slowed, the stranger pulled himself upright and removed the handkerchief, revealing a smile of welcome beneath the golden glint of his black-framed glasses. Big Wu heaved himself out of his seat and threw the side-door wide. Then the two men were lost in a most uncharacteristically emotional embrace.

'This must be Little Brother Wu,' said Mei-Feng to Blossom as the two of them pulled themselves stiffly out of their seats.

'I have never met Mining Engineer Wu,' answered Blossom, made a little formal by obvious nervousness. 'But I know they became very close after their parents died, so I must assume you are correct.'

But Big Wu was back. 'Blossom,' he called. 'Come and meet our baby boy's uncle . . .'

It soon transpired that the prospective Baby Wu had more than an uncle to meet. He had an aunt and several cousins into the bargain. And the simple joy with which the families got together brought a lump to Mei-Feng's throat, even as it compounded her driving desire to get Chopper's helicopter fuelled up and on downriver to see how her own family in Nanjing was surviving the disaster. She soon found herself hoping most fervently that her own family had access to a facility such as this one.

Little Brother Wu had simply opened all the services he possibly could to the people who needed them. He was careful to keep an eye out for freeloaders and sneak-thieves but, in fact, the men and women he put in place to oversee the refugees really had little to do, other than to offer ready sympathy, food and drink; or to perform a simple triage, deciding who needed tending most and soonest.

As he hurried them across the open centre of the compound, Little Brother revealed that he was concerned about the lack of power in the local grid, that the phones were down and radio and TV stations seemed to be off-line, and by the fact that he was unable to communicate with any civil or military authorities. But as he showed them into a big, bright building he calmly explained that he did not doubt help would be coming soon, and in the meantime he had a good supply of almost everything, and he was certain that his bosses at TNMG would want him to do what he could under the circumstances.

He insisted that everyone be fed, and even the driven Mei-Feng saw how unwise it would be to damage the generous young man's *face* by refusing, when she had so much she needed to tell him and so much that she wanted to ask of him. And in any case, Blossom had consumed all the Coke and chips hours since, eating for two, as she said.

So, while the women and children cheerfully gathered around one end of the compound's canteen, discussing a horoscope drawn up to assess the prospective baby's prospects, Mei-Feng joined the men at the other end where more immediate concerns were being discussed.

'Little Brother,' insisted Big Wu round a mouthful of soy cheese, steamed pork and noodles, 'is there no way you can use the radio to broadcast general warnings of the danger? You have no idea of what is coming down on you. A wave and a flood that makes the one you have just experienced look like a passing shower.'

'We could broadcast, I suppose,' allowed Little Brother, cleaning the lenses of his glasses on his tie and frowning with concentration as he thought. 'But we have been broadcasting for some time and the only reply we received was the one from you and your helicopter. Our own machine has been taken to Datong for repairs, but—'

'Datong is gone,' said Chopper baldly.

'I see.' Little Brother put his glasses back on and thought for a second more. Then, 'Just how big is this second wave?' he asked.

'I saw it tear the great bridge at Wuhan apart,' Big Wu answered roundly. 'It will be here long before you can expect any help. Tongling city may have stood up well so far, but if what happened at Wuhan happens here, you will be inundated with refugees even if you don't get flooded with water. You must prepare as best you can. Ask Leading Architect Chang if you don't believe me!'

Mei-Feng looked up warily from her head-brain lamb soup. Little Brother was looking at her, his face folded into an even fiercer frown, his fingers on the arm of his glasses once again. 'It's true,' she said. 'We've been trying to warn as many people as we can as we came downriver – but we haven't found that many this side of Jiujiang because Lake Poyang seems to have flooded too. But there must be more people downstream who need warning. That's why it's so important Chopper and I refuel and get on as soon as we can.'

The glasses came off. The tie came out and started polishing the thick lenses once more. The frown became worthy of Genghis Khan.

'And Leading Architect Chang has family down there herself,' emphasized Chopper helpfully.

'Where?' asked Little Brother, apparently sidetracked, his frown lightening a little.

'In Nanjing,' Mei-Feng answered. 'Nanjing is lower than Tongling. Your city's mean elevation here is between fifteen and fifty-three metres until you get up here to the mine of course. Nanjing's is between twelve and fifteen. And it has extensive subways and an underground railway which are all likely to be flooded, along with the foundations and cellars of most buildings. Even a modest flood might have done untold damage because it is all so low – until you get to the foothills of the Zijinshan. And there are only parks and temples there – as well as the Sun Yat Sen mausoleum. Not well-stocked, fully-powered copper mines.

'Besides, my family live down on Beijing Donglu by the old city walls and the Xuanwu Lake park. Which will all be lake now, as likely as not. Not what you'd call high up. Parents, uncles and aunts, cousins. Thank the sky we moved my husband's parents away from the docks and down to Pudong . . .'

'You are right to be concerned,' allowed Little Brother. 'We will give you all the fuel you want of course. Nanjing is only one hundred miles, say one hundred and fifty kilometres from here. Though, of course, the vagaries of the river add considerably to that distance if one goes by water instead of air.'

'We can do that in less than an hour,' interjected Chopper. 'Then we'll just need to find somewhere to land.'

Mei-Feng forbore to point out that, if push came to shove, there was plenty of room to land a helicopter at the mausoleum.

'Is that all your family?' asked Little Brother solicitously. 'Your husband?'

'My husband is out there somewhere on the river,' said Mei-Feng shortly. 'He's the senior river pilot working out of the Shanghai Port

Authority. He'll be somewhere on the water, doing his best to help, if he's still alive.'

'And that is all?' Little Brother was leading them across the canteen now. 'You have no children?'

'We have one. A daughter. She is the captain of a corvette. The last I heard she was out in the Yellow Sea, trying to help in the search for a sunken submarine.'

'Out at sea, and on a corvette,' said Little Brother Wu, more cheerfully as they stepped out into the sultry night, and the pungent stench of avgas made her nostrils twitch. 'That must be a comfort to you. Your daughter at least must be safe.'

PART THREE
NANJING

TWENTY-ONE
Safe

The pirate who called himself Captain Gan raised his fist to strike Captain Chang again. 'Where are the guns from this armoury?' he screamed, spraying the stony face opposite with spittle. 'Tell me or I'll beat you to pulp!'

Richard eased himself into the doorway and said, 'I wouldn't do that if I were you.'

The pirate turned and gaped. The presence of the huge barbarian was a surprise – but he had no idea what the round-eye gweilo was talking about. Although Richard understood every word he heard, and spoke what he fondly believed to be pretty accurate Mandarin, his accent was terrible. And in any case, Gan himself spoke with a thick Zhenjiang brogue. The communication between them was, therefore, at this juncture at least, as effective as that between a Bluegrass Kentuckian and a French Canadian.

There was no mistaking the clarity of Captain Cai's voice as it boomed over the tannoy just at that moment, however. 'Gan?' it called. 'Gan, where are you? Uncle Zheng's boat is coming out towards us now.'

Bloody hell, thought Richard, swinging round and sprinting back the way he had just come. Another boat! Why hadn't he seen that one coming? Gan and Cai didn't look such buffoons now. Not if Uncle Zheng had more than a couple more well-armed men in whatever vessel he was bringing alongside.

The unwelcome vision of a huge black junk rose in Richard's memory. Up until the moment that the earthquake had changed everything by bringing the motorway bridge down on top of it, that junk, packed with ruthless men and lethal weapons, had been set to do to *Poseidon* what Blackbeard, Flint, Long John Silver and Calico Jack Rackham were said to have done to many an unfortunate vessel in fact and fiction. Not to mention to any poor souls left alive aboard her.

And now here was another pirate vessel ready to take up where the black junk had been forced to leave off.

Where in heaven's name were all the guns from the armoury?

Richard burst out of the port-side bulkhead door on to the weather deck. The early morning was bright, its light flat and clear. There across the swollen lagoon that lapped now at the gates of Yizheng a couple of miles beyond its normal bankside, a long, lean motorboat was sweeping towards them. It had to be the boat that Cai had been talking about – it was the only one other than *Poseidon* on the swollen river. This was no old-fashioned pirate junk. It was much more like one of those dangerous little vessels that had a habit of capturing oil-tankers off Somalia, and then evading half of the navies in the world when they came in pursuit. A rough count convinced Richard that Uncle Zheng must have the better part of twenty men with him.

'Now this is an interesting situation, is it not?' asked an unfamiliar voice in clipped and precise English. *English* English, too, thought Richard as he swung round. Not American English. Not West Point: Sandhurst. Or Sandhurst, near as dammit. The slight but ramrod figure of Paradeground Ping was standing at his shoulder, the black peak of his perfectly straight cap pointing towards Uncle Zheng's boat.

Richard couldn't think of an immediate answer, so, with uncharacteristic wisdom, he said nothing, his mind racing back to that brief conversation with Captain Chang – apparently, she had held Ping and his men in reserve just for the vital moment. A leader worthy of the nickname Mongol indeed.

'These men assume they are, if I may use a Byronic reference, wolves coming down on the fold. But are they, in fact, more Biblical lambs to the slaughter?'

Richard's eyes narrowed. 'Are they? Wolves? Or lambs?' His eyes raked the deck. Ping and he seemed to be utterly alone.

'That rather depends, does it not?' asked Ping easily.

'On who has the guns from the armoury – and how they propose to use them?'

'Oh, I think we may assume you know the answers to both of those questions; though not, perhaps, the *motivation* behind the answers. Or perhaps I should say *motives*.'

'Motivation?' asked Richard, lost.

'We have two *considerable* women aboard do we not?' asked Ping as though this answered everything.

Richard said nothing, as his agile mind began to fill in the blanks while Ping continued his brief lecture.

'Take Captain Mariner, for instance,' persisted Ping. 'One has not come across a lady such as Captain Mariner since one's last party at Camberley.'

So, Ping had, it seemed, been to the Royal Military Academy, thought Richard. Thereby hung a tale. One that would be well worth following up, perhaps at a more opportune moment.

But Lieutenant Ping was proceeding in his monologue about Robin. 'Soaked in blood and cranial-matter when a man mere inches away has his brains blown out; sponged down and ogled, I hear, by lustful pirates in a state of déshabillé. Does she cry for help? Cower? Hide?'

'No. By the sound of things she comes and finds you the instant I left her to her own devices. And if I know her, she had a plan . . .'

'And consider our own commander, the intrepid Captain Chang. Does she hesitate in these dangerous circumstances – dangerous to her person as well as to her command – because she does not know what to do, or dares not do it? The woman who commanded the dock at Zhenjiang like the most warlike of Khans? Who rammed the barrier and met the first wave more intrepidly than even her father the river pilot could have done?'

'No,' answered Richard again. 'She hesitates only because she does not know who she can trust.'

'Indeed,' said Ping. A shot rang out. A single, muffled report from below decks. A masculine scream choked down to a moaning whimper. Then silence. 'Well, perhaps now she does.'

Two streams of marines appeared then, each led by one of the women they had just been discussing. One squad came down from the bridge. Robin, ahead of these men, handed Richard the Simonov sniper rifle Captain Cai had confiscated. As she did so, Captain Chang arrived with the squad from below. 'The ship is yours again, Captain,' said Ping formally, snapping to attention.

'Thank you, Lieutenant,' answered Captain Chang, equally formally. She too came to attention. Their cap-peaks, noses and chins were exactly level, almost touching.

As were their eyes.

And their lips.

'I will return to my bridge,' she announced after an instant.

'We will remain here and prepare to repel boarders,' said Ping. 'I see you have brought up the guards from the engine room, as well as the others deployed by the hold containing the statue below. Good.'

'There's no need for guards any more,' said the Captain roundly.

'We certainly have other priorities at the moment,' said Ping. He glanced out at the pirate boat.

'I don't want them aboard. We've had enough dealings with pirates, Triads and so-forth,' the Captain decided. Then she turned and ran towards the A-deck door into her command-bridge. She paused, her foot raised on the step of the bulkhead door. 'But I don't think I want a slaughter,' she said, and was gone.

Ping's eyes followed her and lingered on the vacancy she had last occupied just for an instant. Long enough for Richard to understand very clearly that, unlike the probably deceased pirate Gan, the Lieutenant at least knew exactly what her sex was.

And the way he purred 'Now . . .' in Mandarin, as he turned back to his observation of the approaching vessel, suddenly made Richard realize that Ping felt that he had a score to settle – on Captain Chang's behalf, as well as his own, perhaps. Her point about the slaughter was well made. But would he pay any attention to it?

'Form a line abreast. Ready your weapons,' ordered Ping quietly, 'and prepare to fire down into the pirate vessel on my order. But stay back. They cannot see us from such a low elevation – the safety rails are perfect camouflage. We can simply wipe them out.'

'Or,' said Richard conversationally, in English in case the exchange might damage Ping's face and authority, 'the Simonov is accurate and powerful enough to blow their outboard off. Or to put a hole through it and smash the works at any rate.'

Lieutenant Ping's eyes narrowed in thought. He was clearly recalling the Captain's last words. And calculating in typically soldierly fashion – would she be more impressed by obedience or by bravery? Was she the kind of woman who appreciated peacemakers or warmakers? And what would she think of a man who stood by and allowed another man to do his dirty work?

Richard had very little doubt about Robin and what her preferences were likely to be in the same situation. He just hoped Ping would make his mind up quickly – one way or another.

But Ping was a quick-thinking, decisive leader. And he was by no means a savage.

'So, what are we talking about here?' he asked, still speaking English, looking at the venerable weapon in Richard's hands. 'Seven point five millimetre load?'

'Just over. But muzzle velocity of seven hundred and fifty metres per second give or take. I zeroed it recently and I can guarantee accuracy to the better part of a mile with the scope. It's calibrated to a thousand metres.' He glanced at the incoming pirate boat. 'Impact like an elephant gun at this range, I'd say.'

'Let's do it, then,' decided Ping. He switched to Mandarin. 'The Captain has requested that we attempt minimum loss of life,' he said formally. 'Do you think you could disable the pirate vessel for me?'

'I believe so, Lieutenant.'

'Very well. Please proceed.'

Richard put the Simonov to his shoulder and screwed the telescopic sight into his right eye, keeping his left eye open for ease of sighting. He swung the sniper rifle round until the incoming pirate boat was in the centre of the magnified circle. It was coming straight on and the close-up magnification of the scope made it seem that the pirates would be aboard in mere moments.

The vertical gauge of the calibrated sight seemed to start at the sharp point of the bow and end at the black box of the outboard. Richard was easily able to read the word TOHATSU stencilled there in white Roman lettering. Richard swept the focus up and down the boat, counting the excited, well-armed men. Uncle Zheng seemed very well supported. So well supported, as to be a little overconfident, in fact. There was no sign of binoculars – there seemed to be no one observing *Poseidon* closely at all. Just a collection of seemingly drunken young men waving a range of weapons, most of which looked much younger and a good deal more dangerous than the Simonov itself. The only person there of any age or authority – Uncle Zheng, therefore – was holding the outboard's control like a long black tiller. Richard focussed on Uncle Zheng and the outboard for a moment longer, pleased to see that the pirate captain was as overconfident as his men, lolling at ease on the aft thwart with the tiller almost at arm's length.

Richard brought the cross-hairs on to the topmost T of TOHATSU, some deep-seated desire for precision satisfied by the way the two came together. He squeezed the trigger and the long gun kicked against his shoulder with an agreeable authority. The report of the shot echoed across the river, amplified at once by a decided THUMP and a range of outraged shouts. Then the shouts themselves were drowned in the controlled cheering of Ping's marines.

The scope had jumped up and Richard had lifted the rifle away a little automatically, careful not to give himself a black eye. He blinked now, refocussing. The pirate boat was rocking dangerously as the men aboard it stood, shouting and waving. One of the pirates squeezed off a wild shot and the men in front of him screamed – deafened and burned – and lucky not to be shot. Where the bullet went, heaven only knew. But the recoil was enough to unbalance the gunman and he went overboard, taking the two men beside him down into the muddy water. Richard got a glimpse of Uncle Zheng, who was also standing and shouting. The outboard beside his right knee was blazing merrily, its top gone and its control hanging like a broken arm.

Suddenly, there was a commotion above Richard's head and he looked up to see Captain Cai jump screaming into the water, followed by something that looked a little like a big bag of dirty washing. When the washing hit the water, Captain Gan's head emerged from it, and he started floundering through the wreckage floating on the surface after Cai, towards Uncle Zheng's boat.

Such was their concentration on what was happening on the river that no one aboard kept any kind of a watch on the low clouds of the sky. So when the helicopter dropped into position immediately above the drifting hulk of the pirates' boat it was a surprise to everyone. Certainly, its sudden arrival completed the undoing of Uncle Zheng and his crew. The last of the pirates still standing up and waving their weapons threateningly at *Poseidon*, dived into the water with such panic that they overturned the boat, so all of them joined Gan and Cai in the icy waters of the swollen river. But the helicopter did not attack them. Instead, it hung in the lower air and an amplified voice bellowed:

'*Poseidon*. This is Lieutenant Commander Tan seconded from the *Luyang* to the command of Deputy General Commissioner Huuk. Is everything all right aboard?'

Poseidon's tannoy bellowed in reply. 'We are all well except for Radio Operator Dung who has been shot and killed by pirates who destroyed our radio,' answered Captain Chang steadily.

'I was ordered by the Deputy General Commissioner to enquire particularly about Captain Robin Mariner.'

'The Captain is well.'

'Thank you. I will report on all matters. Please proceed. We will return to Zhenjiang.'

'Thank you, Lieutenant Commander Tan. Good luck.'

But, as the crowded helicopter span and prepared to carry Tan and his command back towards Zhenjiang, with its flooded docks and empty fuel bowsers, he looked down at the wide brown waters of the river and the upturned hull of the pirate boat, too deeply lost in thought even to register that a massive mooring buoy marked YIZHENG No. 4 swept almost wilfully along the current and smashed the upturned boat to kindling.

Why had the Dragon Head seemed so genuinely worried about the golden-haired western woman? he thought, frowning.

TWENTY-TWO
Dock

Steady Xin eased *Poseidon*'s long, sleek bow past the dangerous swirl of water that had once been dock number one beside the unnaturally widened outwash of the Qinhuai, the river's northern channel, and into what was left of the Nanjing city docks a little less than one hour later.

Richard stood at the solid helmsman's shoulder, looking away left across the flooded area, up the densely urbanized slopes towards the distant Zijinshan. It might be called the Purple Mountain, he thought, but it looked more like a smoky slag heap against the low grey morning sky. The whole vibrant city of Nanjing, capital of China under the great Ming Dynasty, seemed drenched, deserted. Dead. He could see no citizens. There didn't seem to be any cars moving. Though from here it was impossible to guess how many of the streets were underwater. The ranks of tall buildings seemed lightless and lifeless. He shivered suddenly and wondered why they had fought so hard and long to come to this place. But then, of course, he got his answer.

Through the tight-packed high-rises of the modern and usually bustling city away to the south-east, where the land was higher, he caught his first clear glimpse of the great Ming Wall, a massive edifice that wound through the heart of Nanjing. It was twelve metres tall. A hulking presence that brought to Richard's mind the physical reality of the wave that was bound downstream towards them. As he thought, he kept glancing almost unconsciously at his battered old Rolex as he tried to calculate how much time they had in hand before the monster was due to come sweeping over the low island of Meizi Zhou and roaring out of the Nanjingdaqiao river reach.

He kept transposing the imaginary visions of the huge wall into different places closer to the river, especially here, in the city's low point at the waterside. The low point, he thought, except for the lakes further inland where the city's topography pulled it lower still, as a kind of balance to the heights of the Purple Mountain. He did this so that he could estimate against the fronts of the nearest buildings how high a wave, likely to be nearly twice as tall as the great Ming Wall, would come as it rode down the back of the already swollen river.

How many people in the silent city, who fondly believed that they had already faced the worst and survived – that they had nothing to look forward to but help – would simply be doomed without some kind of warning. What he saw in his prophetic imagination made his blood run cold. And the rest of his long, lean frame burn with the need for immediate action.

Si Ji Shi Guan (NCO 4th Class) Steadyhand Xin was also deeply preoccupied. He had been so, indeed, since before the pirates came aboard. But the combination of events during that adventure had made him withdraw deeply into himself, as he sought to examine his own feelings and motivations. However, Steady was naturally a taciturn, not to say withdrawn, individual – so no one noticed. Instead, they had, as ever, relied upon the closest thing the ship had to a boatswain to do his duty steadily and effectively. And so he had.

But the broad, calloused hands that rested steadily on *Poseidon*'s controls burned with the memory of Captain Chang's slim waist, as though when they lifted her off the gangplank in Zhenjiang they had been lifting her into Steady Xin's bed. As though the cool, well-pressed white cotton of her starched uniform had been the thinnest tissue of silk, burning with the white heat of their mutual arousal.

And his arm tingled where it had held her safe. And his right pectoral muscle blazed with the physical memory of one firm breast trapped briefly against it.

The knuckles of his right fist throbbed with bruising from the face he had punched to achieve her rescue. How it had throbbed with an almost uncontrollable desire to punch the pirates Gan and Cai, no matter that it may have cost Xin his life. Only the radio operator's death had made him pause – for the terrible vision of his captain struck by a stray bullet as he fought to protect her *face*, and her honour, had proved too much for him to bear. How it now tingled with an equally powerful desire to punch the supercilious face of Shao Wei Lieutenant Paradeground Ping.

Steady was vaguely aware of the bustle around him during the three-quarters of an hour after the helicopter left and *Poseidon* – though he thought of her as *Yu-quiang*, her original name – had swept with lordly disdain past the floundering, howling pirate scum. He had been aware that the commanders – there seemed to be so many – had been in a huddle at the back of the bridge when the mooring buoy from Yizheng had completed the destruction of the pirate boat. So he was probably the only man aboard who was aware of the incident – apart from Ping, who seemed to have eyes everywhere. Ping. Perhaps he should change his nickname from Paradeground to Punchbag. Yes. That would be entirely satisfactory.

Later, he had become vaguely aware of the gweilo giant, who had a habit of standing beside him, coming and going with increasing regularity. Steady quite liked the Good Luck Giant; felt towards him and the ugly round-eyed golden-haired wife much as a legendary member of the ancient Middle Kingdom in fairy tales might feel about a couple of pet dragons. He kept a distant eye on the unfathomable, conceivably lucky – but probably dangerous – pair.

But he knew where his captain was at every moment she was on the bridge, as though he had an extra set of senses in the back of his head, his shoulders, back and buttocks. She burned like a flame and he could feel the heat of her at all times. Whenever she was close to him, her reflection seemed to fill the clearview in front of him, like the face of an actress on wide-screen in the cinema. And even when she moved away, the reflection seemed to linger.

The tall dark clouds gathered in the waxing morning above the flooded waste that had been the Nanjing Inspection Zone and the Yicheng Oil Tanker Anchorage had somehow assumed the tumble of her pageboy haircut. The way the flooded river widened over the Niaoyu Zhou seemed in his fancy to gain something of the pale ivory of her forehead – until her father the river pilot growled that he should take extra care here because the marker buoys seemed to have broken their moorings. And the river guidance system was down. As dead as the radio that Zong Wei the electrical engineering lieutenant was trying his best to fix. The radio room was festooned with the contents, not only of the damaged set, but also of the ship's entire stock of spare parts. Captain Chang had stopped going in to hurry the lieutenant up when she realized that the pressure she was exerting was having no effect other than to steam up his glasses.

In the meantime, Straightline started calling depths to help him stay in the deeps of the central channel as they came down into the Longtan Shuiado reach. But here at least the flood helped them – they had the better part of thirty metres beneath her keel. All they had to take care of was the increasingly thick flotsam clogging the surface. And soon that became solid enough to register on the collision alarm radar. Especially as they began to ease through the broad southern outflow of the Boata Shuaido reach that flowed round the huge flooded river island of Bagua Zhou. The outflow was normally a couple of hundred feet wide – now it was nearly twice that, and packed with all sorts of rubbish from saturated books to upturned barges, swept out of Jiatong and beyond.

Steady fell back into his thoughts again, unaware how much of what was happening in his head was there because of a weird mare's nest of guilt, confusion, lust and exhaustion. A mile or so ahead, a low bridge spanned the river, seeming to rise out of the water and fall back into it. Like the back of a river dragon. Abruptly, Xin's right side caught fire and the pale oval of his captain's face was reflected on the glass, the straight dark line of her brows seeming to follow the line of the bridge. Beneath it, her eyes flashed briefly as she surveyed the devastation ahead.

'Straightline,' she said quietly. 'I know we have plenty of depth beneath our keel. But do we have clearance to pass the Nanjing Chanjiang second bridge?'

'We should do, Captain. If we stay in the middle of the channel. Under the central span.'

Captain Chang leaned towards Xin. His hands shook on the controls. Her nearness was almost painfully intense. 'The bridge is flat,' she observed. 'It hardly seems to matter where on the river we are. But do as he says, Steady. Take it slowly, though. Let's go down to thirty per cent on revolutions . . .'

She adjusted the engine room telegraph herself. The sleeve of her uniform brushed the entire length of his naked forearm. The side of her hand touched his, only to be jerked away automatically. 'You have given me a shock, Steady,' she said, surprised. Their eyes met in the clearview; hers given added depth and definition by the shadow under the approaching bridge. Then she turned and crossed the bridge to stand between her father and the ubiquitous Lieutenant Ping.

Steady guided *Poseidon* under the central span, his entire conscious-ness caught between the conflicting imperatives of holding the slowly-moving vessel straight against the vagaries of the swirling current between the bridge's piles; of easing the useless whip aerial gently across the underside so that they bent but did not break, and of trying to work out a nickname for Ping that was even more insulting than Punchbag.

'Careful, Steady!' snapped the Captain.

'Careful . . .' he echoed automatically. And, for all his concentration, experience and expertise, *Poseidon* was twisted off-line by a particu-larly vicious cross-current. The top of a radio aerial ten metres above their heads snagged. There was a crack and a judder. And their radio was suddenly doubly dead. Zong Wei actually wailed aloud with sheer frustration. 'Now even if I get this mess sorted out, I shall have to restring the aerial!' he called. 'Captain, this is impossible . . .'

'Helmsman!' snapped Ping officiously. 'The Captain told you to take care!'

'Sorry . . .' started Steady, contritely.

'Sorry, SIR!' snarled Ping.

'Lighten up, Lieutenant,' suggested the Good Luck Giant in his horrific Mandarin. 'If Steady couldn't see that one coming, no one could. He's the best helmsman I've ever worked with.' He swung round, his voice attaining the deep, calming rumble that parents use with warring children. 'And so are you, Zong Wei. You'll have that radio up and working soon. Even if it does mean a quick scramble aloft.'

The gweilo's words were welcome, thought the mutinous helmsman. The balance of *face* was readjusted more fairly. But the words should have come from the Captain's tempting lips, and her silence hurt Steady with unexpected poignancy. The worm of jealousy began to stir deep below the layers of his affections. And, taken all in all, he was a dangerous man to have as an enemy.

Still undecided as to whether he was friend or foe to most of those aboard, Steady Xin, guided *Poseidon* across the flooded docks as the Captain and the pilot stood side by side, straining to see anything that looked like a familiar anchorage. According to the vessel's accurate GPS system, they should have been snugging safely into a berth at the city's number 4 dock, but instead, they seemed to be several metres above it.

'All stop,' ordered the Captain after a moment more. 'Reverse engines please. Father, do we dare drop anchor? Or would it be even more dangerous to risk drifting?'

'Can you trust Mr Xin to hold her steady?' asked the river pilot.

'Of course!' she answered.

'Even after the loss of the whip antenna?' probed Ping.

'Of course. Steady could not help that!' she snapped hotly.

'Then there's your answer,' said Richard decisively. 'Trust Steady to keep her safe and don't risk losing your anchor. And trust Zong Wei to get the radio resurrected with all possible dispatch. But what's the plan, now that we're here? What orders did Deputy General Commissioner Huuk give you?'

'What you would expect. What I suspect you know as well as I do. We must contact Mayor Jaa and find out how the people in the city are holding up, warn them of the second wave and then report back. I understand his offices are in the municipal buildings at Forty-one East Beijing Road. And to do that, we will need to go ashore. Or at least we will need to go into the city, as we aren't precisely sure where the *shore* is any more.'

'If the road, the offices or Mayor Jaa are actually still there, of course,' said Richard.

'Well, unless somebody comes out to tell us – and I don't see anyone around – then we won't know unless we go and look!' announced Robin.

'True,' said Richard. 'But the chopper's gone and so is the radio – courtesy of pirates. And so is the zodiac, come to that, courtesy of that typhoon. Do we have any other smaller vessels aboard that might let us explore a flooded city and look for either contacts, or some means of making contact?'

'Only one that I can see,' said Robin forcefully, looking straight ahead past Steady's square shoulder and out on to the foredeck.

'*Marilyn*?' said Richard, his tone betraying a mixture of outrage and intrigue.

'*Marilyn*,' confirmed Robin.

'You think that what we need in order to explore a flooded city is a flame-red forty-foot kevlar-hulled powerboat, capable of cruising at seventy-five knots?'

'She's all we've got. She'll take a driver and four others in the cockpit – more aboard if you put them below. But if you're careful she'll have no real draft at all. She has a radio if you can get anyone to receive her signals. And she's damn near impossible to miss.'

'Right!' said Richard, who had been at the wheel when she was a target for a disturbingly wide, if varyingly accurate, range of armaments. 'Impossible to miss in all sorts of ways.'

'I will come,' decided the Captain. 'With Straightline and Lieutenant Ping. We will go in the cockpit. Straightline, bring a hand-held GPS and the biggest chart you have. And some kind of map of the city . . .'

'One that shows the topography if possible,' added Richard, remembering his earlier thoughts about the lie of the land in Nanjing, and how the heights of the mountain might be balanced by the depths of the lakes.

'No need. I know the city as well as Father. The topography, as you call it. We will go in up the Qinhuai River and see where we get from there,' continued the Captain decisively. 'As I am sure Captain Mariner has already calculated, the water is likely to be deepest here, so we will be able to get in farthest and swiftest. Lieutenant Ping, please assign your four best men to come with us and get them to bring all the armaments they can carry. Father, you have the ship. Captain Mariner, you will con *Marilyn* for us. I would prefer if your wife would stay aboard to help and advise the pilot as necessary.'

The pilot grunted, but Richard smiled accommodatingly at the Captain's courteous preservation of Robin's *face*. There was clearly something of a bargain being made here. Even so, he thought he had better take Robin aside. 'Come down to the cabin,' he suggested. 'I need to get one or two things . . .' What he needed to get of course was the bundle of information that Daniel Huuk had given him to pass on to Mayor Jaa, as well as the authorities from the Deputy Director and the Dragon Head – just in case.

'Look, Robin . . .'

'What?' she said coolly.

'I don't know . . . A couple of things, I suppose. Are you OK staying aboard while I take *Marilyn* ashore?'

'Lover, I've lost count of the times you've gone swanning off without me. Just be careful. That's all I ask.'

'OK. But, look, now that we're actually here, so to speak . . . Look. You know Daniel Huuk much better than I do . . .'

'Mmmm hmmm . . .' she said, non-committally.

'Well, I don't know, it just seems a bit odd that he should be sending us all the way up to Nanjing, on the off chance that we can convince the Mayor that there's a huge flood coming.' Richard pulled the bundle of documents Huuk had given him out of its rudimentary hiding place and turned to go. 'I mean I know why Captain Chang and her father are happy to be here – they have family they want to get out of the danger zone. But what is Daniel Huuk really up to?'

Robin just shrugged, and followed him back up on to the main deck where the Captain was issuing the complex orders necessary to get the Cigarette go-faster boat ready for lowering.

TWENTY-THREE
Outwash

Daniel glanced across the body of the helicopter, past Leung's dazed profile and out beyond the city as the first wave arrived at last. All the way down to the horizon, ships and boats were racing away like a herd of panicked water buffalo stampeding towards the illusory hope of safety. But they had neither the speed nor the sea-room to stay ahead of the wave as it spread out across the water. Now, he thought, if they could be organized. If he could somehow get them ready to come back in and take people off high points in the city, then there were enough big ships out there to accommodate the bulk of them. A stirring of memory came. Something he had read about years ago. What was it? Dunkirk! Yes, that was it. Dunkirk.

But then Daniel dismissed his thoughts and settled to watch the less hopeful reality of what was actually going on beneath him. In the slow-motion of a badly cranked silent movie, Daniel saw the ships and boats beginning to collide with each other. Smacks and sampans being rolled over, crushed and drowned by the bigger vessels. No one daring to slow and help the men thrown into the water, for fear the wave would catch them.

Then the wave did indeed begin to catch up with them. The first of the fleeing vessels either kicked up their heels and started to pitch as the red wall swept in under their racing counters – or were ridden down and simply swept under, depending on their size, disposition and seaworthiness.

Daniel cursed under his breath, sailor enough still to know in his bones what the terror and the carnage must be like down there – and this was among vessels designed to handle conditions involving waves and walls of water. That would be one of the top priorities he would discuss with the mayor. First, restore power to the flood management system, then move as many people as possible to safety, then organize this gaggle of vessels into sufficient order to start picking the survivors up . . .

As they flew over the carnage, Political Officer Leung gathered himself and began passing on the messages that had come in for the Deputy General Commissioner. Messages from Beijing. From the office of the Mayor of Shanghai, towards whom they were racing. From the Bureau of Public Security and the Bureau of Justice as well as Finance, Civil Affairs and Transport. The District Governor's Office in Pudong, as well as contacts for the relevant Deputy Governors responsible for that side of the river, not to mention the Provincial Governor's office for Shanghai Shi. From the upper echelons of the People's Liberation Army, its air force, its navy, and its special forces. The first demands for comment from national and international news services.

But the Deputy General Commissioner seemed truly interested in only one message – one that came via the *Luyang* anchored off Shanghai. A message that seemed to the political officer a little obscure – and on such a small scale as to seem almost incredibly irrelevant when set against the others. The message was simply to the effect that a couple of gweilos who seemed to have somehow got mixed up with some river pirates were both well. And that the good ship *Yu-quiang* would be docking in Nanjing before noon.

On receipt of the cryptic message, the Deputy General Commissioner gave an unguarded smile wide enough to crease the corners of his eyes and mouth.

By a quirk of fate, as all of this was going on, Daniel caught a distant glimpse of the wave's progress up the Huangpu River towards the heart of Shanghai, as he raced the wall of water towards Number 200, People's Avenue.

What he could not see, however, was how well the sandbag embankments in Huangpu Park had protected the Bund; whether the flood had run back up the Suzhu Creek to flood Hongpu, Yangpu or the Huangpu District whose heart he was racing towards. Whether Mayor Hong and his able teams of civil servants had been able to protect – evacuate and protect – the sections of the city most vulnerable to the flood according to their post-quake plans. Underground car parks, basement-level shopping malls. The subway system.

Then it would just be down to *joss* whether or not the drainage and sewerage systems were still functioning well enough to help, rather than hinder, all their efforts.

And, as the helicopter began to lose height, heading for the helipad on top of the strong, square roof of the mayor's office at Number 200, People's Avenue, Daniel could see that there would still need to be a lot of work done before the big, dangerous and deadly second wave arrived.

A frown replaced the smile on his lean countenance. Why had he not heard directly from the Mariners?

What was going on upriver, now that the irrelevance of the pirate attack had been resolved?

What was the point of sending fact-finding missions upstream if they failed to report on conditions and damage?

To give warning of the second wave – whether it was real or just the figment of night-time panic.

Whether it was actually coming.

What size it was.

And, most crucial of all, when it could be expected to arrive down here.

TWENTY-FOUR
Xuanwu

Marilyn eased down into the water with the eight all safely aboard. Imposing though the bright red Cigarette Top Gun had seemed on *Poseidon*'s foredeck, down here beside the corvette's hull she seemed small and frail.

To all, perhaps, except Richard, who had raced her up the Yangtze weaving in and out between the inbound and outbound freighters and container ships half a dozen times the size of Captain Chang's lean warship, like a Ferrari racing eighteen-wheelers on the freeway. And yet even he was wearing a bright life-jacket – under which, in a waterproof packet, lay the booklet of call signs, wavelengths and passwords that Ping had brought over from Daniel Huuk on the *Luyang*.

As the sleek vessel settled into the water, Richard flicked all the switches and put the settings at optimum for the conditions he reckoned they would be facing. He checked the fuel gauge which read almost full. He flicked the automatic tuner on the Cigarette's two-way radio, but it remained whispering almost silently as no one nearby broke through the static to communicate with them. At the very least that meant the electrical officer Zong Wei hadn't fixed *Poseidon*'s set yet either.

The thoughtful Richard gunned the motors as soon as the falls were free and started easing her confidently forward. Straightline and Ping shared the wide bench seat aft of the two deep pilot's chairs forward. The space between them was filled with Straightline's chart of the Nanjing waterways and another, smaller, tourist map of the city itself. The big squares of paper were held in place by the seamen's thighs and by the weight of the navigator's GPS handset. The day was overcast and gusty. There was rain in the air and the heavy wind was strong enough to keep lifting the stiff cartridge paper of the chart and snatching at the flimsy stuff of the map.

The first thing Richard saw ahead of him on the wide, wide waterway was a series of square grey structures that looked like iron boxes set on stilts. 'What are those?' he flung over his shoulder at Straightline. His narrowed eyes beginning to see what looked like a weir between them where the water behaved strangely.

'Barriers,' came the reply. 'River management system. There are movable barriers under there . . .'

'They don't seem to be managing much at the moment,' observed Richard drily, gunning the motors a little more to drive the sleek, red Kevlar hull over the mill race that was all there was to show of the curved barriers lost beneath the flood. He tried to feel through the hull to work out the water's disposition, like a fisherman exploring the ocean deeps through his fishing line. But the flood made reading the river almost impossible. What should have been little more than two hundred feet wide was more than four hundred now. What should have been perhaps twenty feet deep looked more like fifty. He had been expecting three metres, maybe five, of flood. There was more than that here. Why might that be? he wondered. The topography of the city sloping downwards to the north and the west, away from the purple heights in the south-east?

The buildings on either hand were tall – many almost skyscrapers. None seemed particularly quake-damaged. There had been some first-rate architecture here. But they stood in a sullenly moving lake now, like tree-trunks in a flooded swamp. He was tempted to turn aside and push *Marilyn*'s flame-red nose into the glass-walled waterways that should have been the thoroughfares of Shimao Binjiang New Town. But Straightline was calling directions and warning him about the next upcoming hazard, the double spans of the Huimin road bridge. They all bowed their heads as Richard eased *Marilyn* under the bridge – though there was no real chance of banging them.

The river widened again and they found themselves sailing between illusory green banks that were actually the tops of drowning trees. Low traditional buildings fell back behind the underwater thoroughfares that Captain Chang explained were Zhenghuai Road and Huabin Road that had run along the embankments on the riverside – while the river still had sides.

The next hazard she warned against was the twin span of the Rehe south road bridge, and it was almost immediately after this that things began to get out of hand.

So far, even though the water's edge had been pushed so far back into the blocks of the city itself, it had seemed to Richard that there had to be an end to it. The flow of the river, the way the currents moved beneath *Marilyn*'s shallow draft all seemed to speak of relatively settled and safely contained floodwaters. But as they came out from under the second bridge, the whole aspect of the waterway changed. *Marilyn* started tugging to go left with the relentless persistence of an excited dog.

'Straightline! What's down there?' called Richard, wrestling to keep *Marilyn*'s increasingly wilful length under some kind of control.

'The Hucheng River,' called Straightline.

'It doesn't really go anywhere,' added Captain Chang. 'I mean, it's landlocked. More like a canal.'

'Well it's going to take *Marilyn* away from us unless . . .' grated Richard, and he gunned the motors, sending the hull smashing over the cross-current like a lifeboat being launched from the beach.

Immediately, another bridge pounced down on them like the blade of a guillotine. With no thought other than to escape the mill race threatening to pull them up into the Hucheng River, Richard gunned the massive motors once again and *Marilyn* answered with all the power at her command. Her nose came up as her power plants settled to work. She tore out of the clutch of the cross-currents and powered under the bridge at the better part of sixty miles an hour.

'Mofan West road bridge,' called Straightline helpfully at exactly the same moment as the Captain. Their voices echoed sepulchrally even as they spoke, for the Cigarette went under the span as the words came out of his mouth.

And then things went very badly out of control indeed.

Marilyn came out from under the Mofan road bridge straight into what Captain Chang later explained should have been a gentle southerly reach past the Zigin Tower landmark on one hand, and Bingdongcun on the other, until it reached the span of the Beijing West road bridge.

But there was no gentle southerly reach. Instead, Richard found *Marilyn* was heading at full speed straight on along a wild, wide new rivercourse, that seemed to be heading almost due east. In his mind, he saw at last – if too late – what his subconscious had been trying to warn him about with its fixation on the topography of the city. Everything hard left and dead ahead was lower than everything up on their right. So much lower that the flood water was tearing the city apart in its keenness to get down there.

The Zigin Tower sped by, one amongst a mass of high-rises through which the new river was forcing its white-water way. Treetops thumped against *Marilyn*'s racing keel forcefully enough to make them all shout with shock. Then Ping shouted, 'There's a road down there . . .'

And Straightline called, 'I can't find it! Shit! I can't see . . .'

Captain Chang called out, 'It must be Huju North . . .'

But even as she said the word 'north', the boat's head was wrenched south by the racing current, and *Marilyn* plunged back amongst a heaving maze of reefs and cliffs that were in fact the tops and fronts of buildings.

The Captain, who knew the city well, continued, shouting over the gathering thunder of the water, 'We're going into Gulu! My God! We must be heading for the lake!'

'What lake?' called Ping.

Richard closed his eyes for an instant, even though he was fighting to keep some kind of control of the Cigarette – which was suddenly behaving more like a white-water raft than an ocean-going powerboat. He saw the map and recognized the anglicized version of the name beneath the Chinese character. Lake Xuanwu. The city's lowest point.

'Lake Xuanwu,' shouted the Captain.

'How far?' yelled Richard, who was seriously beginning to doubt his ability to keep them from disaster for any length of time – or much more distance.

He opened his eyes and found that they were at a crossroads of some kind. The frontages of buildings reached right and left, ahead and astern. He glanced right – upslope, hoping to see some hope of escape. Instead, he saw a huge whirlpool at the next crossroads uphill. A funnel of water seemed to stand there, seemingly set in amber glass. From the fleeting look he got, the whole thing seemed to stand three metres high and it must have gaped ten metres across at its terrifying maw.

But then Straightline yelled, 'Look!'

'What?' yelled Richard, as they were hurled through the crossroads.

'There was a fountain! Down on the left, in . . .' he consulted his map '. . . Zhongyang Road, I guess . . . And I mean a fountain. Like a geyser. Four, maybe five metres high . . . It was—'

What it was seemed irrelevant to Richard just at the moment. 'How far to the lake?' he bellowed.

'Three kilometres from the river on the map,' called Straightline.

'But if this is anything to go by, the lake will have grown,' shouted Richard. 'It's where this lot is all heading for! And, given the speed we're doing we must be almost there ourselves!'

'That is true,' called Captain Chang. 'So offer a prayer to your ancestors that we make it!' She leaned forward, her eyes narrow and her face set. Richard focussed fearsomely as buildings heaved and rocked, below and beside them, as the current whirled them onwards. One minute, they were leaping with the wild spray over submerged walls and even houses. The next, they were speeding down canyons as narrow as footpaths between towering skyscrapers. Only the wild waters seemed to know where it – and they – were going.

At last Captain Chang shouted. 'I know this! It's . . .!' and even as she did so, *Marilyn* seemed to jump over another weir that the bemused Richard recognized as the top of the Ming Wall itself, and sped out from under the towers Chang had been talking about into the relative quiet of a great lake.

'Oh, Daddy, that was *fun!*' Richard breathed as he pushed himself back into the depths of the jet-pilot seat and eased his cramping shoulders, remembering many a hair-raising adventure with his twins when they were younger. He pushed the throttles forward and sent *Marilyn* cruising more sedately out into the middle of the water as he looked around.

On the far shore there was a range of buildings that seemed to be standing well above the water, and Richard realized with something of a shock that this was because they were clustered on the lower slopes of the Purple Mountain.

It took *Marilyn* the better part of fifteen minutes to cross the lake, even though Richard, aware of the urgency, powered her up to full speed as soon as he felt it safe to do so. During the last few moments of the trip, the flame-red vessel was surrounded by black-hulled inflatables.

When they first saw these inflatables approaching, Ping called his men to ready their weapons – thoughts of pirates, looters and anarchy stirring in his mind. But Chang surveyed the nearest of the vessels through *Marilyn*'s onboard binoculars and told them to stand down.

'Uniforms,' she said tersely. 'Police or militia. And they don't behave like renegades or deserters. They look as though they have radios . . .'

Richard reached down and started channel surfing on *Marilyn*'s radio. They picked up a broadcast almost at once and assumed that it must be from the approaching vessels. But after a confused and confusing conversation Captain Chang suddenly announced, 'It's not them at all. It's someone in a helicopter. Inbound from Tongling.'

'Nice to know there's life somewhere out there,' said Richard. 'But we have more immediate concerns.'

And he cut the conversation off by switching channels once again.

Immediately, Captain Chang was in communication with the lead inflatable, and by the time the little flotilla reached the new shoreline on the lower slopes of the Purple Mountain, all the relevant formalities had been completed. Mayor Jaa, they were informed, knew they were coming and would see them. But he was far too busy to talk to them just at the moment. If and when they made it to his new headquarters in the Sun Yat Sen Memorial Park at the top of the Zijinshan Purple Mountain, he would be glad to hear what they had to say, accept what they had to offer and offer in turn whatever help, experience or advice he had, or could command.

TWENTY-FIVE
Zijinshan

For some reason, which neither Chang nor Richard could quite fathom at first, the water seemed to stop at Ningqi Street, and the little flotilla of inflatables, having picked its way through the upper stories of the flooded university buildings, came ashore at the post office. Only when they saw the men standing on the roadway that formed the new shoreline did it become obvious how steeply the land was beginning to slope upwards here. That was why the water stopped. This was effectively the foothill of the Purple Mountain.

But the lead inflatable did not stop. It held back and ordered *Marilyn* to do so, as well as the others beached on the pavement. Then it turned downtown and led *Marilyn* onwards, round the foot of the mountain and through the complexes of roadway and rooftop that represented the variously inundated areas of Gangzicun, Chouchengmu and Pipazhu to the Huning Expressway. Here they sailed just above the roofs, doors and wheels of cars, estates, four-by-fours, vans, trucks and lorries all scattered hither and yon by the combination of earthquake and flood. As it turned out, the plan was to proceed until they reached Laoguoyuan where they could come ashore.

Leaving *Marilyn* in the hands of the Nanjing police, Richard hurried after the others up the hill towards the Sun Yat Sen Memorial park fifteen minutes later, past the first large building they had seen so far that was not flooded. 'Where's that?' asked Richard, intrigued.

'It's Nanjing Underwater World,' Chang informed him drily. And he stopped dead, looking down at her, wondering if, amid all this mayhem she had found a sense of humour that was almost the match of his own.

The captain of the floating police contingent led the way with three of his uniformed crew behind him; then came Richard carrying Daniel Huuk's booklet of call-signs, still in its waterproof package.

Chang and Straightline walked beside him, with Ping and his men formed up behind. And that was just as well. The military phalanx was not needed for protection, but it was useful to aid speed of movement. For the mountain slopes were packed with people. Mostly in family groups surrounded by possessions, using the woodland of the wild slopes as fuel to heat food and keep warm; it seemed that the millions of Nanjing inhabitants had gathered here, in the illusory safety of their mountain, just above the tideline of the flood. It was the smoke from their fires, Richard realized, as much as the overcast and stormy day that made the Zijinshan seem like a slag heap instead of a purple mountain.

How many people lived in Nanjing? Richard cudgelled his brain. Well over six million. But that was in the entire urban area. They couldn't have got six million people up here. Still, there was one hell of a crowd on the purple mountain.

What was almost shocking was the fact that the thousands – maybe millions – were so quiet and orderly. There seemed to be no panic. There had been – and was – no sign of lawlessness. Only resigned acceptance, and a couple of million souls doing their best to stay safe and alive as they waited for orders. Or news. Or rescue.

The Sun Yat Sen Memorial gardens were packed as well, but at least the central square was kept clear. It seemed to Richard that much of what he thought of as 'city hall' was assembled in the buildings around the Paifang gate, at the foot of the flights of steps leading up to the ornate building itself. Here, at the top of a brisk climb, Mayor Jaa sat at the hub of a small but effective communications centre. However, the best he had in the way of radio equipment seemed to be the police and militia's short-range two-ways. And he did not sit for long.

Jaa turned out to be a tall, lean, athletic Han. He was dressed in a dark business suit of Western cut, though the jacket lay folded over the back of a chair. White shirt, open at the collar. Thick, black-rimmed glasses. Hair like thick black lacquer over the broad dome of his head. There was something about him that, obscurely, reminded Richard of Daniel Huuk. He sparked with restless energy clearly intensified by the crisis he was trying to deal with. He seemed to speak in a continuous controlled bellow, for the noise made by the restless wind, the rumbling of the petrol-fuelled generators and the conversations of a couple of million people nearby added to quite a high level of background noise.

Even as Richard and Captain Chang waited to speak with him – and they did not wait long – he had thrown the walkie-talkie to an aid with orders to keep on top of communications. Quite an order – they might not have much in the way of range, but the airwaves that they controlled seemed tight-packed with masses of information.

Unaware of Richard's arrival, Mayor Jaa was demanding a report as to how the search for a proper radio was going, and hurried up some unfortunates who were not being quick enough at finding either an undamaged radio store, or a well-equipped Ham radio enthusiast.

The fleets of inflatables were bringing in food and medication from the flooded areas of the city – and the militia patrols were bringing more from the higher, dryer areas. The emergency services were scouring all the districts they could reach as they searched for victims of the earthquake and people trapped by flood waters. The Mayor and his team clearly had a plan – even in the face of this magnitude of disaster – and it was a plan that seemed to be working. Richard thought, I must talk this over with Daniel Huuk as soon as we have radio contact. It reminded him of something. What was it? Operation Dynamo. Yes, that was it. Operation Dynamo. The miracle of Dunkirk.

'But we are blind and deaf and dumb!' cried Jaa at last with perfectly understandable frustration. 'We know nothing about what else is happening in the country, or what Beijing is doing. And now we have these people warning that there may be more floods coming before any sort of rescue can get to us! Where are they? Where are these people who have come from Shanghai to help us?'

Suddenly, the background noise reached a new level as a helicopter roared low over the Mausoleum and settled down the long flights of steps – clearly with every intention of landing on the open area outside the Paifang gate.

'What now?' bellowed the Mayor. 'Can anyone tell me what is going on now?'

And Richard at last stepped forward.

'The helicopter has come up from Tongling,' he said in his quarterdeck voice, easily overcoming the hubbub. His voice was clear though his Mandarin accent was less so. 'They contacted us aboard our vessel but we hadn't time for a detailed conversation. Like us, I am sure they are here to bring news and offer help.'

'And who are you?' demanded Jaa.

Richard stepped forward and offered his credentials – literally, like an ambassador showing his documents of appointment, signed by the sovereign and the sovereign's ministers of state. But the documents Richard showed the Mayor with such careful discretion were signed by the Deputy General Commissioner of the Institute of Public Security, and by the Dragon Head of the Invisible Power Triad.

Mayor Jaa looked down at the papers and then up at the man. His eyes narrowed suddenly, becoming almost invisible behind the lenses of his spectacles. 'This is quite a wide range of qualifications,' he said, in Harvard-Law English. 'Someone has almost absolute faith in you. Who are you? And why should I trust you?'

'Mayor Jaa. My name is Richard Mariner. I have brought a booklet of codes and contacts entrusted to me by Deputy General Commissioner Huuk of the Institute of Public Security, who has known me for many years. But more urgently, I have news. The Deputy General Commissioner is certain that the Three Gorges Dam burst when the earthquake struck at about eighteen hundred hours yesterday. We are certain that there is a wall of water coming down the Yangtze towards you. You must move your people even higher up the mountain if possible, and call back anyone you have out in the city now.' He stood back a little, having delivered himself of the speech, suddenly deflated. His mind jumping back to the hurried conversation with Robin. There was more to this than there seemed to be, he was certain. There was another part to Daniel Huuk's plan that he didn't know about yet.

Jaa stood silent, his mind clearly racing. 'Are you sure?' he asked at last. 'How big is this wave? When will it get here? Where is it now?'

Richard turned back to look at Captain Chang, his mind racing with calculations that he suddenly realized he should have prepared long since. Answers he should have had at his fingertips now.

And there at the door of the mausoleum stood a tall, strikingly beautiful woman whose Han blood was obviously tinged with a little Mongol. 'The wave is real, Mayor Jaa,' she called, her voice as loud and clear as Richard's. Her Mandarin accent flawless. 'It was big enough to tear down the High Bridge at Wuhan as I watched it, and I am reliably informed that it has just reached Tongling.'

At the sound of the clear, ringing voice, Captain Chang swung round. And she whispered the word that seemed so unlikely to Richard that he thought his Mandarin was letting him down at last. '*Mother!*' The Captain turned towards Richard, her face almost vacant with shock and surprise. 'It is Leading Architect Chang Mei-Feng. My mother!'

But Richard didn't really hear her. His mind was racing. His near-photographic memory dredged up a chart that seemed clear enough to give him a good idea of distances and times. The river wound about a bit between here and Tongling. There were side-channels, marshes, islands. It must be between 150 and 200 miles in all. If the flood was still coming at a mean speed of fifty miles per hour . . .

'You have between three and four hours, Mayor Jaa. And if the water was powerful enough to destroy the bridge at Wuhan then it will do a great deal more damage to your city. Still,' he looked around, 'you should be safe enough up here and higher up towards the peak. Can you move your people up there in that time?'

'With luck,' answered the Mayor tersely. 'We have them organized into groups by family and area. Like the old communes. Each group has a leader. Each leader has a walkie-talkie . . . But what I wouldn't give for a good powerful radio transceiver. Preferably with a satellite link!' he added.

'I believe I can help you,' said the beautiful, crystal tones once more.

Richard turned back. The extraordinary woman was standing beside the Captain and their arms were round each other. There were tears in both pairs of eyes. The impact of the Captain's words hit him then. This lovely woman was the plain sailor's mother. 'I have a present from the management of the Tongling Non-Ferrous Metals Group in my helicopter,' she said with a dazzling smile.

Mei-Feng's present was a big Shenzen commercial CB AM/FM/Digital Transciever with more than 240 channels and 6 bands.

It plugged into the Mayor's power supply with an adaptor. It took only a couple of moments to get the thing working – Richard was able to help for the equipment was not all that different to the big Hagenuk marine transceivers he had used in the past. But he was happy to hand over to the far more competent young man from the Mayor's communications unit who showed up almost immediately.

Mayor Jaa was on the air within minutes, clutching the booklet of codes that Richard had brought from Huuk. With these and the Shenzen transceiver he was able to make contact first with the man who had given it to him – Director Wu at the Tongling Non-Ferrous Metals compound. Wu was able to pass on vital – if distantly observed – information about the arrival, size and destructive force of the wave as it came past Tongling.

Then Jaa made contact with the office of his opposite number, Mayor Hong of Shanghai, passing on an initial warning – and the news that the corvette *Poseidon* would be returning downriver with all possible dispatch. Bringing the items that Deputy General Commissioner Huuk requested – if Mayor Hong could pass the message on at his earliest convenience . . .

Then, little more than eighteen hours after the original quake, he finally made contact with Beijing and started to report what he knew – and what he feared.

'This could take some time,' said Richard, his mind racing at the Mayor's obscure words. 'What are our next priorities?'

And, on the point of the question itself, Mayor Jaa looked up. 'Your priority is Wen-Qi,' he said, as though Richard would know exactly what he was talking about. 'You have been sent here to fetch her, after all. She goes back with you, of course.'

And the fact that he had interrupted a conversation with the Politburo Standing Committee to say this emphasized how massively important he thought it was.

'Wen-Qi?' said Richard, his mind racing. 'Who or what is Wen-Qi?'

'It is a woman's name,' said Captain Chang, turning back from her conversation with the tall, stunning woman at her side. 'It means "glittering green like jade".'

'Jade,' said Richard, irresistibly reminded of the members of pop groups in England, of youthful models revealing far too much of themselves in tabloid newspapers and of reality TV shows. Feeling like the last of the dinosaurs in the blink of an eye, he could almost hear his daughter Mary hooting with outraged laughter at his antediluvian sexist snobbery.

'Me,' said another voice. Low but determined. Youthful but somehow forceful. Speaking in American-accented English. 'I am Wen-Qi. Don't you *dare* call me Jade!'

Richard swung round and found himself confronted by another female stranger. This one was a young woman – little more than a girl. Her hair was cut square across the forehead just above her level eyebrows and round below the ears in bangs, like Captain Chang's. Her face was oval, her cheekbones sharp and wide. But her nose was long and straight, while her lips, like her chin, were square and determined. She stood about five foot six, but probably had more growing to do. Her slim young figure was dressed in a school uniform – with white socks and black patent shoes that gleamed like lacquer. On the ground beside them stood an expensive designer suitcase, and she was straightening from having placed it there as she spoke.

But everything that Richard noticed about her was secondary to one overwhelming impression. Her eyes. They were long, sloping above the wide cheekbones, and unusually wide for a Han. Wide enough to reveal mixed race. And they were green. Moss-green under downcast lashes. But when she glanced up at Richard as she straightened, not at all discomfited by the way he towered over her, they gleamed pure, clear jade.

'My name is Wen-Qi Huuk,' she announced, still speaking English like a princess addressing a group of lackeys, and putting her name into the Western form as a mark of her superiority. 'And you have all come here to take me back to my father, at last.'

PART FOUR
SHANGHAI

TWENTY-SIX
Run

*P*oseidon began her run back downriver little more than an hour later, with the great wave between two and three hours behind her. Under normal circumstances, any vessel less fleet than *Marilyn* would have been hard put to stay ahead of something moving at a mean velocity of fifty miles per hour, but *Poseidon* was fast and the river helped her head for the sea as effectively as it had slowed her progress upstream.

Poseidon herself was capable of thirty-five knots and the flood was running out beneath her keel at the better part of another thirty. There were points at which her mean speed measured against the shore came close to *Marilyn*'s seventy knots, therefore, but they were few and far between. For the swollen river, running at spate though it was, was also full of flotsam from the wreckage it had caused inland and Steady Xin had to keep a sharp eye out – even beyond the dictates of Straightline and his collision alarm radar, the constant imprecations of a captain as tense as a cat on a hot tin roof and the growled commands of her father the river pilot.

And, of course, Steady was as exhausted as they all were. Preoccupied in ways neither his captain nor anyone else on the bridge would ever have conceived – torn between thoughts of lust and murder, mutiny and piracy. But worst of all, he was constantly distracted by Wen-Qi, the Little Empress, and her demands to have this demonstrated and that explained. To hold this, to touch that. To switch this on or off. To control. To power.

To steer.

The tempestuous demands of the spoilt girl were in marked contrast with the attitudes of her elders. And there were several generations of Chinese families aboard now. The dazzling Mei-Feng had joined her daughter and husband, though she had had limited opportunity for anything like intimate conversation with either. She had brought Chopper with her and he had parked his helicopter on the helipad at the stern of the corvette, after he had lowered *Marilyn* into the water beside her so that the Cigarette could be winched back on to the foredeck beside *Neptune*. He was down there now with Zong Wei, overseeing the helicopter's refuelling from

Poseidon's avgas reservoir, untouched since the corvette's own helicopter had been lost overboard.

It was fortunate that Chopper's helicopter was sturdy and quite roomy, for as *Marilyn*'s commander and crew – including Ping and his men – had enjoyed an aerial adventure flying low above the city's flooded suburbs while slung beneath the helicopter's belly, the cabin had been packed not only with Daniel Huuk's daughter but with Mei-Feng's mother and father as well.

These last were a pair of almost ghostly stooped figures in their eighties whose joy at being reunited with their family was expressed in silence and minimal movement. So similar to the understated reunion of Mei-Feng and the Captain her daughter at the Sun Yat Sen mausoleum. So different to the strident and self-centred demands of the twelve-year-old Wen-Qi Huuk. They had been easy enough to find, even amongst the millions on the Purple Mountain, for, as Mayor Jaa had explained, he had organized his refugees in little ersatz communes by family and district.

Now, they were below with most of the rest of the new passengers – including Mei-Feng herself who had paused only to share some solic-itous words about the modest boxing-glove of bandage that swathed her husband's hand where he had been wounded in the shooting earlier, seemingly satisfied with his dismissive words that it was little more than a scratch. They were all apparently snatching some much needed rest in preparation for who knew what rigours to come.

Robin had gone below too, making a show of guiding the relieved Mei-Feng and her parents, but Richard knew that she had done so because Wen-Qi's behaviour was making her palms itch to slap the importunate child. 'I'm going before I do the little monster some permanent damage!' hissed Robin in passing, herself the mother of twins who had been far from perfect in their younger years.

Richard remained, fascinated by the shifting moods and atmospheres on the bridge around him. Simply awed by the cheerful indulgence with which everyone else was willing to treat the girl. It was a whole different mindset, he thought. Where Robin saw only grating over-indulgence of a spoilt and demanding child, they seemed to see a precious mind exploring the limits of its new experience. He had a moment of almost dreamlike insight. Wen-Qi as a younger girl pulling one of her dolls apart, as Mary, his own daughter, had done on more than one occasion. Where Robin and he had seen only the almost mindless destructiveness of an angry little girl, no doubt the beaming Chinese all around him would see the potential surgeon hard at work.

But there was more to it than that. For the radio was working now.

The Assistant Radio Operator Non-commissioned Officer Chu, simply known as FM – replacement for the deceased Broadband Dung – was in contact with the mayor's office in Shanghai. And Daniel Huuk was there, busily engaged in plans to restore power to the flood management system and meet the wave when it arrived – now that Mei-Feng had given them both a timescale and an idea of its potential destructiveness. And Daniel, it seemed, was the one grown-up who was not prepared to indulge young Wen-Qi. She had demanded to talk to him on the radio. She had received short shrift.

Short shrift in spades, in fact.

Poor old FM had paled as he passed the Deputy General Commissioner's fatherly message to her. 'Tell Jade I am far too busy to talk to children now. I am pleased Captain Mariner has brought her aboard and I will see her when she arrives if I have time. In the meantime, she should do what she is told, sit quiet and not make a nuisance of herself . . .'

The abrupt parental orders drove home in Richard's mind the fact that Huuk had been a member of the Hong Kong Naval contingent at one time – son in turn of an English naval officer. He could almost hear himself speaking in the abrupt and insensitive words. And it wasn't just the radio operator FM who blenched at them. All the Chinese on the bridge did too. To have created something as precious as a child under the one-child policy – even if it was by bad *joss* a girl – and to treat it with such brutality. To cost it so much *face* . . .

Especially as, immediately afterwards, Daniel had spent some minutes in conversation with Richard himself – someone Wen-Qi clearly thought of as some kind of subhuman ogre, as opposed to the more positive Good Luck Giant the rest of the Chinese crew supposed him to be.

Daniel had been preoccupied and terse, but he knew he owed Richard some kind of explanation and was willing to give him the basic minimum. He remained wilfully obscure as to her mother's identity, for instance. But he was clear about his desire to keep her existence secure – if not precisely secret – and about the way he had housed her with his friend Mayor Jaa (close friend and senior Triad officer, thought Richard, reading between the lines and remembering the Mayor's reaction to his letters of introduction). He explained she had been placed in the boarding-house of the famous Nanjing International School. This had several benefits – not least of which was the fact that since a series of attacks in 2010, schools had a level of security normally granted only to international banks.

The recent repeated attempts on Daniel's own life almost certainly would be widened to include threats to his only living relative now that they had proved unsuccessful – for the time being. And in any case, absolutely though he trusted the social system of the People's Republic in the face of disasters such as these, there might well be lawlessness that could conceivably get out of hand.

All in all, it seemed to Daniel that the safest place for Wen-Qi was at her father's side. Though there were several risks involved of course. He was busy – to put it mildly – and he was under threat.

Richard grunted grudging agreement and changed the subject. 'Daniel,' he said, 'what do you remember about Operation Dynamo? What the British code-named the relief of Dunkirk . . .'

Half an hour later, Daniel was replaced on the radio by a young-sounding official from the Shanghai Port Authority called Bing, who demanded a quick word with the river pilot. Richard called the pilot through, his spirit lightening suddenly. His conversation with Daniel had established that they were both thinking along the same lines. Things were getting back to normal in Shanghai at least; Daniel Huuk and Mayor Hong seemed to be getting a grip if they had restored power to the Port Authority and were soon to restore it also to the flood management system for the whole Shanghai Shi. Maybe they would have their own version of Operation Dynamo in place for when the wave arrived.

But then things went downhill. The 'quick word' that developed into a detailed update on the vessel, her disposition, and everyone – indeed *everything* – aboard. A suspiciously detailed report, thought Richard, slipping back into paranoid mode as he moved back towards the clearview to loom behind Wen-Qi, who seemed to be conning them downstream at full speed in place of Steady, and in spite of Straightline.

But Richard did not stay standing behind the child like a disapproving schoolmaster for long. Partway through the report, River Pilot Chang gestured a little wildly for his daughter to join him and the bemused FM Chu was ejected from the radio room. Everyone else on the bridge seemed to be focussed on Wen-Qi and her demands, but Richard picked up on a subtle change in the atmosphere, so he drifted apparently casually back towards the firmly closed radio-room door.

'This man Bing Yusheng from the Port Authority,' Pilot Chang was whispering fiercely. 'He is Green Gang Triad. He keeps using coded phrases to me because I am – *used to be* – Green Gang too. There is something going on. Something I do not like or trust.'

'Keep talking,' decided his daughter. 'Use your Green Gang codes in reply. If we plan well, we can get him to reveal something of what is going on.'

'I will try. But I do not want to warn him that I have changed my allegiance.'

'Then take great care, Father!'

It occurred to neither of them, nor to the eavesdropping Richard, that Mei-Feng also wore on the smallest finger of her left hand the tell-tale tattoo in the Chinese figure signifying green. That she was still a member of the Green Gang herself – and as yet she knew nothing of her daughter's allegiance to Daniel Huuk's Invisible Power organization, nor of her husband's defection to her daughter's secret society.

The Captain came out of the radio room in a very much less indulgent mood than when she had gone in. Her cold gaze raked her command bridge and her square face settled into a disapproving frown. 'Lieutenant Jiang!' she snapped. 'What do you mean by running at full speed in conditions such as this? What kind of a navigator are you? What kind of a watch officer? Helmsman! Why under the sky have you allowed that *child* access to the helm? What is going on here? My command is not a toy! Will someone kindly remove this schoolgirl from my bridge before she sinks us all!'

'That'll be me,' said Richard easily in Mandarin. Then he switched into English for his calmest, most irresistible rumble. 'Come along please, Wen-Qi. I have something I want to show you . . .'

Wen-Qi swung round, her face pale with shock, her expression darkening mutinously.

TWENTY-SEVEN
Wen-Qi

Wen-Qi was entranced by Genghis.

As Richard had guessed it would, the strange statue's combination of gold, jewellery, mystery and antiquity appealed to almost every aspect of her passionate intelligence and current enthusiasm. It clearly did so right from the first moment he performed the courtly presentation in his most flowery Mandarin, as though he was introducing a visiting Empress and the golden Khan to each other. An introduction ridiculously courtly enough to elicit a promising giggle from her.

'And where did the Great Khan come from?' she asked, touching Genghis's golden shoulder with a hesitant fingertip, as though fearful that a museum guard would appear and berate her importunate enthusiasm. Or, perhaps, that the fearsome little golden warrior would spring to life and attack her. And Richard answered with the whole truth this time, in some detail, though he knew she was hardly listening – as she tried to digest the information about the half-imaginary father whom she hardly knew.

But as it turned out, Wen-Qi was paying close enough attention to the story to ask if she could see the wonderful deep-sea remote explorer that had found and recovered the priceless artefact in the icy abysses of the Yellow Sea, and brought it aboard *Poseidon* from Kublai Khan's own sunken treasure ship.

As Richard, suddenly entrapped in nets of his own making, was preparing to spend a great deal more time with the girl than he had intended to, Robin and Mei-Feng appeared. This was a considerable relief to him, because he had suddenly been struck by something that should have been more obvious, more quickly, to his increasingly exhausted mind. That, now that this stage of his involvement in events was over – the codes delivered to Nanjing and the Deputy General Commissioner and Dragon Head's secret daughter retrieved – together with sundry members of the Chang family – he really needed to turn his attention to the future. To the implications of everything he had been able to achieve, discover, confirm. To the Shanghai endgame. For he had no intention of being either a passenger or a bystander, if he could help it.

The two women had somehow become fast friends, almost at the instant of their first meeting, and now the Leading Architect also, apparently, wanted to see the golden statue. And, as chance would have it, they were a perfect replacement for Richard.

Mei-Feng took an instant, almost overwhelming, shine to Wen-Qi, announcing that the girl reminded her most forcefully of her own daughter. A fact that impressed her three listeners variously – as the daughter in question was now the captain of the ship. And, as it turned out, Robin had not only been partner with Richard in the recovery of the statue, and was therefore just as competent as he to describe and discuss the events – perhaps demonstrate the remote vehicle *Neptune* – but she was also even more closely acquainted with the girl's enigmatic father.

Although, perhaps as well for everyone's peace of mind, Robin had no real idea of the borderline psychotic level of Daniel Huuk's actual erotic fixation with her. Any more than anyone had thought through the implications of letting a member of the Green Gang – albeit a reluctant, almost theoretical member – have free access to the daughter of the rival Invisible Power Triad's acting Dragon Head.

Richard returned to the bridge, therefore, with both dispatch and relief. One of them not particularly well placed. He joined the Changs, father and daughter, and watched the three figures exploring *Neptune* and *Marilyn*, as they carefully observed their instruments, their heading – and the state of water and weather ahead.

As Richard's mind began to wrestle with the problems he was now free to consider, the wild blue dazzle of his eyes narrowed, taking in almost automatically the full panorama offered by the clearview and by the instruments surrounding it. The river was full and running fast, of course – though nothing compared to how it would be when the big wave arrived. The early afternoon was still overcast, but there was some hope that the clouds would yield to the sun that was burning somewhere high above them. The heavy, humid wind was gusting fitfully enough to stir the hair of the women on the foredeck, but little more than that.

Richard was on an almost dreamlike level of reality, the exhaustion that was a reaction to the relentless action of the last thirty-six hours really beginning to get a grip on him. What he could see had an almost unnatural intensity, even under the restless leaden skies; as though the three figures and the red and yellow machines they were moving over and under had been part of one of the Disney/Pixar animations so beloved of the twins in their youth. And, to be fair, both *Marilyn* and

Neptune had more than enough character to grace a *Toy Story* or a *Wall-E*.

The full-throttle thrumming of the motors and the thudding wash of *Poseidon*'s progress down the racing river – through the flotsam beneath her cutwater – seemed almost intrusive, and yet it was nowhere near enough to drown out the sibilants of the whispered conversation that the pilot was having with his daughter.

'Let her amuse herself with the child and the gweilo woman for a while. She has been through a terrible adventure.'

'We all have, Father. And there is worse to come. That is my point. And she is in a position to help, I am sure. She should be in contact with the mayor's office, with the district architect's office. If anyone can assess the likely impact of the wave on the structure of the buildings in both Shanghai and Pudong, then it is she.'

'Don't you think she knows that, Jiang-Quing?'

'If she knows it then she should be doing something about it, Pappi! It is not like her to be playing with a child when there is work to be done. Especially someone else's child!'

There was a little silence as the river pilot digested these bitter words. Consumed, no doubt, by the guilt of every overworked parent in the face of a lonely offspring's need for that most precious of commodities – time. Then he whispered so quietly that even the dreaming Richard had to strain to hear. 'Do you think she is up to something? Could she know who Wen-Qi *is*?'

'She does not know about this, does she?' breathed the Captain, gesturing to her father's hand. 'Not the truth of it – the implications.'

'No! We are seeing ghosts!' decided the pilot more loudly. 'In a few minutes, I will go and get her, explain my new situation.' He waved his bandaged hand vaguely like a sleepy panda. 'Then, when she understands we are no longer Green Gang – and nor should she be – we will get her in contact with the authorities. Put her to work.'

Silence fell then, not least because Paradeground Ping arrived on the bridge and stood beside the Captain like an honour guard beside a queen. The smart marine officer's presence brought all speech to a halt for several reasons. He was an unknown quantity. His political allegiances were not clear – even if his emotional ones were becoming more so. And that fact, too, gave the Captain and her father something more to think about than Mei-Feng and the tell-tale tattoo on her finger. Richard's focus moved away from what he could hear and back to what he could see.

They were in the Yizheng Shaido reach now, speeding past the flooded flats on the river side of Zhenjiang where the pirate captains

Gan and Cai had come aboard. Moving at a velocity that would simply have torn them from their boarding ropes and sent them screaming, sprawling and splashing to their doom. Richard wondered briefly what had happened to them, and to Uncle Zheng and his men. Then he dismissed the pirates from his mind.

Pirates, Green Gang, everything except what *Poseidon* was doing now and what she would be expected to do in the near future.

In four hours' time, in fact, when the wave reached Shanghai.

Richard's mind ran with the thoughts that the Captain and the pilot had been discussing. Inevitably, he leaped far ahead of anything the father and daughter had been envisaging. As far as Richard could see, there was little alternative to a Dunkirk-style evacuation. But even on the best day of Operation Dynamo, 31 May 1940, they had taken less than 70,000 men off the French beaches in more than twelve hours. How many Shanghaiese they could get on to the relative safety of what shipping might be available in four hours – if they hadn't got things under way already – was beyond his calculation.

But, as with Nanjing, he was pretty well aware of how many people they were likely to need to move. The threatened city was the most populous on earth. In the whole of the Shanghai Shi there were reckoned to be in the region of twenty million souls. And, if he remembered his topography correctly, it was mostly less than half a dozen metres above the high water mark.

And to make matters worse, the whole area was flat. Flat as in the phrase 'river flats' or 'coastal flats'. As in 'flat: a large stretch of low-lying level ground'.

Whereas Nanjing had maybe one tenth of the number of inhabitants, it also had a genuine mountain tall enough to protect them from the flood and – apparently – roomy enough to house them all, if only temporarily. Shanghai in contrast, had no real high points that close by. The Shanghai Hills were hills in little more than name. Really and truly, the only points in the city that were likely to stand above the new water level were those buildings – like those of Nanjing University and the others *Marilyn* had all but white-water-rafted through – which had been so strongly built that they could withstand the immense forces of the water's massive surge.

A lesser man would have been put off by the enormity of what he was trying to get his head round, but it was one of Richard's most deeply ingrained characteristics that he never gave up. If he saw a challenge he rose to it. Though to be fair, Robin was getting increasingly worried about the habit. It was always 'Do or Die' with him. So far he had always got things done. One day, she feared, he would simply die trying.

But not today, he thought, feeling adrenaline flood his system.

And his mind went into overdrive.

How many people could be put aboard all the ships that had fled downriver into the rivermouth, he wondered, if they could all be recalled and docked along the Huangpu? And how many of the rest might be safely – if temporarily – housed in the upper floors of the sturdiest skyscrapers in Shanghai and Pudong? If they could get to the buildings of course, through the floods that were already flowing through the streets – as they had been flowing over those of Gangzicun, Chouchengmu and Pipazhu, and the Huning Expressway in Nanjing.

He had no idea.

But, of course, he knew a woman who did.

And, with that extra card in his hand, his position was strengthened immeasurably. For, as the proud husband and daughter had been keen to explain – even when they thought they were probably talking of a dead woman – Chang Mei-Feng was a leading expert in the architecture of tall buildings and large structures. She, if anybody, would know which of the buildings in Shanghai and Pudong were the most likely to survive the dual assault of earthquake and wave shock. With Mei-Feng's knowledge at his disposal, he could really start putting some proper plans together.

TWENTY-EIGHT
Xin

The wreckage of Uncle Zheng's pirate boat was not far down river from Zhenjiang. It formed part of an almost completely submerged jumble of flotsam bunched around the bulk of the marker buoy that had completed its destruction. The whole lot had become tangled round another one of the river's marker buoys whose chain remained strongly attached to the river-bed. The buoy had once sat proud of the surface, marking the edge of a navigable channel. Now it was just a ripple on the rushing surface, somewhere in the midst of the bewildering panorama of the flood.

To Steady Xin's tired eyes it looked like nothing more than yet another cross-current making the pattern of the racing river buckle and twist. Straightline's radar was fooled by the clutter below the surface of the broad expanse of littered floodwater dead ahead. Treacherously, at the moment they needed its warning most, it remained stubbornly silent. And even had the exhausted helmsman been alert enough to read the racing water more accurately, his preoccupation with the Captain was becoming so fixated that he would hardly have registered the significance of what he saw. And, finally, the Captain and her father were also – almost fatally – distracted by their own thoughts. While Ping, the cause of at least some of those thoughts, would not have recognized the danger even had he been looking out at the river instead of at the way the Captain's hair curled just at the nape of her neck.

And so it was left to Richard to glance down from his dreamy observation of Robin and her two companions clambering about like monkeys on the two bright vessels *Poseidon* carried on her foredeck, and see dead ahead a tell-tale shading of the water that made his blood run cold. Like the first apparently innocent cloudlet in a clear blue sky, warning of a hurricane coming. That made him shout out, almost too late, 'Steady! Hard over! Obstruction dead ahead!'

Straightline's radar shrilled suddenly, as though the shouting had woken up the sleepy machine. It was this as much as anything that made Steady react as swiftly – and as strongly – as he did. *Poseidon* went into a racing turn to starboard, slewing round hard right. Her whole hull tilted, rolling in a way it had not done since the earthquake itself. There were distant sounds of crewmen, equipment, odds and ends being tossed about below. The obstruction vanished behind a wall of water thrown up by the racing hull.

Richard had seen the manoeuvre coming the instant he had seen the tell-tale rippling over the obstruction – and he held on for dear life. Steady, hanging on to the con, managed to live up to his nickname too. Everyone else on the bridge went staggering. Straightline crashed into the river pilot, and the Captain somehow ended up in the sturdy arms of Paradeground Ping. And she remained there as the vessel swung back on to its original heading and came erect again, pitching and rolling in reaction to the unaccustomed severity of the movement – amid yet more tumbling, crashing, shouting and swearing from below.

It was the complex of emotions arising from the simple accident of her safe soft landing in Ping's strong arms that made the Captain over-react in the way she did. And that in turn, made all the difference later.

'Xin Si Ji Shi Guan,' she spat as she pulled herself perhaps a little reluctantly out of Ping's embrace. 'Get off my bridge! You are relieved of your duty. Go below at once and send up a replacement. In the meantime, Jiang Zhong Wei, you may replace him at the helm. I will be holding a captain's enquiry into this at the earliest opportunity.'

Richard followed Steady Xin off the bridge, even as Straightline, crestfallen, stepped forward to take up the menial duty of helmsman. His priorities were very different to those of the enraged commander. For he had seen more than she had. 'Steady, follow me,' he called. 'On to the foredeck! Quickly!'

And Xin, mutinous already, was happy to obey the giant if it meant disobeying his ugly bitch of a captain.

Whereas below decks the violence of the vessel's movements had caused a certain amount of damage and upset, on the foredeck it had caused much more potentially serious consequences. The three figures which had been clambering between the cartoon-bright shapes of *Neptune* and *Marilyn* a moment before, were lost to sight now. Indeed, both the remote deep-sea explorer and the long Cigarette powerboat were testing their fastenings to the limit of their specifications. And beyond.

Richard's cheek had been cut to the bone at the beginning of this whole adventure by *Neptune*'s attempts to tear free from her cradle in a typhoon, so he did not trust her now. And *Marilyn* herself had abandoned ship and slid overboard at the height of the earthquake – so she too needed careful watching when the going got tough.

And what danger the pair of these all-too heavy and solid vessels would present to any all-too breakable body caught between, beside or beneath them as they moved, hardly bore thinking about.

Richard and Steady came through the starboard A-deck door, out on to the foredeck side by side and went pounding forward. The walkway was narrow and, in spite of the fact that his concern was the greatest, Richard fell in behind the slighter, shorter figure of Steady Xin, whose rage and outrage gave him wings. And that fact came close to saving his life.

The starboard walkway brought them immediately beneath *Marilyn* and the helmsman was lucky not to be beheaded as the Cigarette's twin screws swung past like executioners' axes less than six feet above the deck. Richard, given that life-saving instant of warning, dived head-long – running far too fast to slow or stop on the slippery deck. The razor-sharp curves of steel swung back again as the dangerously beautiful vessel continued to fight herself free of her restraints. He felt the wind of their passage on the back of his neck and shoulders. Heard the groaning of the straining lashings. Knew there was little time to secure her.

He rolled sideways as he landed and found himself face to face with Robin, so intimately close that they might have been in bed at home. '*Neptune*'s coming loose,' she said. 'Better hope she doesn't chop your other cheek open. One duelling scar is enough.'

'*Neptune*,' he said. 'What about *Marilyn*?'

'I don't know what you see in her,' said Robin baldly, rolling over and beginning to pick herself up. 'At heart she's a two-timing bitch!'

Steady Xin's command of English was basic to put it mildly. But that was a phrase he recognized. And he knew just who it best applied to. But the thought was one that lay at the back of his mind, for he had more immediate concerns. The bow of the Cigarette was better secured than her stern – it was lighter, and was not burdened by two huge motors. Furthermore, it was held high by the fact that it was secured to the big crane-like gantry of the winch designed to lower and raise *Neptune*. So he was able to stay on his feet without risking his head as he ran forward beneath the up-tilted hull and the angular gantry-arm it was hanging from.

Mei-Feng and Wen-Qi were on the deck beneath the Cigarette's red bow in the winch's skeletal shadow. Half on the deck, rather. The older woman was sprawling face down, her silk skirt bunched around her waist, revealing all too much in the way of upper thigh and lower buttock, especially as her legs were spread for purchase. Her chest was at the point where the scuppers would have been in a more old-fashioned vessel and her head and shoulders were beneath the safety rail as she clung on like grim death to the hands of the terrified schoolgirl who was dangling helplessly over the side.

Steady threw himself on his knees and reached down to help the schoolgirl, aware only of the older woman's thankful gasp.

But had Richard and Robin not been there, his simple act of unthinking gallantry would have been the death of them all. For just at the moment he reached down for Wen-Qi, *Neptune* tore loose and started to roll down on their heads.

Richard had picked himself up at the same time as Robin had, and although he had spared his two-timing Ferrari-red passion a second glance, he had followed his decisive spouse to the restless deep-sea remote explorer. They were there side by side when that vital line parted, therefore. And this time it was the line that went – not the metal clip. So Richard's other cheek remained safe. The woven steel retainer whipped hissing upwards with terrible force, however. Both of the Mariners leaped back as though they were one being, then saw the massive explorer beginning to roll, and they leaped forward again.

On this side of the vessel was a ladder riveted to the round side which gave access to the hatches on the top. Richard leaped for this and clung there, throwing all his weight back to counter the vessel's weighty roll. 'Robin!' he yelled and she leaped as well, hitting him on the back like a rugby forward tackling him round the waist. Her added weight threatened to wrench his fingers loose from the rungs and his shoulders out of their sockets. But their combined weight held the stirring vessel still – for the moment at least.

Straightline saw what was happening then and had the wit to swing to starboard so that the deck tilted back. Combined with the Mariners' weight, that was enough to settle *Neptune* squarely into her cradle. Then Richard was reaching up for the frayed end of the parted line as Robin dropped catlike back on to the deck.

Zong Wei the electrical engineer and Chopper appeared, and the four of them managed to re-secure *Neptune* in the time it took for Mei-Feng and Steady to pull Wen-Qi safely back aboard. Mei-Feng then fell to readjusting her clothing in a belated attempt to make herself decent. Steady stood, seemingly a little overwhelmed as Wen-Qi hugged him tearfully, apparently overcome by her near-death experience.

The Captain and the river pilot came out on to the deck as well then, and were just about to hurry forward to make sure that Mei-Feng was all right when *Marilyn* jumped ship once again. The counter-roll to Straightline's left turn swung the Cigarette's twin screws out well clear of the starboard side, and the strain on the retaining ropes simply became too much. The rear lines parted. For an instant, the whole of the Cigarette's weight came on to the one line running through the gantry to the winch. And, as it did so, the ratchet slipped as though the winch itself had been seduced into complicity with *Marilyn*'s desertion. The Cigarette fell free of the corvette's side and splashed down into the water beside her, pulling cable off the whirling winch like a huge fish stripping line off a fisherman's reel as it dived for freedom. The sound was overwhelming as the woven steel tore through the straining wheels of the winch's block.

Robin ran to the crane's controls and released the swivel so that the arm swung round to face the angle of the screaming line. The line ran more freely at once and the sound faded. But even as Robin was leaping one way, Richard was leaping the other, reaching for the override. He had the experience and the simple native wit to put the break on slowly, so at least they managed to avoid a bird's nest of tangled steel.

Then a kind of peace settled on the still-racing *Poseidon*. *Neptune* was settled and secure. *Marilyn* was snugged against her starboard aft quarter like a calf at its mother's side. Richard crossed to stand beside the tall woman, the sobbing child and the solid seaman so that he could look back down along the thrumming line to where the go-faster boat sat, as sweet and innocent as the best-trained and most obedient of dogs out for a walk at her master's heel.

He straightened. Looked around more widely. The corvette was racing straight and true towards Shanghai through the Kou'an Shuidao reach, with the river running fast, wide and flat before her. Flat over the deserted ruins of Kou'an town itself on the distant port-side bank, he noted grimly, his blue eyes narrowed thoughtfully.

'Are you all right, Mother?' asked Captain Chang.

'I am. Thanks to this young man.' Mei-Feng turned to Steady Xin.

There was an instant of uncomfortable silence broken by the whooping sobs of the still-shocked Wen-Qi.

'He saved both of us,' Mei-Feng persisted. 'He really deserves some kind of recognition. A reward perhaps . . .'

'This too will be mentioned in my report of the incident,' announced the Captain stiffly. Xin did not appear to have heard her.

'Huh,' grunted her mother, spectacularly unimpressed. 'Now little one,' she turned to the sobbing girl, 'are you all right, dear?'

'Thanks to this man,' announced Wen-Qi, still clutching the embarrassed sailor. 'And no thanks to you!'

'I beg your pardon?' said Mei-Feng, apparently nonplussed at the child's rudeness.

'You know!' hissed Wen-Qi, hugging Xin more tightly still, seeming to use his sturdy body as some kind of protective shield. '*You know! You pushed me!* But I hung on – you know I did.'

She swung round, her blazing green gaze sweeping over all of them as her voice rang out across the water. 'When the boat swerved, she pushed me. Hard. On purpose. She tried to push me overboard!'

TWENTY-NINE
Trial

As *Poseidon* raced on downriver through the *shuidao* river reaches of Jiangyin and Rugao, towards the broad bays marked as *Cao*s on the charts, which were the gateways to the estuary itself to the mouth of the Huangpu and to Shanghai, Mongol Chang held her captain's enquiry.

When the confused and enraged commander had threatened the enquiry in the first place, it had been with the simple objective of disciplining Steady Xin for a moment's unaccustomed inattention to his duty. Especially as that lapse had nearly cost her her command and had certainly cost her a great deal of *face*. Especially in the eyes of a man with whom she wished to stand in high regard. But now, the very nature of the enquiry had been changed by the accusations of a frightened and tearful little girl.

Xin was dealt with swiftly enough, given at once an official reprimand and an official commendation, and dismissed. But then the enquiry had to continue, for the Captain found herself in the most painful of situations. One which her hesitation in informing her mother of the new, changed Triad circumstances, seemed to have caused. One which the stubborn, wilful and all too public persistence of a spoilt little girl made inevitably public and official. For now Captain Chang Jiang Quing had to try and find out whether leading Architect Chang Mei-Feng, as a loyal Green Gang member, had in fact tried to damage the daughter of the rival Invisible Power Triad's Dragon Head, Wen-Qi Huuk.

As far as Richard, as a distant, disinterested observer, could see, the only positive element from the Captain's point of view was the fact that the situation meant that she held the enquiry alone. No other officers could be released from duty to assist. Not even, for some reason he couldn't quite fathom, the redoubtable Lieutenant Ping. So, he assumed, cynically, if things went too terribly wrong, then the records could be doctored, lost or destroyed. But, knowing the Captain as well as he did – or believed he did – he doubted that the die-straight young officer would stoop to such depths, unless things came to the most terrible pass.

Although Robin was involved in this enquiry, as the witness who had been nearest to the incident itself, Richard withdrew from the proceedings soon after Steady Xin, and went back up on to the bridge while Xin went angrily about some business of his own below.

On the bridge, Richard discovered that both the helmsman and the navigator had been replaced with crewmen Richard did not recognize. The pilot, who seemingly held the watch, was deep in a perfectly understandable brown study. Richard therefore quickly returned to the thoughts he had been examining just before the vessel swerved with such near-fatal consequences. But the distraction of thinking about that swerve – albeit briefly – took Richard to the clearview where his eyes swept the expanse of the widening river's mouth and noted in passing that a small team of seamen was working on the forepeak – checking that *Neptune* was secure, no doubt. Ensuring *Marilyn* had done no real damage to the hull, the winch, the crane, the block or tackle. Or to the hull itself as she went over the side, come to that.

But the distraction was little more than momentary. Richard was soon immersed in his thoughts once again, and he drifted through into the chart room to see whether the big white-, sand- and blue-coloured cartridge paper squares would allow his thoughts to take more tangible form. He was still deeply immersed in close study of the chart detailing the waters around Nanjing and the English Language Pilot for the area, when the ship's alarms went off and he was called to frantic action once again.

Wen-Qi was released from the captain's enquiry after about half an hour and she wandered into the vaguely familiar corridors still frightened and outraged. To be brutally honest she was not a hundred per cent certain the old woman Mei-Feng had meant to push her overboard. It was just conceivable – as the ugly captain had suggested time and again – that the shove which sent her tumbling over the safety rail might indeed have been a clumsy attempt to catch hold of her and pull her back.

But Wen-Qi had spent the short span of her young life all too well aware that the daughter of a father such as hers might be the target of an infinite variety of dangers. Which was, of course, why the father she loved to distraction – and who loved her equally in return – stayed so far out of her life. Left her in the care of others. Placed her in the restrictive security of boarding schools in cities so far-distant from his own. Such a daughter, so deeply motivated, was not about to allow an incident that threatened her life to be merely accidental.

And, brutally frank with herself again, she knew she was in a foul mood. Had been for days in fact, for reasons she could not begin to fathom. The only moments when the dark clouds haunting her had lightened at all, were that brief one when the cheerful gweilo giant had introduced her to the great golden Khan in that barbarous semblance of courtly Mandarin. And, of course, that literally uplifting minute when the square-faced, fatherly figure of Steady Xin had pulled her back to safety after that ancient bitch, the ugly captain's mother, had pushed her overboard. Had *probably* pushed her overboard. Perhaps.

So deep and dark were these thoughts that Wen-Qi did not even register either the sound of the ship's emergency alarm or the bustle that resulted from it. Instead, she wandered, confused, disconsolate and unobserved down towards the place where she had felt safe and amused.

'Hello, Great Khan,' she said as she walked in through the unguarded door. 'It is I, the Empress Wen-Qi. I have come to grace you with another personal visit. Shall we remain here and converse? Or would you rather venture forth so that we may survey that huge section of the Middle Kingdom which pays tribute and homage to our greatness?'

She reached out to touch the golden shoulder, but just as she did so, something made her hesitate. She remembered that childish fear she had felt when she touched the statue last. That there was a museum attendant or a guard who would come and punish her for her transgression. She looked guiltily over her shoulder. And started with fright. For there was, in fact, someone standing just inside the door. And there were several more behind him. She gasped in air to shout, but the stranger stepped forward, smiling, and she recognized him. And gave a hesitant smile in return.

It was her friend and saviour Steady Xin.

Richard came out of the chart room and on to the command bridge at a flat run. 'What is it?' he called to the pilot. River Pilot Chang simply pointed forward. There was a thick plume of smoke pouring upwards from a point in the deck just forward of *Neptune*. 'On my ship that was the paint locker,' he said. 'And on most others I have worked aboard.'

'Mine too,' agreed Richard tersely. 'And it certainly is aboard *Poseidon*. We had it open after the typhoon when the whole ship needed sprucing up. That could be nasty. Better get to work.'

Richard met Robin at the main A-deck door and this time it was he who took the lead, running beneath the empty air where *Marylyn* had swung like a headsman's axe so recently. Both of them had been aboard through sufficient adventures and drills to be sure where the fire-fighting equipment was, and to be able to fit easily into the routine of getting it out and employed. So much so, that it was not immediately obvious that there were crewmen missing from their allotted places in the teams. A fact further obscured at first by the arrival of Ping and his men – most of whom were as able to help as Richard and Robin were themselves. And, finally, by the fact that several of the sharp-edge firefighters were dressed in flameproof suits and masks that hid their faces entirely. Something further complicated by the fact that the super-efficient Captain, in the endlessly repeated drills of happier and less busy times, had ensured that each white-suited firefighter had a buddy who could take his place at a moment's notice if something unexpected held him up.

But to be fair the emergency was sufficiently immediate, dangerous and critical to make clear thought and head-counting impossible. The paint locker was a lethally dangerous place in which to have a fire. It was full of oil-based paints, alcohol-based thinners, varnishes and polishes of all sorts. It was also the workshop where such sections and lengths of timber that needed aboard were stored. Linoleum. Carpeting. Cable, made of strands of Kevlar and polypropylene. All incredibly combustible.

And, if that were not enough, the paint-locker filled that tight triangular bow-space between *Neptune* secured above and her control room situated below. Both the deep-sea explorer and the banks of computers needed to manage it were terribly susceptible to heat – where icy cold and unimaginable pressure could be shrugged off as next to nothing. And the control room, of course, would be rendered useless – making *Neptune* useless too – if any liquid used in fire-fighting leaked down into its labyrinthine mazes of circuitry.

Captain Chang was there almost as quickly as Richard and Robin, smoothly taking control, confident of her father's command of the bridge. Confident, also, that she was in command of an efficient and well-practised crew. The four firefighters were suited up already and so her first order was to open the access trap in the deck. 'Slowly! Carefully!' she called. 'No. Wait! I'll do it myself. Stand by with the retardant foam, back-up teams. But wait for my word. We will do this all with the dry-powder equipment if we can.'

The hatch was raised by an electric mechanism which the fire had not yet damaged. Chang pushed the control buttons with careful fingers, as Richard and Robin both stood ready with the canisters of retardant foam, looking over the white-suited shoulders of the first team. Behind them, emergency – emergency *only* – teams stood ready with hoses ready to flood the locker out if the fire was too far out of control to be conquered by retardant foam or by powder. If the whole ship was so severely at risk that the preservation of *Neptune* and her control systems became of secondary importance.

The hatch opened an inch or two, smoke billowing more thickly yet. There was a gentle rumbling sound. Richard strained to peer beyond the white figures of the first team and the Stygian darkness of the fumes to see if there was a tell-tale brightness that would reveal actual flames burning down there. He guessed Chang would be doing the same. Bright hot flames in the middle of all that potential explosiveness would be the signal to send in the first jet of water, no matter what the cost.

But there was nothing. The hatch came up a foot. Then a metre. If anything, the smoke began to thin. 'Fire teams,' called Chang. 'Fire teams in with the powder canisters. Stand by with the foam, the rest of you. Stand back the hose teams.'

The steady headwind carried the fumes back to Richard then, and his sensitive nostrils twitched. The black smoke stank of rags and rubber. In his bones he already knew the truth before the first team disappeared into the fuming black pit of the paint-locker. By the time that the four of them returned with a big steel dustbin packed with smoking rubbish, he had put his foam canister back on its hook at the fire point and was looking around, frowning.

The first thing he noticed was that the line which had been tautly pulling *Marilyn* alongside the racing ship was slack now, whipping desultorily as the wind took the length of it and the wake toyed with the lower end. He knew the Cigarette was gone before he looked back and down.

He turned back to look at the Captain's thunderous face as the penny dropped with her as well. 'Call to stations!' she bellowed. 'Everyone to their emergency station! Now! Not you, Lieutenant Ping. You take four men and check on the statue in the hold. Detail two more to check the gun-locker.'

Everyone aboard was formed up obediently, even before the emergency siren was switched off. This was another drill Mongol Chang had insisted on holding with exacting regularity. The team leaders detailed to head up each contingent did a quick headcount, followed by a namecheck. It took little more than five minutes to establish that Zong Wei Lieutenant Straightline Jiang was not there to head his team. That Si Ji Shi Guan NCO 4th Class Steadyhand Xin was not there either. That there were four other men gone with them.

Within six minutes, Ping and his men were back before the livid Captain to report that the golden statue and several guns were gone.

That there was a ladder left clipped to the aft port quarter, immediately above where the Cigarette had been. That there was also some Kevlar-strand rope wrapped in a makeshift pulley on the safety rail.

Within ten minutes, therefore, the fuming Captain was certain that she had a full picture of the scale of the theft, mutiny and piracy that her missing crewmen had perpetrated under cover of the fire they had set in the paint locker.

Or she did, until Robin Mariner, who had been looking around the crew members assembled at their stations on the foredeck asked, her voice shaking a little with unaccustomed apprehension, 'Has anybody here seen Wen-Qi Huuk?'

THIRTY
Error

'There!' called Richard. 'There she is!' He leaned forward until his seat belt creaked, gesturing to Chopper, who gave a terse nod and brought the helicopter round in a lazy curve, losing height and gaining speed as the pursuit got properly under way.

During the moments after Robin's simple question about Wen-Qi's whereabouts, the whole of *Poseidon* had become a bustle of frenetic activity, much of it overlapping. Several teams of people had sprung into action at the same time, each fixated on achieving one particular vital objective. Robin had rushed off with two trusted men from the bespectacled electrical engineer Zong Wei's team to comb the vessel from stem to stern and make sure Wen-Qi was not simply hiding somewhere aboard.

Mei-Feng would have gone with her, but her daughter simply ordered her on to the bridge where she was given a short, clear explanation of the new situation with regard to her family's Triad affiliations. And, therefore, if she had actually tried to push Wen-Qi overboard, of the almost unimaginable error of her ways. The shocked and shaken woman had convinced her unsettlingly forceful daughter that she had not pushed Wen-Qi overboard. That her Green Gang membership was a matter of form. That she would do anything short of chopping off her little finger to put her family's mind at rest.

Richard in the meantime ran back to look at the point where the deserters had gone aboard *Marilyn*. It was exactly as had been reported – ladder clipped in place, makeshift pulley for lowering the priceless statue, dancing end of rope leaping from wavetop to wavetop in the corvette's wake where the Cigarette had been snapped free. He scanned the distant banks of the racing river but he could see nothing immediately. The flood had pushed the river margins so far back he needed binoculars to see anything clearly.

They must have loaded up, he thought, as he brought his attention to more immediate matters, cut loose, and then simply sat there, using *Poseidon*'s speed to help their escape by waiting until they could steer away towards one bank or the other as they fell further and further behind. Certainly, there was only one broad wake obvious in the rush of water astern of the corvette. They wouldn't have dared power up those massively noisy motors until they were certain the rumble of *Poseidon*'s own engines was more than enough to drown out the all too distinctive snarl. So, logic dictated, they couldn't be all that far away. Yet.

Richard swung round, his eyes raking over the helicopter in whose shadow he was standing. That was the obvious way forward. The helicopter would find *Marilyn* in moments. And even as he realized this, Chopper himself appeared, with Mei-Feng just behind him. The chastened woman had been dispatched by her still-raging daughter to rouse the pilot and get the helicopter ready for hot pursuit. To lose Genghis would mean the end of her career. To lose Wen-Qi might mean the end of a great deal more than that.

'The Captain says we are to take the helicopter up at once and go after the boat with all dispatch,' said Chopper.

'I am to go also,' said the architect quietly. 'At the least I can try and convince the child I never tried to harm her. . And my daughter feels Wen-Qi may need a woman . . . The men may have . . .'

Richard frowned. It simply had not occurred to him that Steady and Straightline might have taken the girl as anything more than a bargaining counter. An insurance policy. 'If that's what you think, then we'd better get straight on to the authorities,' he said.

'No!' gasped Mei-Feng. 'Not yet. Not until we have had a chance to retrieve the . . . the situation . . .'

And Richard understood the other part of her mission then. She, as perfect Chinese parent, was here to preserve – at any cost – the face of her little empress offspring.

He'd have to keep an eye on that situation too, he thought. For there was wide room for trouble there. 'OK,' he allowed, grudgingly.

The pair of them turned towards the helicopter, apparently expecting to take off at once. But Richard's sharp eyes and quick mind had seen and understood more than they, and understood the more immediate error in their plans. He noticed scratches on the helicopter's door and he guessed that both Steady and Straightline would readily appreciate the danger of pursuit. 'Chopper,' he called, therefore. 'Check for damage . . .' He paused, struggling unsuccessfully to conjure up the Mandarin phrase for 'sabotage'. Then he turned and ran back down to the cabin he shared with Robin. It was empty. But he hadn't come for company. He had come for the powerful binoculars he had left down there earlier after the incident with the pirates.

Chopper had just discovered a bunch of wires torn free behind the helicopter's dashboard – as though this had been a car in a crime drama

– when Richard returned. He had just used the helicopter's radio to ask for Zong Wei to come up from the electrical department when Ping and a squad of four armed men arrived into the bargain.

The marine lieutenant too had orders to pursue the powerboat and to return with the girl, no matter what the cost. And they were as certain as they could be now that she was aboard *Marilyn*, for Robin and her team had found no sign of her aboard *Poseidon*. But Richard was as well aware as anyone aboard of the burgeoning relationship between the commander and the precise young officer. He, like Mei-Feng, would be more likely to put Captain Chang's career before Wen-Qi's safety – up to a point at least.

And that was likely to rob them of one of the most powerful weapons in their armoury – calling on Daniel Huuk for help in apprehending the fleeing thieves. Calling on anyone, indeed, who might be likely to tell Daniel Huuk that *Poseidon*, her owner, commander, officers and crew, had let his beloved daughter fall into the hands of a gang of desperate, stop-at-nothing kidnappers.

But the immediate focus remained the helicopter. Unless they could fix that then they would have no real choice, no matter how angry Huuk would be when he learned the truth. But it soon transpired that the deserters, too, had made mistakes. With the main imperative being silence, and no one really clear about the best way to disable a helicopter, the departing men had managed only limited damage. Chopper had the wires reattached in a few moments and the electrical engineering officer Zong Wei had approved the work in a very few minutes after that. The Civil Airworthiness Authorities – or whatever the Chinese called them – might have been less than happy with the idea of taking the helicopter up with the makeshift repairs and the damaged door, thought Richard grimly. But there was little choice if they were going to get after the mutineers. And so he clambered aboard and went without thinking to the co-pilot's seat.

Chopper heaved himself aboard as Zong Wei departed, satisfied, then Mei-Feng, Ping and his men all clambered into the seats in the cabin behind. Chopper contacted the bridge and they were off.

There was no more thought or planning to it than that.

As the helicopter swooped up through the gusty air, Richard pressed the binoculars to his eyes and began to sweep the box of enhanced vision from side to side of the river. Although he was focussed on his search for the bright red Cigarette, he couldn't help but notice a huge mass of apparently incidental detail. The helicopter had soon climbed high enough to make both riverbanks easily visible, and Richard found himself struck by the way the detritus spread by the first wave was scattered much more widely on the north bank than the south. It took less than a second's reasoning to understand that this was because the north bank was lower than the south. Because it spread back on flats and ridges to the flood-damaged cities and towns towards Jingjiang. Further east, the problem got worse as the raised water level of the lingering flood still covered a huge area that had been marshes and mazes of low islands – now a great shallow lagoon. But then the river turned south and it was the turn of what had been the southern shore to be littered with debris and sluggishly awash.

And yet the trend was unmistakable, thought Richard. The bank that would eventually lead to the mouth of the Huangpu and the southern tongue of the Shanghai Shi was higher, sheerer, more robust – and consequently much less damaged than its opposite. All along this section at least. Clearly the wave itself had reached farther inland there – as the jetsam evidenced. And even the lingering flood water seemed deeper – wider – over there.

Fascinated, Richard swung the letter box of vision over to the southern bank – though it was rapidly becoming the western bank as the river turned south. Here the flooded swamps were rapidly giving way to a wide bay, backed at first by marshes seemingly awash, and then quite suddenly by much more solid cliffs. And, as the helicopter soared up towards the base of the low overcast, the Shanghai-Nanjing expressway came into view, snaking along the raised river-bank, heading determinedly inland. Quiet for the most part, of course, for it had been broken ten miles closer to Shanghai when the bridge across one of the bays had come down in the earth tremor. Still . . .

And it was at this point, mid-thought, that Richard saw *Marilyn.* 'There!' he called. 'There she is!' He leaned forward until his seat-belt creaked, pulling the binoculars away from his eyes and gesturing to Chopper, who gave a terse nod and brought the helicopter round in a lazy curve, losing height and gaining speed as the pursuit got properly under way.

But the binoculars had fooled Richard a little, and forced him into an uncharacteristic error of judgement. In their enhanced focus, the Cigarette had seemed quite close. But now he was simply shocked by how far away she seemed as he sought her with his naked eye. He glanced at his Rolex. It must have been well over half an hour since they discovered that the Cigarette was missing. Say half an hour since Steady or Straightline had dared to open the throttles. And those throttles had been opened to the max and then some by the look of things. The speedboat was sitting high, her bow well out of the water and she was powering forward at seventy-five mph. With the speed of the river's spate beneath her, she must be passing the shore-line at the better part of a hundred mph – twice as fast as the corvette, and damn near as fast as the helicopter.

Richard realized with a start that the racing vessel was already sweeping past the bay he had been thinking of – the bay whose bed was littered with the remains of the shattered motorway bridge. At that speed, with the waterway surging behind and the river wide open before her, *Marilyn* would be in the mouth of the Huangpu well before they caught up with her, and probably in Shanghai itself before they got in any kind of a position to slow her or to stop her.

Now Mei-Feng's presence as her daughter's representative – not to mention Lieutenant Ping's – began to weigh more heavily on him. Had the fleeing vessel contained no more than a gang of thieves and a stolen statue, he would have been ordering Chopper to call the author-ities for help. Clearly, as things stood, however, he dare not call on the mayor or the police. They would certainly be in close contact with Daniel Huuk. But, he thought a little desperately, perhaps the Port Authority.

Richard leaned across to Chopper. 'Can you open a channel to the Port Authority?' he asked. 'If I remember correctly, the Captain and the pilot have both been in contact with a man called Bing Yusheng who is employed there.'

Chopper nodded accommodatingly and no one in the rear cabin seemed to have any objections. Chopper put the reception on broad-cast and almost immediately, the Port Authority answered. But the switchboard was terse. 'We are extremely busy. It is our job to oversee the disposition of all the vessels in the Changjiang Kou. There are hundreds – thousands – large and small. Everything from fishing smacks to supertankers. This had better be very important indeed.'

Richard simply read out the phrase on one of the sheets of paper given to him by Daniel Huuk. It was the Deputy General Commissioner of the Institute of Public Security's personal authority. The switchboard patched them through immediately . . .

. . . into the middle of a conversation that Bing Yusheng was obvi-ously having with someone else. And it took Richard only an instant to realize who that 'someone else' was.

And Mei-Feng leaned forward after the first few words to whisper urgently, 'They are talking of Triad matters!'

'I am a mere forty-niner,' Bing was saying.

'A junior member,' breathed Mei-Feng.

'I have neither the seniority nor the authority to accept such a thing or to cancel anyone's debts. You must talk to White Fan, Vanguard or Deputy Mountain Master,' he continued.

'Senior officers. Mountain Master and Dragon Head are the same thing. It varies from Triad to Triad,' breathed Mei-Feng.

'But who are these people? And where can I find them?' demanded the all-too-familiar voice of Steady Xin.

'I can ask White Fan to contact you as soon as you dock. But things are very confused here. It is not merely the floods. There is talk of the Mountain Master meeting . . . You are certain you are Green Gang?'

'I have given you the word,' came another voice, Straightline's. 'I am no Blue Lantern, like my friend here. I have drunk the black cock's blood, passed the arch of swords and seen my promises burned.'

'It is the ritual,' breathed Mei-Feng. 'Then he will have been marked . . .' She held up her little finger revealing its tattoo.

'Very well,' continued Bing Yusheng's voice. 'There is talk of the Mountain Master being among the dead. But I will call White Fan and he will meet you where you dock. He will bring Red Pole and other Four-Two-Six fighters to look after what you are bringing. Have you planned where you will come ashore?'

'Where is there, after the floods?' asked Steady Xin.

'Do you know the Nanjianglu ferry pier?'

'Yes.'

'It isn't there any more, but there is a good spot opposite. The bridge over the Bailianjing Road. It is now at water level. It would make a good dock.'

'I know the place,' came Straightline's voice. 'It is beside the 2010 World Expo buildings . . .'

'Indeed,' said the garrulous Bing Yusheng. 'It was renovated then as part of the massive upgrade of the city's flood defences. The main pumping station is there. Consequently, there is much coming and going as Mayor Hong and his men fight the floods in preparation for what is coming next. Those pumping stations are our only hope of controlling the second wave, apparently. So there is a great deal of preparation work – traffic and personnel as well as of shipping – small boats such as yours. You should not stand out too badly there.'

'And Red Pole and his foot soldiers will fit right in,' whispered Richard. He gestured to Chopper to turn the radio off.

He turned to face Mei-Feng and Lieutenant Ping. 'I'm sorry,' he said. 'This situation is escalating far beyond our control. We could maybe catch up with the Cigarette and conceivably get Genghis and Wen-Qi back, if we had time. But we don't. And we simply daren't risk taking on the Green Gang with an innocent schoolgirl's life at risk. I'm calling this in to the authorities.'

THIRTY-ONE
Huangpu

Daniel Huuk was as enraged as Richard had feared he would be. But, like an old-fashioned paterfamilias in Victorian England, he allowed a great deal of his wrath to go towards his inconveniently distracting daughter. Even before Richard's radio-report was completed, he could be heard passing immediate authority for the resolution of the situation, the recovery of the statue and the rescue of Wen-Qi briskly down the chain of command to Commodore Shan on the *Luyang*.

'Mayor Hong and I have millions of lives to preserve here!' he snarled. 'The flood defence system for the whole Taihu Basin, which includes Shanghai, Pudong, the Shanghai Shi and all adjoining areas south of the Yangtze, is already overwhelmed; but thanks to the work of the city authorities over the last few years it is state-of-the-art and will pump much of this water out of the area given time. But whether it will be able to handle the wave and flood you predict is another matter. I will get a clearer estimate of what is coming within the next few minutes, however. Mayor Jaa informs me that the wave is about to hit Nanjing, and he has his best scientists from the university waiting to give us precise measurements.'

Richard half closed his eyes, remembering the towers of the university buildings standing above the tearing maelstrom *Marilyn* had powered through on the way to the Purple Mountain. Could Huuk mean that there were men and women still in there, ready to assess the power of the deluge that was about to hit them? Such heroic self-sacrifice seemed almost inconceivable, even in a society such as this. But Huuk's next words left no more room for doubt.

'They have petrol-powered generators there, apparently,' he continued thoughtfully. 'Enough power for some of their instruments to be working. As long as the buildings remain standing.'

Richard swung round. 'Mei-Feng, are there buildings in Nanjing strong enough to take that sort of battering?'

She nodded. 'The latest structures are all earthquake stressed. Enormously strong. It depends how much force the wave has lost since it destroyed the bridge in Wuhan.'

'The best estimate we have so far has come from Tongling. A man called Wu gave us some vital detail,' Huuk proceeded, unaware of the whispered question and answer session. 'And that was distant observation; lacking in scientific precision. However . . .'

As the one-sided conversation proceeded, Chopper swung the helicopter on to the course of the flood-widened River Huangpu and settled down, still half in pursuit of the bright red Cigarette, because he had not been directed to do anything else. Richard looked out and down, looking at the passing conurbation almost as though he were using Google Earth on his computer. Though they had been shaken as well as swamped, a surprising number of buildings still stood proud of the roiling brown surface. Perhaps the poor souls in Nanjing University might stand a chance after all, he thought. On both sides, the Huangpu was spread wide, far beyond the normal confines of its banks and embankments – even those updated and improved during the last few years.

On the right, in the Shanghai City area itself, the margin of detritus showed the limits of where the wave had reached among the increasingly tight-packed buildings. But then down nearer the river, the water still swirled along streets and thoroughfares. The difference, Richard supposed, was down to the flood defence system and the work of the massive pumps that were trying to move the water out of the city and into the distant sea.

On the left, away over Pudong towards the lower-lying Shanghai Shi there seemed to be no edge to the water – merely a distant grey-brown line that was at once the horizon and the Chanhjang Kou, whither the flood water was bound in its complex of drains, pipes and channels.

And in and out from the wall of big ships lined up just this side of that grey-brown line, there bustled a numberless fleet of little boats – some even smaller than *Marilyn*, taking as many souls as they could out of the flooded city and on to the distant flotilla. But the water was too shallow to allow direct access over the flooded land. The little ships were picking their way along channels, canals and riverways of slightly deeper water as they bustled in and out. It was almost as Richard had imagined it, and he realized that in a strange way, the next wave would be a liberation – all the boats and some sizeable ships should be able to sail over the top of the flood. Straight through the Shanghai Shi, into Pudong and even across to Shanghai itself, for a little while at least. If there was anyone left in Shanghai to rescue. If there was anywhere they could be rescued *from*. Still it was certainly the first stage of Operation Dynamo for the twenty-first century. The Dunkirk evacuation on an unimaginable scale.

But realistically, even this immense effort could not hope to move the millions of Shanghaiese to safety within the time frame dictated by the oncoming wave. Almost disconsolately, he raked the flat landscape, in the faint hope that his phenomenal memory had let him down and there was, somewhere, a Purple Mountain that might offer safety to the last million or so. But there was nothing.

Nothing at all.

'Which buildings in Nanjing might survive?' he asked idly, his binoculars once again striving to follow *Marilyn* amid the bustle that Bing Yusheng had already warned them about. 'Which ones would stand the best chance?'

Mei-Feng leaned forward readily. 'Greenland Financial Centre,' she said. 'Half a dozen others spring immediately to mind. They should all have withstood the earthquake well and should be strong enough to take a considerable hit from the wave. On the assumption, of course, that it has lost a good deal of its original power, as I say. New Century Plaza, the JinLing building, Langshi City Plaza, Galaxy International, Nanjing International . . .'

Richard lowered the binoculars, struck by her immediate certainty. He pulled himself right round, frowning. 'And, all things being equal, which buildings in Shanghai stand the best chance? Say ten or a dozen?'

But before Mei-Feng could answer, the radio came alive again. 'Richard,' said Daniel Huuk. 'I think you had better land on the *Luyang* and report to Commodore Shan. The *Luyang* is one of my major communications centres. And it is where we propose to launch the recovery of your pirated speedboat from. You will see it easily, I think. It is the only large vessel left on the Huangpu. Have you the call-sign and wavelength?'

The familiar shape of the big destroyer was indeed easy to see. It was facing downstream, seemingly anchored off the Shanghai shipyards. Their dry docks weren't dry any longer, thought Richard grimly. And they were due to get wetter still.

It was that thought that took him out of the helicopter, with Mei-Feng close behind, and up to the bridge through all the bustle going on aboard. Here Commodore Shan stood with Political Officer Leung beside him. Both men were standing stock-still, seemingly turned to stone by the gabble of words coming through the crackly ether and out of the radio.

'As near as we can judge,' said an unfamiliar female voice, which seemed to be trembling with something more than excitement or apprehension, 'the mean speed of approach is forty miles per hour. The leading edge seems to be in the region of twelve metres but the shape is almost ballistic rather than sheer. A roller rather than a big surf. There is all sorts of detritus being carried within it, and it is this that is likely to do the damage when it impacts. Some of the power seems to be turned aside by Qian Zhou, though the island itself is underwater now. But that appears to be good for us. Bad for Pukou on the far shore.

'The general disturbance according to our equipment is equivalent to a quake measuring high six on the Richter scale. Seven now. Ah! I see it clearly. Jiangshan Square has gone under. Can you hear me? The sound is becoming worse. Zonghai has gone under too. Yuhuatai. Qinhai. Mochu Lake. Jianye! Baixia. The Zixia lake. The big post-first-flood Zixia lake. Here it comes!'

There was an overwhelming noise through which it was just possible to hear the nameless, heroic scientist call out, 'That's eight! Eight on the Richter—'

Then, suddenly, stunningly, a whispering near-silence.

'We're still here,' the scientist said, her voice shaking with simple awe. 'The building has withstood the impact. I have no idea what damage has been done to the lower floors but the upper sections are still standing and seem to be safe.

'I am looking north now, following the trail of the wave. And I can see that other buildings have survived. The Greenland Financial Centre up in Goulou beyond Drum Tower Park. The Langshi Plaza building down in Jiangshan. The Jin Ling. Nanjing International—'

And the line went dead.

Richard swung round to face Mei-Feng. 'You named them all,' he said. 'All the buildings that survived. You were right!'

'They were the most modern, I think. The most likely to be stressed against earthquake. And against the impact of the wave, obviously.'

'And did you hear what she said about the speed? If it has slowed to forty miles per hour then that gives us six hours before the wave can get here. Six hours! That gives us more of a chance. What do you think?'

But before Mei-Feng could answer or he could say anything further, Lieutenant Ping appeared at her shoulder like a frowning ghost. 'May I speak?' he said. 'Urgently. In private.'

The bridge-wing served Ping's purpose well enough, and allowed Richard to look across the Huangpu towards Pudong as they talked. And so what the worried marine described to him was easy enough to visualize.

'I don't know whether the Deputy General Commissioner's orders were passed on in sufficient detail. And there seems hardly time or opportunity to check . . .'

'But?' Richard was looking past the slight officer's square shoulder, down the wide river towards the site which had housed the famous 2010 World Expo – where *Marilyn* was heading. To the Bailianjing road bridge that was now, with the raised water-level, a convenient dock. Where Red Pole and his Green Gang thugs were waiting . . .

'I know the officer Commodore Shan has detailed to go out after *Marilyn*,' Ping whispered, torn by an almost incalculable range of conflicting loyalties. 'His name is Lieutenant Kung. His nickname is *Butcher*.' The lieutenant paused meaningfully. He knew Richard would not suppose the name came from Lieutenant Kung's great passion for meat.

'But he may have been given orders to take great care . . .' said Richard after a moment.

'He is taking his most ruthless men,' persisted Ping.

'He's taking on the Green Gang,' reasoned Richard, but he was not really convinced by his own half-hearted counter-argument. It was based on the assumption that Commodore Shan was capable of far greater forethought than Richard actually thought he was capable of.

'He's taking a couple of J201s.' Ping added the final fact like a poker player laying down the fourth ace.

'J201s! But they're anti-tank weapons . . .' Richard was simply horrified.

'Precisely. Not really designed for surgical extraction in delicate hostage situations. More *wham bam – sorry ma'am!*'

'Couldn't have put it better myself. And these orders come from Commodore Shan himself?'

'Apparently so. Directly from the Commodore. Like the Deputy General Commissioner, he has more important things to do. Bigger fish to fry.'

'Hell's teeth.' There was an instant of silence. Then Richard snapped, 'Where's Chopper?'

THIRTY-TWO
Bridge

Short of placing a man carrying the personal authority of the General Commissioner and of the Dragon Head under arrest, there was nothing Shan could do to stop Richard taking his helicopter and flying upriver. The Commodore was a diplomat as much as a commander and so he remained aloof – as did Political Officer Leung. Richard had little trouble in commandeering what – and who – he wanted.

As the helicopter lifted off, carrying exactly the same contingent as had come in from *Poseidon* – guns and all – Robin came through from the corvette's bridge. 'We're just about to turn into the Huangpu,' she said. 'But it's like turning in from a deserted country freeway on to a city street at rush-hour. Where did all these boats come from?'

Richard had little time to explain. 'How are things going?' he countered.

'Fine, apart from the crowds. How about you?'

'Fine. I think your best bet is to come upriver until you can berth by the *Luyang*. You'll find her by the old dry docks. Tell Captain Chang.'

'I hear you Captain Mariner,' came Chang's voice speaking English. 'Old dry docks? I thought they'd been refurbished.'

'I meant that it's been a while since they were dry.'

'Most amusing.' Captain Chang did not sound amused in the slightest. 'But I know precisely where you mean. Or rather, my father does.'

'Good. Estimated time of arrival?'

'Fifteen miles? We've had to cut speed with all this clutter. Say an hour. Maybe less.'

Marilyn might be pretty easy to spot even among the 'clutter' on the river, as Captain Chang put it. But the helicopter was just one among many in the sky. Just as Mayor Hong and Daniel Huuk had begun to get a firm grip on organizing the ships and boats into an effective evacuation force to rival Mayor Jaa's inflatables in Nanjing, so they had commandeered every helicopter they could and were putting them all to work. Chopper began to remark on identification marks from as far afield as Beijing, as the central government got the first of the relief supplies in. Beijing might be the crown of China; but Shanghai was the jewel in the crown, and even those few in Tiannenman Square who had not cut their political teeth down here knew that. But the long and the short of it was that, while Richard had a very good idea of where *Marilyn* was as well as where she was bound for, he reckoned that no one aboard the Cigarette was likely to have any idea that one of the helicopters in the lower sky above them was close on their tail and closing fast.

The Bailianjing bridge joined the two halves of the Bailianjing Road running north and south of the Bailianjing River, which itself wandered away through Pudong until it joined the Chuanyang River at the heart of the Taihu Basin flood management system. Chopper allowed the helicopter to settle on the northern spur which heaved itself out of the flood waters somewhere in front of the Jiang Tan hotel, whose smart reception area seemed still to be awash. There was no way to go north from here – except by boat; nor east or west, come to that, thought Richard as he unbuckled and prepared to climb down. So it was hardly surprising that the roadway was utterly deserted. Deserted of people at any rate. There was a battered old yellow school bus abandoned half in and half out of the water.

A swift circular recce on their way down had shown that this desolation was not the case on the south side of the bridge, where the Bailianjing Road ran safely through the modest hillock of Dongshufang – where a sizeable section of the 2010 Expo had been erected – to the raised section of Pudong South Road, a twelve-lane highway elevated clear of the floods and consequently fairly busy. That would be the way Red Pole and his men were likely to be coming. And he assumed that Butcher Kung, his anti-tank missiles and his murderous marines would, true to their type, come in over the water.

'We really have only one realistic objective,' he said to Ping, as they stood side by side surveying the slight up-slope towards the bridge, as the helicopter lifted off behind them, with Mei-Feng still mutinously aboard. Only acquiescent to Richard's terse decision, because she would be coming back with Chopper to take care of Wen-Qi when the fighting was all over. If everything went to plan. And if they achieved the objective Richard and Ping were discussing. 'Get Wen-Qi out of there if we can.'

'And the statue?' asked the marine quietly.

'Too heavy to carry unless we can take the boat as a whole – or commandeer whatever Red Pole and the Triad boys have brought to transport him away. Which would be a bridge too far, I think. As the saying goes.' He glanced speculatively over his shoulder. 'Or unless we can get that bus started up? Take the old boy back to school . . .'

Ping gestured and one of his men doubled across for a closer look at the abandoned vehicle. 'And the boat? *Marilyn*?' he asked.

'Let her sink or swim, I'm afraid. She'll have to take her chances with everyone aboard her, except Wen-Qi.'

'I agree,' the spruce marine nodded approvingly. 'Let's get to work.'

A swift battlefield survey revealed good news and bad. They had arrived first. But there was nowhere to hide, to set up a defensive position or to engineer a decent field of fire. Even on the south side of the bridge, the closest thing to a redoubt was a partially flooded building a little way down the Bailianjing River – accessible only after a quick swim. 'That must be the pump station for the drainage section of the main flood defence system,' Richard observed. 'So near and yet so far . . .'

'The same could be said for that,' added Ping, gesturing south down the Huangpu to where the American Expo Pavilion still stood, its grey steel structure looking like an eagle spreading its wings in welcome. A sea-eagle currently, rather than a bald eagle.

It was at this point that Ping's man reported back. 'The bus is dead, sir. It's not going anywhere without a tow-truck.'

'Hmmm,' said Richard brightening up. 'Let's have a closer look at that.'

The school bus was a long solid yellow box with a luggage rack secured to its roof. In their haste to escape the rising water, several passengers had left bits and pieces up there. Hardly surprising. It looked as though whatever happened had been a close call. Its front wheels, bumper and much of its radiator grille were under water, but its door was open and it was easy enough to climb aboard.

The angle of its long body gave a good view from the rear windows along the outer edge of the bridge, looking down towards the water rather than up towards the road. 'That's handy,' said Richard. 'If we can hide away in here unsuspected we'll have ringside seats for when *Marilyn* pulls in, and anything that happens on this side of the span. We'll be blind if they go to the far side, though. And we can't see over the bridge itself.'

'Unless we put a man up on the roof,' said Ping thoughtfully. 'Unless they're coming in by chopper – and I don't think they will be – then no one's going to look up there.'

'And I suppose whoever's up there could use that luggage as

camouflage, in any case,' added Richard. Then he repeated to himself, 'In any *case* . . .'

'We need a sharp-eyed observer up there,' said Ping. 'Someone who's hard to unsettle; who's good with decisions. And accurate with one of these . . .' As he spoke, he held out his hand and one of the marines stepped smartly forward and handed over Richard's Simonov sniper rifle.

'Ah,' said Richard, surprised that he hadn't seen the long, lean gun go on or off the helicopter. 'I thought you'd never ask.'

The luggage rack was basically a ten-foot cradle of wooden slats. It was possibly the least comfortable thing Richard had ever lain on. His knee-caps and elbow joints kept sliding into the gaps between the slats and more than once as he struggled to get into the best position, he thought he had crippled himself. But after five minutes he was lying flat behind a modest fortification of backpacks, hopefully all but invisible in his increasingly creased and baggy black suit. One of the backpacks was full of large books and these were spread beneath his elbows so that he could look over the wall of bags, through the Simonov's sniper sight like Nelson scanning the waters off Cape Trafalgar with his telescope. They'll almost certainly do their business on this side of the bridge, he was thinking as his tactical sense kicked in, tightening his scrotum and belly, shortening his breath and raising the hairs on the back of his neck. As far as they know, they're likely to be unobserved here. Different matter over the other side with all that traffic up on the flyover and whatnot . . .

The early afternoon settled to a sort of calm. The breeze fell light. A muddy, oily river scent thickened . The clouds seemed to thin a little and the whole bleak scene brightened. A kind of silence fell, against the constant backdrop of road and river traffic, the busy hissing trickle of the water and the whisper of the wind. The emergency exit window in the back of the bus immediately beneath him slammed open with a crash that made him jump. 'What can you see?' demanded Ping.

'Nothing. Yet.' From here Richard could see over the flat-topped bridge and down the far slope to the increasingly busy bustle on the raised sections and the flyover beyond. The scene was deeply disturbing because the flood waters made the roads seem like causeways reaching out into a wide brown seascape littered with islands that were the Expo pavilions in various states of repair. On the water of the Huangpu proper, the busy boats seemed to prefer sticking to the recognized waterways. Very few of them were venturing into the flooded areas at this point, even to see what pickings the departed Expo exhibitors might have left.

'You've got a better view of the river,' Richard said quietly. 'Anything coming our way?'

'Not yet,' answered Ping, equally quietly. 'They'll be easy enough to spot. Most of the traffic is out in the main channel.'

Richard could see the reasoning behind this. Many of the exhibition halls from Expo 2010 had been long closed, and others were in the process of being taken down and moved away, even before the flood arrived. Only the American pavilion seemed to be standing proud. Apart from that, the area in front of him was not heavily populated. On the contrary. It was regressing to an open industrial site. There was no one calling for help. Quite the opposite. The men and women in the vehicles coming and going down there all seemed confidently purposeful.

'Same up here,' he said. 'Most of the traffic's at the far end of the road . . .'

But then he caught his breath. A big old lorry was pulling out of the throng and easing its way up the slope towards the bridge. It was taking its time; in no hurry. Behind the battered square cab, the high back seemed to be covered with canvas. Through the sniper scope he could see two men on the seat in front. How many men were packed behind and beneath the dusty canvas it was impossible to say. 'Looks like we have visitors,' he whispered.

And, even before he could think the game's afoot, things started to move much more rapidly.

Marilyn came out of the throng midstream at three-quarters speed, snarling round in a wide curve towards the bridge. As she came, the way fell off her and her nose settled on to the sluggishly heaving water. Whoever was at the throttles cut the power and the snarl became a growl, and then a rumble as she coasted in. Someone aboard the truck must have seen her – she was by no means hard to spot – and the ancient motor roared as the vehicle revved up and came more quickly, spewing clouds of grey exhaust. Richard kept the scope on the truck. He could only see *Marilyn* by glancing carefully over his shoulder. Any attempt to move the whole long rifle would have given him away immediately. And once the truck crested the low rise on to the flat top of the bridge, any movement at all became out of the question.

'She's at the bank. Foot of the bridge this side,' whispered Ping, his voice disguised by the growling of the two motors. 'Lieutenant Jiang is getting out and walking up on to the roadway. Xin is out ashore and holding her in place . . .'

Straightline walked into Richard's field of vision then. Into his field of fire, too. In the middle of the bridge he stopped uncertainly. The door of the truck opened and a huge man climbed down. He turned back and slapped the dusty side of the canvas. The better part of a dozen men piled out and formed up behind him, becoming a tight wall between him and the truck itself. They seemed to Richard to be carrying clubs and knives. The big man was carrying a gun. For once in his life Richard had no idea what kind of gun it was, beyond that it was a handgun. An automatic like an old World War Two Browning. The big man was dressed in jeans and a T-shirt that was moulded to his massive torso like a layer of black paint. He was as bald as a bullet, with a neck as thick as a shell casing. His ears stood out like those of an enraged elephant. This, thought Richard, must be Red Pole, head of the Green Gang's enforcement unit. The big man ambled up to Straightline and they began to talk. His men stayed beside the truck.

Then the screaming started. Richard tensed to turn, his automatic reactions taking over. But he held himself still by a sheer effort of will. The screams were shouts of rage, not of fear or pain.

'It's the girl,' hissed Ping. 'She's on *Marilyn*'s deck. She's jumped ashore. Xin's let go of the rope. He's coming after her. *Marilyn*'s drifting into the Bailianjing river. She'll be under the bridge in a minute . . .'

Wen-Qi and Xin ran on to the bridge, and into Richard's view. As they did so, the schoolgirl's screams became words. 'Help! You must help me! I've been kidnapped! These men are Green Gang Triad. My father is Daniel Huuk, Dragon Head of the Invisible Power!'

Red Pole's massive head came up, his eyes narrowed speculatively. He turned back to Straightline, frowning suspiciously. Clearly the negotiations had not included the children of rival Triad leaders. Until now.

Wen-Qi's words faltered into silence as she realized the enormity of what she had done.

Everything seemed to stop.

And Lieutenant Ping screamed something at the top of his voice.

Richard didn't really register what the marine lieutenant shouted, he was so surprised that the officer should have given them all away so unexpectedly. He tore his eyes from the sniper scope and looked round. What he saw froze into a kind of still photograph in his mind, seen in an instant and remembered for a lifetime.

Out on the river, a naval-looking cutter had pulled clear of the throng of shipping. Its lean bow was pointing this way. It was packed with men in uniform. One of whom was kneeling in the forecastle, frozen in the act of firing something from a tube on a tripod secured at the point of the cutwater. And there, just above the flat brown surface, halfway between the cutter and the bridge there was some kind of a missile.

Richard realized in that instant what Ping had shouted. '*Incoming!*'

Butcher Kung's J201 missile took *Marilyn* directly on the stern as she drifted in the current beneath the bridge. It did to the Cigarette what it was designed to do to a tank. But the beautiful vessel had no armour. Had it not had such massive motors, the impact-warhead might even have failed to fire. But the simple weight of those huge motors set the whole thing off. The kilograms of shaped high-explosive not only destroyed the speedboat, vaporizing everyone aboard except Genghis, it took out a sizeable section of the bridge into the bargain. The bus was simply lifted into the air, pushed deeper into the water and allowed to fall back like a felled tree. Its back wheels came down on the roadway hard enough to burst the tyres.

Richard nearly lost the Simonov, and had cause to bless the sturdy wooden slats that kept him safely in place. He jammed the scope to his eye and surveyed the scene through a cloud of smoke and concrete dust. All he could see at first was the truck, also blown awry by the explosion, its canvas gone, its windscreen shattered, its driver's face a mask of blood. He began to sweep the enhanced vision closer and closer still, feverishly seeking a slim, girlish form amongst the confusing jumble which seemed to be all that was left of the roadway. He found that he was praying Wen-Qi had not been killed. And his prayers were answered. A mixed blessing, as it turned out.

Wen-Qi was on the far side of a considerable crater which seemed to be floored by the heaving surface of the racing river. As Richard's sniper scope found her, she was just picking herself up, shaking her head, beginning to look around, apparently with all the unthinking resilience of the young. At first glance she seemed to be alone, but then several jumbles of rubble resolved themselves into dust-covered figures and suddenly she was surrounded. Straightline picked himself up and staggered towards the gigantic Red Pole, who shot him in the face as he rose to his full height. As simply, as unthinkingly as that. The bullet entered the lieutenant's cheekbone and burst out at the point above the nape of his neck. Straightline collapsed like a puppet with its strings cut.

Red Pole continued, striding purposefully forward as the men round the truck behind him began to pick themselves up and reach for their weapons. Red Pole came on regardless, taking aim at the girl.

Richard drew a bead on the massive man, but before he could fire, Steady Xin threw himself in the way. Protecting the child with his sturdy body he shouted, 'Don't kill her! She was telling the truth . . .'

Red Pole's second bullet took Xin in the shoulder. His whole body flinched, but he remained in front of the girl. 'Don't,' he shouted again. 'She's worth more than the statue! Alive, she's worth more! *Alive . . .*'

'Bastard!' Wen-Qi threw herself on her would-be protector. Under normal circumstances, the sturdy seaman would simply have shrugged her off, but his shoulder was shattered and his arm useless. He fell to his knees. Red Pole put the pistol to the top of his stubbled head and pulled the trigger. The bullet shattered the top of Steady's skull like a spoon hitting a hard-boiled egg.

Then, catching Wen-Qi in his huge left hand even as the sailor's corpse slumped to the ground, Red Pole strode forward once again. The Green Gang enforcer held the schoolgirl up in front of him like a shield as he looked around, clearly trying to work out what on earth was going on here. His left forearm crushed her lower ribs to his belly. Her shoulders were on a level with his. The back of her head banged against his chin as she writhed helplessly and screamed insults. She wriggled and kicked, her heels drumming against his thighs completely unnoticed. She was so small and he was so huge.

All in all, thought Richard, she was not much use as body armour. The cross-hairs of the sniper scope settled on the flap of his right ear, well clear of Wen-Qi's head. He squeezed the trigger and felt the Simonov kick against his shoulder.

Ping's scream of warning was all but lost in the whip crack of the report.

The bullet took Red Pole's ear off. It shattered his cheekbone, exploded his eardrum and deafened him so completely that he fell to his knees, totally incapacitated. Given another instant, it would have been easy enough for Wen-Qi to tear herself from his grip as the enormity of disorientating agony claimed him. But Richard's simple plan was superseded by Butcher Kung.

The second J201 took the truck in the side and blew it away as effectively as the first one had destroyed *Marilyn*. Wen-Qi was lucky indeed that she had not quite managed to wriggle free of Red Pole's failing grasp. For, if – as Richard had observed – she was too slight to make effective body armour for him, he was more than big enough to be adequate protection for her. The blast from the explosion blew the huge enforcer flat, killing him at once, and his massive torso covered Wen-Qi as effectively as an air-raid shelter.

It took Richard's help for Ping to move the dead man off the unconscious girl, five minutes later. As they did so, Richard looked around at the carnage. 'This looks like work for Butcher Kung and his men,' he said grimly, but his words were all-but lost beneath the sound of the approaching helicopter.

It was Richard who carried Wen-Qi to the helicopter when Chopper, who had been made to hover as near as possible to the scene by the increasingly frantic Mei-Feng, landed back on the same spot as before. He handed the battered child over to the worried woman, then they all took their seats as Mei-Feng exhausted her store of first aid experience checking Wen-Qi's stirring form for any signs of serious physical damage. But at no stage in their brisk evacuation of the battleground did they hang around. They were so quick, in fact, that they were lifting off even as Butcher Kung and his men came ashore to see what damage they had done. And to start to clear some of it up.

'I think, under the circumstances, we had better go back to *Poseidon*,' decided Richard. 'We've quite a complicated report to make to Captain Chang. And I cannot begin to imagine what she's going to write in her ship's log about all this. It'll give us all something to do while she comes downriver and ties up by the *Luyang*.'

As he spoke, Wen-Qi's eyes opened and she grasped Mei-Feng with all her might. '*I want my pappi!*' whispered the little girl.

As Richard's helicopter lifted off and the bow of Kung's cutter slid on to the groin of masonry and mud where *Marilyn* had come ashore, the solid golden statue that they had christened Genghis Khan settled on to the bed of the Bailianjing River. On to the concrete apron of the first great pipe of the flood defence drainage system. It settled massively, with a clang loud enough to make Kung look up on the bridge above. It weighed more than seventy-five kilos and there was nothing in its solid frame but pure gold, except for the jewels that decorated its solidly cast armour.

It was battered, twisted, part-melted by the J201 ATM's blast, but it fell upright and stood erect. What was left of its seared and damaged face looked straight ahead upriver, towards where the Bailianjing River became a carefully controlled, crucially important, central part of the major drainage system for the whole Taihu Basin. And, less than five metres in front of it, stood the great whirling fan of the huge turbine pump that controlled the whole complex of the flood defences.

THIRTY-THREE
Dynamo

During the next six hours, as the great wave rushed downriver from Nanjing, Richard, Robin and Mei-Feng became ever more intimately involved with the deceptively simple two-pronged plan to protect the people of the Shanghai Shi.

Had it not been for the Mariners' relationship with the Deputy General Commissioner – and his unusually potent presence here – then a couple of gweilo visitors would never have been allowed access to the relevant airwaves, let alone being permitted to offer suggestions, or the simple honour of having them listened to. And, on occasion, acted upon.

Mei-Feng was another matter. Her reputation and position assured her of attention, even though, at first, what she seemed to be suggesting raised eyebrows from Shanghai City Hall to Tiannenman Square. Especially as she seemed to be suggesting a course of action she had first planned with the gweilo Richard Mariner.

But, what with one thing and another, by the time *Poseidon* reached the Shanghai dry dock and secured herself to the *Luyang*'s towering side, it was taken for granted that Richard, Robin and Mei-Feng would transfer back across on to the destroyer's command bridge, which remained one of the central communications hubs of the whole desperate enterprise. The only fly in the ointment was that Mei-Feng insisted on bringing the shocked and frightened Wen-Qi with her. And Robin, taxing even Daniel's unique combination of Chinese civility and British Naval Officer sangfroid, insisted that the distant father spend a little time in soothing his terrified child. Even over a video-link, it was better than nothing, she said. And she was right, but only partially so. And the immediate outcome was that the still-shaken child was passed into the world-weary ambit of Political Officer Leung, whose allegiances were now clear and whose position in the Invisible Power Triad assured. But, at the end of the day, Wen-Qi still wanted her father. She wanted to hug him while he held her safe and told her everything was going to be all right.

*　　*　　*

The evacuation of the Shanghai Shi, which Richard would forever think of as Dynamo, was already under way. The little ships were coming and going between the flooded city and the huge – and growing – flotilla waiting just offshore. In the flooded areas of the city, inflatables such as Mayor Jaa had employed in Nanjing were supplemented by sampans, skiffs, rowing boats, punts – anything that could move in the shallow flood waters between the buildings and handle the occasional surges and rips.

But as time passed, more and more areas of the city, on their little ridges and hillocks, became passable on foot as the flood control system pumped millions of gallons of water through, past and beneath Pudong, across the Shi and out into the bay. And those who could get about were ordered to report to rescue stations, carefully placed – at Mai-Feng's insistence – in the tall buildings most likely to survive the onslaught of the second wave.

While the little boats with their negligible drafts picked their way between the buildings and people slopped on foot in their thousands, tens of thousands, to each of the twenty or so rescue stations, and as the drainage system laboured to breaking point pushing the flood water out to sea, even bigger plans were being drawn up.

Taking Daniel's observations of the way the first wave had moved across the estuary as his template, Richard was calculating how the second wave would behave. Estimating, with the input of the army of experts the Mayor had assembled and the further, more distant advisory panels waiting at the far end of the conferencing facilities, how much damage would be done on its first arrival. How deep the flood would be after it departed. What larger vessels would therefore be able to sail safely straight across the Shanghai Shi and start to rescue those waiting on the 'high ground'. On the upper floors of the Waitan Gate Towers, the Shanghai World Financial Centre, of the Jin Mao Tower, of the Shimao International Plaza and its adjacent Financial Centre, from Tomorrow Square where Daniel Huuk's personal luggage was still in his room at the Marriott Hotel. And a dozen more that Mei-Feng listed as most likely to survive the impact of the second wave.

Chopper was among the first to see it, four hours later, as it burst out of the narrow mouth of the Dongzhou Cao Yangtze river section, like a dragon escaping from a cave, and exploded across the Baimaosha Caio in a welter of foam; the sheer cliff-face of it seeming to ease back even as he watched it spread exponentially across the low flat banks to the north and south.

His helicopter was one of half a dozen detailed to fly sorties upriver and try to give warning of the wave's approach, but it had never occurred to him that, having fled the monster all along the Yangtze from the wreckage of Three Gorges, he would be amongst the first to face it here. Or now. But at least his experiences during the last day allowed him to get a firm perspective. While the other helicopter pilots were sending back apocalyptic messages to the various command and communication centres in the city, he was thinking, this is no longer the wave that obliterated Yichang and destroyed the great bridge at Wusan. And he calmly contacted the *Luyang*, asking to be put through directly to Captain Mariner.

'We have little more than two hours' warning, but that should be enough,' said Richard, his deep voice at its calmest and most reasonable as he addressed the party-line that accessed Daniel, Mayor Hong, the distant Committee in Beijing and all the experts they had assembled. 'The wave is lower than it was. Certainly, it is much more like the wave that came through Nanjing rather than the one that destroyed Wuhan. An ocean roller, as the intrepid scientist at Nanjing University had described it; not a big surf. And according to my information it is spreading north, tending away from us.

'As we observed off Nanjing, the islands are pushing the wave away. The Chongming Dao is completely flooded, more a massive mud reef than an island at the moment, but it seems to be pushing the weight of the water up into the Haimen Shuidao reach and with any luck it will spread across the lower areas of the estuary bank to the north, past Qidong, and leave us relatively unscathed. It's a tough call, I know. But Qidong is less than a twentieth of the size of Shanghai. And, like Shanghai, it's been getting its people clear for some time now. And when I say we'll be relatively unscathed, I mean just that. Relatively.

'The cliffs along the southern shore will serve to push the weight of the water north until it reaches the southern arm of the estuary, the Baoshan Cao and the Wusong Kou where the Yangtze and the Huangpu have their confluence. Then the wave will come down to us. But, again, with luck, the island of Chanxing Dao, which is just north of the bay where the rivers join will push some of the water north again. Though what comes down the Huangpu itself will be extended immensely by the wash of water across the Shanghai Shi.

'Which of course is part of our calculation, because we're relying on the Shi being flooded from Pudong to the sea deeply enough to let the larger boats join our fleet of little ships to access our skyscraper islands. Our high ground.'

'In the meantime, though,' Robin chimed in, still frowning with concern. 'It is time to tell all the little boats to drop off the last of their passengers at the nearest designated rescue station and then get out to sea, where they'll be saf*er* if not exactly as *safe* as we'd like.'

'And in *my* meantime,' added in Mei-Feng, not to be outdone, 'we rely on those pumps to keep dropping the water level so the wave does not start out from such a high base when it does arrive. And we rely on them to keep pumping even harder when it does come, to ease the immediate impact on the lower structures of our buildings as much as possible . . .' She had commandeered the chart room, but instead of charts she was using maps of the city, road maps, tourist guides, anything they could scare up for her.

'And you, Deputy General Commissioner,' said Richard finally, formally. 'Where are you?'

'We are at the mayor's office, Two Hundred People's Avenue. Where we have been throughout the bulk of this incident so far,' answered Daniel shortly.

Richard looked at Mei-Feng, his eyebrows raised. She shook her head. 'The mayor's office is not one of the buildings we recommend,' she said quietly. 'It is not one of the most modern. It is not high-rise. It was lucky to survive the earthquake . . .'

'Where is the nearest one on the recommended list?' interrupted Richard.

'Shimao International,' Mei-Feng answered at once.

'No,' said Daniel. 'We have our own plans in hand. We have boats waiting to take us to the elevated expressway and transport down to the Waitan Gate Towers. It is one of your listed buildings. Perhaps not the highest on the tally because it is right on the river bank beside Waitan – the Bund, as you call it – but from there we will be able to see the progress of the flood. It could hardly be more central, and will certainly be the perfect place to coordinate . . . What did you call it . . .? Dynamo. Yes. It will be the perfect place for us to coordinate Dynamo.

'We're planning on having the communications equipment moved. We will be back in contact with you as soon as we are settled and everything is all set up. And we have two hours you say? Then we'd better get on with it!'

Amid all the bustle that resulted from Huuk's pronouncement – on the *Luyang*'s bridge as much as at 200 People's Avenue – no one noticed the slight figure of Wen-Qi. Her trembling chin firmed up and her green eyes began to shine with determination rather than tears. For she had heard what Huuk had said the same as everyone else had done. Now she knew where her father was going to be. All she had to do was to work out a way of getting to him. Of getting to the Waitan Gate Towers on the river's edge before the great wall of water arrived.

THIRTY-FOUR
Wall

Ninety minutes later, the wave swept down the Baoshan Cao and into the Wusong Kou, where the Huangpu empties into the Yangtze itself. At the mouth of the Baoshan Cou the estuary proper began and the river course widened from less than five miles to more than twenty-five. The wave seemed to lower its head as its width spread exponentially, but somehow it seemed to lose little of its overwhelming power. The wall of water simply seemed to exult in its new-found freedom and it swept forward, its speed and its potential for destruction undiminished.

Chopper Quing's helicopter was following the southern crest of it as closely as he dared as he reported every detail he could see to Richard Mariner aboard the *Luyang*.

The southern edge of the monster was soaring up the sheer walls of the river cliffs below the Shanghai–Nanjing expressway, spitting foam and vomiting jetsam over the deserted highway.

An easterly wind had sprung up, forceful enough to tear spray off of its round, brown shoulder, as though the elements themselves were desirous of pushing the monster back where it had come. Of putting the genie back in the bottle. But all the wind could do was tear off that derisory spray of foam. The cloud cover moved at last, releasing a westering sun, whose beams turned the foaming, brown roller red. For an instant, the whole river, as far as the eye could see, was as red as blood. Just as it had been up in Yichang, at the very start.

The only sound Chopper could hear clearly was Richard's voice in the headphones of his radio, and beyond that there was a muted rumble from his helicopter's rotors. But he knew that had he been able to hear the sounds of nature outside the cabin, to take the headphones off and to stick his head out through the window, the whole of the shaking air through which he was flying would have been filled with the thunderous roaring of the monster.

It seemed to Chopper then that the mouth of the Huangpu appeared with unbelievable suddenness. One moment the forty-foot roller had been pounding along the mud cliff upriver of Liuhezhen, then it was sweeping over the low-lying township itself. Five minutes later, the deserted suburb of Baoshan was swept under and the wave was at the Huangpu, throwing off a huge southbound tongue of watery destruction. It took Chopper an instant, then he realized what he was seeing. 'Its there!' he shouted into the microphone beside his lips. 'It's in the Huangpu! It'll be with you in minutes!'

But the wave was already having an effect on the Huangpu. Although the Taihu Basin drainage system was designed to pump flood waters away through the complex of channels, canals and sewers into the ocean beyond the eastern edges of the Shanghai Shi, it was part of the Huangpu's job to carry water away north into the Yangtze. And this is what it had been doing ever since the first flood ran upstream against the north-flowing impulse of its current.

The second wave effectively dammed the flow. More than that, it forced the northward impulse of the river's current back on itself. The river's currents went wild, twisting in watery frustration, forming mill races and rapids out of nowhere. The water level began to rise at once, not just at the point where the wave was sweeping upstream, but all along the Huangpu and its tributaries. The flood waters as far apart as Huangpu Park and Century Park began to deepen exponentially. The drains in recently dried-out areas began to overflow again. Fountains of filthy water erupted mysteriously and unexpectedly from the Shanghaiside subway stations.

Had Shanghai been human, had the Huangpu been its aorta, then its blood pressure would be soaring off the scale.

Heart-attack time.

The first people to notice the change in the river were Political Officer Leung and Wen-Qi. They were in the cutter Lieutenant Kung had used to bring the bodies back to *Luyang* from what was left of the Bailianjing Bridge. Kung had left the cutter unguarded, lashed to a landing stage, and once Leung had given in to the child's tearful insistence, it had been easy enough for the pair to sneak down to the cutter and to take it. Leung was content to do so, for he was certain he would gain forgiveness – not to say preferment – from the girl's grateful father when he delivered her safely to the Waitan Gate Towers.

Now the naval officer was beginning to regret his decision. Wen-Qi sat slumped silently in the cutter's bow. She had hardly spoken since they had set out. On the one hand he could appreciate that the child had been through a lot in the last few hours – most of it severely traumatic, from what he could understand. On the other, she had seemed lively enough when discussing the plan – and suckering him into it – and keen enough at the outset to make sure her father would appreciate what Leung had done for her and, through her, for Huuk himself. But now the whole atmosphere seemed to have changed in line with the traumatized child's mood swing. The red of the westering sun was not bringing out the best in the flooded landscape. The soaring towers of Pudong and Shanghai had taken on the grim aspect of blood-boltered dragons' teeth chewing at the afternoon sky. Tearing the low clouds to rags and releasing an enervating humidity so powerful that it seemed to flow through the flooded city.

Even the sight of the newly refurbished Bund failed to lift Leung's spirits, for it required a great deal of concentration to stop the cutter from wandering across the flooded Huangpu Park and on to the legendary thoroughfare itself. Lost in thoughts, though lacking the insight to see any real irony in the fact that he was now looking for preferment to a man he had once considered killing, Leung throttled the cutter's motor up and took the little vessel's speed towards its maximum.

At least their objective was in view, he thought. The triangular edifice of the Waitan Gate Towers stood on its massive plinth the size of a soccer field at the end of the Bund, like the prow of some soaring glass-hulled ship that happened to have docked there between the cavernous gapes of the Yan'an Road tunnels. 'Almost there,' he called to the sulky child, feigning a cheeriness he was nowhere near to feeling. 'The water is deep enough to take us over the top of the road tunnel, I think, and it looks as though the topmost steps up to the hotel are still dry. That means the reception will be. Once we're there it should be easy to find him . . .'

But even as Leung spoke, the surface of the river ahead of him seemed to rise up in a hill. He gaped. A steep-sided, white-hearted hill of water, perhaps a metre high, several metres across. Leung had never seen anything like it. For a moment he was carried back to the stories of his childhood and he expected a dragon to burst forth into the air. Or a sea-deity to rise. Perhaps this was Tin Hau, goddess of the sea, come to claim her rights.

The hill of water burst open and a fountain of foaming filth soared up into the sky. Just for an instant, Leung saw something square and metallic go flying upwards, and then explode down into the heaving surface close by.

'What is it?' screamed Wen-Qi, overcome with yet more stark terror.

'The tunnel!' he shouted, scarcely able to believe what he was seeing – or what he was saying. 'It's the road tunnel. It's blowing open!'

As he spoke, Leung gunned the cutter's motor to the max and pushed

her wildly towards the Waitan Gate Towers. But somehow, unbeliev-
ably, he seemed to be sailing uphill. Not as though he were breasting
an oncoming wave, but as though all the water ahead of him were
rising. As though the whole of the Huangpu River had chosen this
very moment to overflow. At the heart of the heaving fountain which
must, thought the reeling sailor, be immediately above one of the air
vents in the roof of the road tunnel, a bright red bonnet suddenly burst
through the surface like a big blood-bubble. 'It's a Geely!' he shouted
in amazement.

'What?' screamed Wen-Qi, to whom he might as well have been
speaking Greek.

'A car! A Geely Panda! What the hell else is coming up? My God!'

The car turned sluggishly on its side and slid back under the surface
like a drowned man. Leung watched it, simply awestruck. And on its
heels, a Volvo reared like an attacking shark. Wen-Qi screamed, and
he assumed the bizarre sight of the floating cars was terrifying her
until he felt the cutter leap upwards and he swung round to look where
he was going.

The cutter was heaving across the raised plaza outside the steel and
crystal prow of the Waitan Gate Towers. The water level had leaped
up maybe three metres – ten feet – since the top had blown off the
tunnel beneath them. Very near to panic, Leung cut the racing motor,
but he was far too late. The heaving, boiling Huangpu simply threw
the *Luyang*'s cutter, the political officer and the Deputy General
Commissioner's daughter against the main entrance doors with sufficient force to shatter them.

THIRTY-FIVE
Water

aniel Huuk was one of the first people in Shanghai to know that the pumps had stopped. He was on the fifth floor of the Waitan Gate Towers, in a haphazardly cleared open space amongst partition-walled shops and stalls, surrounded by the equipment that he, Mayor Hong and their teams had brought from 200 People's Avenue, along with the generators required to keep it all running. Equipment that they had had to carry up stairway after stairway because the lifts had no power. Which was why they had only come this high. There were fifty-five more stories above. But they were packed with people praying that Shanghai's 'Purple Mountain' was as safe as Nanjing's. Furthermore, this had been the first floor with spaces they could clear easily to set up their equipment. And they had been running out of time in any case, a fact emphasized by Richard's reports via walkie-talkie of what Chopper Quing could see.

One of the most important pieces of equipment was the pump-system monitor, a computer constantly updated by radio feeds from remote sensors in all of the new and refurbished pumping stations. Under normal circumstances this – and its far larger cousin, the full flood defence system monitor – would simply be unregarded somewhere in the depths of the hydro-engineering section of the city architect's office. Now, it was like Cinderella, unexpectedly the fairy-tale belle of the ball.

The news that the Bailianjing pump had gone down was so catastrophic that it caused Daniel to totally disregard the horrified reports that the river level had leaped up by a good three metres. And that some sort of vessel had smashed through the main doors below and all but destroyed reception, aided by a considerable wash of water.

Huuk and Hong stood shoulder to shoulder, looking down at the screen of the young hydro-engineer's computer. 'It's not just the Bailianjing pump,' he was saying. 'You see how it controls the whole of that section south of Pudong? It is the main drainage area if the Huangpu backs up as it is doing now. That one pump here,' his rag-nailed, well-chewed, finger shook as it stabbed towards the red square of the schematic marked with the Chinese character for

Bailianjing. 'It is the lead station for the Sanba River system to the north and the Chuanyang system to the south. It was upgraded and refurbished for the 2010 Expo, of course, because so many of the pavilions were just beside it. But given this state of affairs it is even more important still! That part of the system, under these circumstances, is all that can relieve the pressure downriver. The pressure *here*!' And on the final word, he made a fist and punched the screen, right in the centre of Shanghai, where Pudong reached out as though trying to become one with Huangpu Park and the Bund behind it.

'What is wrong with it?' Mayor Hong asked the twitching engineer.

'I can only suppose that something must have blocked it, or become wedged in the mechanism somehow. It was working perfectly until only a moment ago. What might be able to do so, I cannot begin to imagine. There is a short tunnel section at a carefully calculated angle, then a strong metal mesh, also angled to make it harder for rubbish to clog it up. It has been so very carefully constructed, so carefully reconditioned, as I say . . .'

'But something must have caused this malfunction,' insisted Hong, his voice gentle, calm.

'I guess so. As I say . . .'

Hong looked Huuk straight in the eye. 'Have you any idea how we can find out what is going on at this pump? We have no time to get a diver ready, under these circumstances. And in any case, what could a diver do? Especially with the big wave coming. It would be yet another useless death! What under the sky are we going to do?'

Such was the shock of the unexpected disaster that neither Huuk nor Hong had thought to close down the laboriously resurrected conference call facilities. So when Richard's voice boomed out of the ether, they both jumped almost as much as the nervous young hydro-engineer.

'Wait!' shouted Richard suddenly, 'I think I have an idea!'

Political Officer Leung awoke with a start, to find himself lying, of all places, on the reception counter of the Waitan Gate Towers building. He recognized the famously reconstructed Bauhaus design of the three-story atrium, which stood all around him like something out of 1930s Berlin – but he simply did not believe what he was seeing. He lay there for a moment longer, gazing up at the famous stained glass ceiling, so cleverly lit from above that it seemed eternally like an evening sky just at the moment after sunset. It was absolutely incredible, he thought, that such a seemingly fragile construction should have survived the earthquake that had rocked the city thirty-six hours or so ago. It certainly spoke well for the solid construction of the whole building itself. Then the pain came, chopping through the dangerously dreamlike reverie, and with it, a memory.

'Where is she?' he demanded, sitting up, though there was no one nearby. Still dazed and disorientated, he swung his legs over the edge of the counter, unconsciously expecting to jump easily down on to the marble floor and go in search of Wen-Qi, or someone who could give him news of her. But the action was less like rising from a tall bed than like stepping into an icy swimming pool. Shocked, he looked down. The whole of the massive reception area was awash. And deserted. With a shout, more of disgust than of fear, he jumped down into the water, then went wading through the filthy, sucking heave of it, looking for the stairs, and calling across the echoing, sloshing, sinister near-silence as he went, 'Wen-Qi? Wen-Qi, where are you?'

Poseidon pulled away from the side of the *Luyang* with a great deal of dispatch. After Richard and Robin had arrived aboard, it required nothing more than the slipping of the lines and the powering-up of the engines. It was only when Richard ran up on to the bridge and saw two strangers guiding the corvette upstream, one at the helm and one at the collision alarm radar, that the enormity of what he had witnessed earlier that day really hit home. During the last few, action-packed days aboard this vessel, he had come to know, trust and like almost everyone aboard. Fair enough, he hadn't known either Steady or Straightline as well as he had believed, for he would have trusted either of them with his life, or his wallet, without a second thought – but the affection and respect had lasted after their desertion with Genghis, and it lingered now most poignantly after their brutal deaths. So much so that it entirely eclipsed his frustration at the loss of the Cigarette speed-boat *Marilyn*.

These thoughts were enough to take *Poseidon* along the flooded north bank, past the inundated ferry piers at Qinhuangdo and Gongpinglu, before the river turned south and Richard was distracted from his sad thoughts by the sight of the buildings of the Bund standing with their feet in the water, behind the little green islands made by the treetops in Huangpu Park. He watched the refurbished frontages stream by, from the Asia Building to the Peninsular Hotel, in their varied styles from Romanesque to Art Deco, then stirred himself as the shadow of the Waitan Gate Tower fell across the frantic bustle on the foredeck.

The line that had held *Marilyn* until her desertion with Steady, Straightline, Genghis and the kidnapped Wen-Qi was recovered now, and the foredeck gantry was back to being used for the purpose its designers envisaged. *Neptune* was ready to go over the side. Although the remote explorer was designed to work in the ocean, at great depths and under massive pressures, there was no reason why she should not be able to work in a shallow river. And her strengths, designed to handle the kinds of conditions which might be expected to present themselves several kilometres down, would only help her handle the kind of situation she would find herself facing if she was still working when the wave arrived.

And that possibility seemed very real. While the great wave's entry into the Huangpu had caused the river to rise and run wild, it had also caused the flood-wave to steepen and, crucially, to slow. For the first time since it had broken free of the crumbling Three Gorges Dam, the great wave had found something running counter to it. And, like a gigantic bully confronted by a small but determined opponent, it seemed to hesitate. At the best estimate, they had a little more than half an hour until the crest of the monster managed to throw itself across the fifteen miles between Baoshan and the Bund.

The Bailianjing Bridge was four miles south of the Bund – a little more than six miles from the shipyard dock where the *Luyang* was anchored. Captain Chang called for full ahead at once, and, as *Poseidon* was facing upriver still, she got it. At once. The river pilot was firmly in command of their course as he guided them up the middle of the central channel, tending a little to the Shanghai side where the river ran faster – and deeper in the days when it had been contained by its natural banks. *Poseidon* was moving forward faster than the wave within five minutes of slipping her cables.

By the time Richard came on to the foredeck, five minutes later, they were passing the mouth of the Sanba River, which was currently flooding Century Park south of Pudong, and only five minutes or so from the mouth of the Bailianjing.

Richard stayed on deck only just long enough to see the remote explorer being lowered into the racing river. Then, with Robin at his side, he ran down to the control room in the corvette's bulbous bow, as Captain Chang and her father called for engines to slow and then to reverse, as the corvette performed the naval equivalent of an emergency stop. It was always claustrophobic and stressful being down here. The control room was at the forward end of a long, narrow corridor with very restricted headroom. It was a small space, crowded with computers, so that the two control-chairs seemed to preclude any chance of anyone actually sitting in them. And it was an unlucky place. The first two trained controllers had been the victims of shark attack. Their main replacement had been Steady Xin. Other than those men – all variously *hors de combat* – only Richard and Robin had any kind of competence at controlling *Neptune* at all. But both of them were navigating officers, command-bridge sailors, unused to the cramped conditions that seemed so much at risk at the end of the fragile bow. Even when *Poseidon* had been sailing safely through the Yellow Sea while *Neptune* explored the ocean depths with not a hazard in sight, the experience had been unnerving. Now, under these circumstances, with so much resting on success and such a huge wave so close behind and getting closer by the second, it was simply terrifying.

'You ready?' asked Richard as he settled himself into the right-hand seat and reached for *Neptune*'s controls.

'Ready as I'll ever be,' answered Robin.

'You can't fool me,' he said. 'You were *born* ready.'

There was quite a complicated start-up sequence, not unlike the pre-flight checks on an airliner. They disregarded it.

'Cameras on,' said Richard, and the computer screens in front of them lit up with pictures of what *Neptune* could see. At the moment, this consisted largely of foaming brown water rearing in vicious cross-currents as the rising river-level forced the Huangpu up above the wreckage of the Bailianjing Bridge.

'Flooding ballast,' said Robin, and instantly the pictures began to show the surface rising rapidly as the explorer began to sink.

Richard keyed in *Neptune*'s inbuilt GPS locator to the schematic of the river system held in *Poseidon*'s computer memories. He would rather have gone live to the Internet but that had been down for days, ever since a massive cable had been cut out in the Yellow Sea. Still this would do, he thought.

Neptune sank so rapidly through the relative shallows of the flooding river that she bounced off the bottom a minute later. All Richard's screens could see was a grey green soup of agitated river water, full of glittering bubbles and a bewildering whirl of rubbish. He switched on the headlights – but, as with a car going through a fog bank, they weren't a lot of help. He tried the heat sensors and the sonar – to little greater effect. But in the corner of the main screen, like one of his children's computer games, there was a window that gave a map showing pretty accurately where *Neptune* was in relation to the shores, the bridge and – crucially – the pumping station.

As Richard and Robin moved the remote vessel forward along the river bed and into the mouth of the concrete-sided drainage tunnel, they tested the articulated arms, especially those ones ending in grabs and claws, for their initial plan was simply to get hold of whatever was blocking the pump and pull it free.

They came up against the grill first. At first it looked as though the woven metal mesh would prove an obstacle, but as they came closer it was clear to see that the damage done to it was sufficient to allow *Neptune* access. So, slowing down and taking ever more care, they guided the robot submarine onward into the short tunnel behind the twisted wire. And there, the brightness of the headlights at last paid dividends. For the screens in front of Richard and Robin alike showed the soles of a pair of boots, a stiff armoured skirt around stubby legs and a pair of tight-clenched buttocks clad in calf-length trousers, all cast out of pure, gleaming gold.

'Now there,' said Robin wryly, 'is a face I'd know anywhere!'

THIRTY-SIX
Gate

I t was oddly appropriate that Mei-Feng, who had seen the wave born at Yicheng, should be amongst the first to see it arrive in the heart of Shanghai. And also, perhaps, that it was Chopper, her companion through those adventures, who signalled its approach.

Chopper had been following the wave down the Huangpu from Baoshan for nearly twenty minutes when he saw it surge over the suspended roadway of the beautiful Yangpu Bridge, leaving for a heart-stopping moment, only the towering stilettos of the uprights with their spiders' webs of cables, like the masts of a sinking schooner above the water. Unaware that Richard and Robin were aboard *Poseidon*, he called the *Luyang* with his warning: 'Here it comes! Watch out, Captain Mariner!'

Mei-Feng looked at Commodore Shan, who was senior officer on the bridge. On the vessel, in fact. 'You must warn *Poseidon*,' she ordered, but he was staring open-mouthed through the clearview. Her gaze, inevitably, followed his. Just in time to see the wave come round the slight bend that lay between the Shanghai shipyard dry dock and the bridge. They were on the command bridge of a destroyer a little more than 150 metres long. The sloping clearview window stood about forty feet above the deck, so the only added height they had over the wave-crest was the height of the freeboard above the river's surface. And suddenly that didn't seem to be very much at all.

The wave swept round the bend, overwhelming the already flooded Dandonglu ferry pier on Shanghaiside and sweeping out over Misheng Road ferry, and indeed Misheng Road itself and Pudong Avenue behind it on the other bank. Commodore Shan shouted something inarticulate and Mei-Feng swore in a deeply unladylike fashion. Then it was on them.

The destroyer had faced bigger waves at sea. But then she had been well clear of land, surrounded by nothing but ocean, and powering forward at speed, under full control. Here she was being held at a very uneasy anchor, her anchor chain already put under a great deal of strain by the rise in the height of the river beneath her. Her bridge was manned by little more than a harbour watch – and her slow-thinking commanding officer. And, fatally, her mighty 57,000 horsepower combined diesel or gas engines were utterly at rest.

When the wave hit her, with all the force of half a million tons or so of hydraulic force moving at forty miles an hour, her mere 7,000 tons displacement, inert in the water, became nothing more to the wild river than the little boat of the Fuhi family in the ancient legend of the Flood.

The ballistic curve of the leading slope tossed the ship's bow into the air so swiftly it hardly seemed the boat had cut into the flank of the thing at all. A filthy crest of foam and flotsam washed up the fore-deck, threatening to tear the gun off its mountings, crashing into the first step of the bridge house, then smashing its way up the second towards the overhang of the clearview. The upward force tore the straining anchors free and the impact threw the ship backwards, like a stray surfboard being tossed shorewards out of control.

Somewhere near the beginning of this process Mei-Feng was thrown to the deck, and it was only by sheer will, combined with a sudden concern about the well-being of her parents below-decks and a burning desire to witness what was happening, that pulled her to her feet again.

By the time she had staggered upright, the clearviews had performed their function and she was able to watch, awestruck as the *Luyang* reversed at its normal flank speed past the suddenly extremely aptly named Ocean Hotel. They passed half-familiar landmarks, hesitating in the wild ride only once, as the anchors tore the Gonglingpu ferry pier off its mountings, thirty feet below the keel. Then there, before her unbelieving eyes, was the shipping building. A brace of banks, seemingly close enough to touch, racing past like speedboats. And, incredibly, when she looked to her right, there was the Hyatt Hotel on the outside of them, between the rearing destroyer and the raging river itself.

Then Mei-Feng was thrown sideways to her knees again as the *Luyang*'s port beam was hit by the outflow of the Wusong River. The whole vessel reeled and dipped sideways, thrown back towards the main stream. She went see-sawing wildly to the outside of the Astor House and swept on clear of both the bridges that leaped north across the Wusong from the Bund – one under water, the other only just clear. Then the anchors became entangled with the trees in Huangpu Park and the destroyer slewed round dangerously, almost – but not quite – going sideways-on to the wave. Had she gone a degree or two further, she would have rolled under. But, miraculously, she didn't. Instead she hung on grimly, sliding back inland at an angle across the Bund.

And at last, inevitably, she hit something. A juddering collision, full on, stern first. The whole length of the hull leaped and shuddered, yawed, pitched wildly, rolled and ground to a halt in an unbelievable cacophony of sound.

Then there was stillness. And silence.

Mei-Feng lay breathlessly on the deck, too overcome to move. Her first thought was for her husband, her next for her daughter, in their helpless little cockleshell of a corvette somewhere just down-river, just about at the point that the wave must be reaching right about now . . .

Then she remembered her parents once more. They were some-where below. She had snatched them off the safety of the Purple Mountain and brought them to this! Were they all right? She gathered the strength to pick herself up and go to look for them. But just at that moment they found her. The two resilient, whip-strong old people, who had witnessed the Rape of Nanjing, lived through more than one war and survived the Cultural Revolution, came solicitously and silently to pick their daughter up off the deck and show her a wonder among the greatest they had experienced.

For there, on what was left of the *Luyang*'s afterdeck, just as though it had fallen from the sky, was a clock in a clock-tower exactly like London's famous Big Ben.

Mei-Feng realized then that the *Luyang* had smashed into the old Custom House, and come to rest in the wreck of the building. But even so, she shared her wonder with her parents before she turned, frowning, to the river. For the stirring of the trapped hull warned her that the water behind the wave was still rising fast.

Even after everything that had happened to her, her mouth went dry with tension. 'Come on,' she said. 'You can do it. But get a move on or we're all in so much trouble!'

'Who are you speaking to, dear?' asked her mother gently.

'To some people I know who are trying to make all this better,' she said, gesturing to the flooded city. 'The clock made me think of them.'

'They will need to be exceptional people indeed,' said her father, nodding wisely, 'to make all this better!'

'They are, I think,' said Mei-Feng.

'Well, Fu, Lu, and Shou be with them,' said Mei-Feng's mother.

'Luck and prosperity they already have,' said Mei-Feng, her face folding into a worried frown. 'But *Shou* . . . I don't know how much *longevity* they can expect at the moment. Or how much any of us can expect, if things go wrong for them.'

'Wen-Qi is *here*?' Daniel Huuk looked at Lieutenant Leung, simply horrified. 'My daughter is in *this building*?'

'She's looking for you, sir,' said Leung, suddenly aware that he may have made an error of truly nightmarish proportions. 'She's had some simply terrible experiences . . .'

'Where is she? *Exactly*?'

'I don't know, sir . . .' Leung gave the outraged father a brief outline of his daughter's plan and their experiences since entering the stolen cutter.

Huuk looked at the sopping sailor with his mind simply reeling. He had so much to do here! So many responsibilities! So many calls on his time with a flood to overcome and a city to save. But his little girl was out there. Lost. Alone. In danger. He could feel the normally icy calm of his blood pressure spiralling upwards to apoplectic pressures.

'We have to find her,' he said. 'Before the wave arrives.'

And even as he made the decision, helicopter pilot Chopper Quing came through on an open channel. 'The wave is here,' he said baldly, his voice booming across the vacancy of Waitan Gate Towers fifth floor. 'It's at the Yangpu Bridge . . .'

Daniel Huuk came closer to simple panic than he had ever come in his life. All the failures that he had kept screwed down with that peculiar combination of Sino-British sangfroid came boiling to the surface. That he had kept her from her mother, that he had sworn to look after her – but had merely used his elevated positions in his various lives as an excuse to keep her away, to pass her off to others. Every forgotten birthday, missed New Year, unattended concert, un-answered letter, email and text rose up to accuse him. And in her moment of direst agony, his child had turned to him. She was lost out there somewhere looking for him. Possibly in the most terrible danger. If she was anywhere below here, she was certainly in the most dreadful danger. All because she had, as always, turned to him.

This time he wouldn't let her down. No matter what. Not this time.

Such was Daniel Huuk's preoccupation with his new mission that not only did he not delegate, he didn't even issue any orders. He simply turned his back on Leung and pounded out of the makeshift command centre and into the nearest stairwell, calling, as Leung himself had done, 'Wen-Qi!'

Leung looked around the open space, at the shocked faces of Mayor Hong and his crisis management team, at the screens in front of them, covered in figures, schematics, and – in one case – bright red symbols. Then he headed for the next nearest stairwell. And when he got there the political officer went upwards, thinking that if the girl was up here, all well and good; if she wasn't, then he would stand a better chance of getting through this alive.

Had Daniel Huuk been thinking clearly and logically, he would have gone down, for it was the lower floors that were going to be most at risk when the wave arrived. He wasn't thinking clearly at all, for he was overcome with guilt and emotion. But he still went down.

The stairwell echoed with a strange whispering susurration as though there were millions of giant insects somewhere close at hand. It took him an instant to realize that this was the conversations of the tens of thousands of refugees packed into the fifty floors above him. The stair-wells from the sixth floor up would be packed in any case – the steps would offer comfortable seating. But although he understood where the sound was coming from, it was still disturbing. And he started shouting 'Wen-Qi!' on almost every breath, as much to shut it out of his head, as for any other reason.

The fourth floor was deserted. It consisted of the more permanent concessions, making it a kind of shopping mall immediately above the three-level vastness of the atrium and the management and storage facilities packed behind it. In fact, he knew, the mall went up for four more floors above his head, many open with balconies and yet more spacious Art Nouveau-style atriums. Down here was the food hall.

Huuk stepped out of the stairwell, through a sizeable area walled with lift-doors, through a teak double swing-door and into the vast mall. The smell of cooking overwhelmed him at once, reminding him that he hadn't eaten in a long while. But the rich aromas were cold on the still silent air. And slightly nauseating in their intensity. No cooking had been done here since the earthquake. And there was no air-con to clear the smells since the power all went out. The food hall, normally a fairyland of neon, was gloomy and, like the stairwell, vaguely threatening.

Immediately in front of him was, prophetically as it turned out, a Subway. *Submarine Rolls* said a poster in the window. *Fresh Filled For You. Try our Breakfast Sub Today!* Then there was a McDonald's. A Pizza parlour. More distantly, a KFC. Down one lane, M&S Food. Down another, behind a noodle shop and a tea emporium, there was a distant Starbucks.

Daniel looked around, dazed by it all. 'Wen-Qi!' he bellowed, tearing his throat, feeling the hopelessness washing over him. Wishing he had taken the time to know the child better, so that he would have some idea at least of what there might be down here to attract her attention.

Beyond the food hall, there was another vast open space leading to a balcony lined with shatter-proof glass that reached from floor to ceiling. Designed to stop patrons throwing anything – including no doubt, them-selves – down on to the glass roof below. For in the square immediately below, there was the night-sky stained glass of the decorative ceiling to the reception area, seemingly half the size of a soccer pitch.

Somehow, even in the absence of electricity, the light gathered here, shining downwards as though there were a system of mirrors some-where, designed to guide the sunbeams like the mirrors the Egyptians were supposed to have used to illuminate the recesses of their pyramids.

A movement!

Huuk froze.

There, immediately opposite him, on the far side of the glass-walled, glass-floored column of light, the slight figure of his daughter drifted, seemingly floating in the grip of a dream.

'Wen-Qi! Wen-Qi!' he bellowed, tearing his throat once again and spraying the glass with spittle and breath. She gave no sign of having heard him. Instead, she turned, and began to wander away towards the front of the building, framed in light from the distant windows, wandering down an avenue of sweet shops so brightly coloured that they and their contents seemed to glow magically in the gloom.

Huuk was off. A lean, fit man who followed a careful exercise regime, he was well able to run a marathon. But the speed at which he ran round the three sides of the walled space robbed him of breath so swiftly that when he at last arrived at the end of the avenue of sweet shops he had no breath left to call her name. So, silently, he charged forward, his eyes made almost tearful by the pain in his heaving chest, the gathering brightness from the windows and the sharpness of his terror that he would lose her again.

But no. He found her quite easily, standing looking out of a vast panoramic window with wide views up towards the Bund and Huangpu Park, sucking on an enormous sugar lollipop shaped like a red, green and orange dragon. He recognized it – a brand she had loved from their brief time together during her childhood. It was a Luck Dragon lollipop. Then his eyes did overflow, with a combination of relief and unfamiliar parental emotion that she should be so untouched, so inno-cent, so beautiful. He hesitated, with eyes for no one – nothing – but her. Wondering whether someone sucking on a Luck Dragon lollipop was too old to be hugged like a baby and crushed to his heaving chest, to his racing heart.

Her green eyes, wide to him, coloured like jade, and, with the powdering of freckles across the bridge of her nose, a poignant reflec-tion of her mother, turned trustingly towards him.

'Daddy,' she said quietly, 'why is that boat flying?'

THIRTY-SEVEN
Eagle

'It's no good,' said Richard bitterly. 'We'll never shift it like this. We have to think of something different. Better.'

'I don't believe you have a lot of time,' warned Captain Chang through the intercom.

'Do tell,' said Richard bitterly under his breath.

'This isn't like you,' said Robin gently. 'I've never known you admit defeat before. Especially when there's so much at stake. I mean, the flood control system for the whole heart of the Shanghai Shi! And you're talking like you think it's time to give up!'

'First time for everything, I guess,' he answered through clenched teeth. 'Be fair, though, it was a pretty big ask in the first place.'

'It was,' she agreed. 'But you were the silly sod who suggested it!'

On the screen in front of him, Genghis lay still with his head and shoulders wedged into the blade of the great turbine which drove the Bailianjing River central pump. *Neptune*'s claws had firm hold of the statue's golden feet – and their purchase could hardly have been better. In the top left corner of the screen, opposite the stubbornly static GPS reading on the schematic in the right, red figures displayed that the AUV's systems were at maximum lift. Had it just been a matter of hauling Genghis to the surface, the job would have been done by now, but the added problem of the wedged head and shoulders simply put the situation beyond the rugged little vessel's capability.

'Is there time to get *Neptune* back to the surface so we can reattach her cable? Then we could latch her back on to that and drag both her and Genghis up using the deck winch.'

As Richard considered Robin's suggestion for an instant, he was pumping his left hand, trying to flood and empty the buoyancy tanks fast enough to jerk *Neptune* – and Genghis – free. To no avail. The safety systems were designed to stop abrupt changes such as these.

'I could run up to the foredeck and dive down with it, I suppose,' he said. 'It looks like the only hope we've got.'

'No!'

Both Robin and Captain Chang shouted the word at once. The effect was more than a little disorientating. Not least because they were shouting the same word at different people.

Robin, outraged by the foolhardiness of the thoughtless plan was shouting at her husband.

Chang – for much the same reasons – was shouting at Lieutenant Ping.

But Ping was in action. 'Free the cable drum,' he yelled. 'I'll pull it down with me!' He pounded off the bridge, tearing his uniform open as he ran.

'Lieutenant . . .' shouted Chang, a little desperately. Especially when she realized she couldn't remember his name. Like the men, she had always thought of him as Paradeground.

'What's happening?' demanded Richard, still working on jerking *Neptune* and the statue free.

'It's what you suggested!' snarled the captain. 'Lieutenant Ping is taking the cable down!'

'Oh shit,' whispered Richard.

'You and your big mouth!' hissed Robin. 'It's going to get you in *real* trouble one day!'

'Right!' said Richard, but to her dying day Robin never knew whether he was agreeing with her – or getting ready to accommodate the plan to the new element. 'Everything on, full beam,' he continued. 'Ping won't see much in that filthy soup. So the more light we can throw on the subject the better for him! And I'd better get the rear cameras working as well so we can watch for him coming in. It'd be a bit of a bummer if he did all this and still failed to get the hook on to the lowering point!'

'Much more to the point,' said Robin dryly, 'how long has he got before the wave arrives?'

'Mayor Hong is on the radio now,' answered Chang, her voice dead. 'The wave has just come past the Yangpu Bridge.'

'How long does that give him?' asked Robin.

'Five minutes? Ten, tops,' answered Richard, his eyes straining to make out Ping's shape in *Neptune*'s rear-pointing cameras.

'Oh shit,' she said.

'Oh shit!' said Daniel Huuk.

His eyes and mind could all too readily comprehend what his daughter simply could not. The wave reached higher than the floor they were standing on; perhaps even higher than the floor above. It stretched from the heart of Pudong on their right to well behind the Bund on their left. It was coming between the towering buildings there with such focus and force that it didn't even seem to be breaking into foam as it hit them. And sliding wildly across the left-hand upper face of it, apparently in full reverse, was the *Luyang* destroyer he had last seen well downriver in the Shanghai shipyards.

For a stomach-churning instant he thought the hundred and fifty metres of steel and explosives, all seven thousand tons of it, was going to come through the panoramic window on top of them. But then he realized it was sliding sideways towards the buildings in the Bund. Which was not a lot of comfort, under the circumstances, because the rest of the massive wave was hurling down towards them at a simply unbelievable velocity. He grabbed Wen-Qi by her left hand and whirled her round. 'RUN!' he screamed.

Side by side they sprinted along that wide, sweet-lined alley towards the column of light that was the heart of the building. The floor beneath their pounding feet began to tremble as though the earthquake were returning with redoubled force. The whole building seemed to be heaving and shaking. The sound was suddenly there, incapacitatingly loud. Daniel realized that he was screaming as he ran, and fought to turn the bellows of distress and fear into articulated words. But all he could come up with was 'Run! Don't look back! Run!'

Then the entire building flinched. It was the most amazing sensation. The floor moved forward, seemingly several inches – enough to make them stumble as they ran. The very air seemed to jump and shudder. Daniel and Wen-Qi were blasted forward in turn, as though by an explosion just behind them. And, in front of them, terrifyingly close in front of them, what had been a column of light reaching down through the stained glass ceiling of the reception area became a column of thick brown water shooting up like the greatest of geysers. The glass walls seemed to contain it for an instant, to make the wild fluidity of it conform to geometric laws. The column of water had flat sides. Square edges. Like some kind of gargantuan ice-cube.

For an instant, it seemed that the enormity of it was going to be contained. But then a fine mist started falling, and Daniel glanced upwards even as he pounded past the strange phenomenon. Water was pouring through the ceiling. And he realized that the strangely constricted fountain had torn through the ceiling and was flooding the mayor's command centre up above.

Still he and Wen-Qi kept on running.

They made it to M&S before the glass all gave way. Oddly the glass in the centre held longer than the panoramic window did. But when the window went and the water started thundering in a brown wall through the sweet shops, it was only a matter of time. And not much time at that.

The wall of water coming in through the panoramic window stretched from floor to ceiling. It ripped out the partition walls of the sweet emporiums and threw them at the glass column in the centre, shattering it immediately. Then, with redoubled force the wall of water swept onwards. One minute Daniel and Wen-Qi were running for the stairwell, the next they were swimming. With only that automatic reflex action that let them gasp in a huge lungful of air each.

Daniel was still holding on to his daughter just as tightly as she was holding on to her Luck Dragon lollipop as the water hurled them forward, between the more solid fronts of the shops; past Starbucks and McDonald's. Past the Subway store, whose rolls were submarine now, in more ways than one. Holding his breath in spite of the agony in his chest, Daniel blinked, stretching his eyes wide, hoping to see through the murky water surrounding him, praying that he would discern something that would give him hope.

But all he could see – vaguely and well out of focus – was the gape of a door-less portal out into the lift lobby. And the wild current carried them through as helplessly as any of the other pieces of flotsam it had snatched from the food hall. And there it held them, jammed against the ceiling, wedged in the corner above the lintel above the doorway out into the stairwell.

All sorts of thoughts flashed through Daniel's mind. Not least that this should not be happening. The wave should be past. The water should be falling away. There should be air coming into the building this high up. They were forty feet in the air and drowning for Christ's sake. What the hell was going on?

But in the back of his mind he saw that nameless hydro-engineer's computer schematic. With the Bailianjing river pump on red. And he knew the answer well enough.

With an enormous effort of will, he pulled Wen-Qi to him and pressed his mouth to hers. She tasted of Luck Dragon lollipops – a flavour he hadn't tasted himself since he kissed her goodbye after her fifth birthday party – the last one he had attended – seven years ago.

With all the care that he was capable of, he slowly and gently emptied his lungs into hers.

'There he is!' shouted Richard. He cut the power to *Neptune*'s motors so that Ping would find it easier to get closer to her. Safer, too – not that safety was a major concern here, under the circumstances.

The marine was half-walking, half-swimming – one handed, with the loop of cable in his other hand. The weight of the woven steel was enough to keep him under the water, and yet it didn't seem to be encumbering him at all. It suddenly struck Richard how slight the marine was, in fact. Had he gone down himself, Richard would never have fitted so neatly into the tunnel mouth. And as for pulling himself up the ladder on *Neptune*'s side, it would simply have been out of the question. But Ping made it. At least, he vanished up off Richard's screen for thirty heart-stopping seconds, then reappeared with no cable and made a 'thumbs up' gesture, before turning and swimming back the way he had come.

'He's hooked it on! Tension the cable.' Richard called.

'No!' snapped the captain. 'Not until he's clear. Can anybody see him yet?'

Richard nodded, answering the first part of the captain's message and hoping somebody else would answer the second part soon. He gritted his teeth until the muscles of his great square jaw stood out like tensioned cables themselves. His huge hands were as tight on the controls as they would go. So tight, they were beginning to cramp. But the enormous power of that grip was transferred directly to the claws at the end of *Neptune*'s arms. Clutching on to Genghis's golden feet. Robin looked indulgently at him.

Robin glanced across at her husband. His face was beaded with sweat, his whole huge frame was shaking with tension and concentration. The definition of his jaw muscles in the strange green light was matched only by the thews in his forearms. Abruptly, Robin wanted those arms wrapped safely round her. Wanted that intense, glistening face to be raining kisses down on her.

'Got him!' yelled the Captain, triumphantly. The phrase fitted right in with what Robin was thinking.

'Richard,' she said gently, 'I love . . .'

And then the wave hit.

They had been so concerned with getting Ping back aboard that they hadn't really seen it coming. To be fair it was disguised by a bend in the river, as well as by the Neihuan road bridge and the elevated freeway on either side of it.

The wave took the stiletto-bowed corvette just as it had taken the *Luyang*. But there were several vital differences, not all of which were obvious to Richard and Robin down in the tiny control room contained within the bulbous bottom of the dagger-topped cutwater.

Because they were sitting down, Richard and Robin were not thrown to the deck, like Mei-Feng had been on the *Luyang*, and like her husband and daughter were now. Instead, they were tossed around the restrictive little room as though they were in the cockpit of his E-Type Jaguar in the most violent of multiple pile-ups. They were hurled back into their seats as the bow whipped up. Neither of them recognized the terrible noise from immediately above as the foredeck crane being torn over the side by the suddenness of the motion.

They were thrown forward as the vessel took off backwards like the *Luyang* had done when the wave swept over her. But Chang was far faster thinking than Commodore Shan and *Poseidon*'s motors, warmed and ready, were racing at full ahead immediately, keeping the reeling vessel under some kind of control, even as those on the bridge started picking themselves up to assess the damage done to their vessel so far.

Richard and Robin were slammed down again as the screaming cable tore free. Robin's head smashed on the console in front of her and the computer screen above it went wild. Richard's too was slammed down, but his face impacted on the set solidity of his forearms, which simply refused to ease their grip. It was this and this alone that stopped the wound on his cheekbone from bursting wide again. Even so, it sprayed blood across his computer screen – no clearer than Robin's, though it was undamaged – which only showed a golden square of formless light and whirling mud suspended in rushing water.

Poseidon reared backwards as the cable came free at last and began to slide down the front of the wave, despite her racing motors, as she was carried upriver, dragging the cable behind her.

Richard and Robin were thrown right as *Poseidon* jerked across the front of the racing wave, and then left as she fought back, pitching and yawing wildly as the Mariners were tossed back and forth like a pair of dice in the cup of an energetic gambler.

But then the crisis was over. The disposition of the corvette eased, she settled into level sailing, and began to fight back against the massive motion of the water. Richard's monitor cleared to show Genghis bumping along between the remains of a strange array of half-constructed, half-deconstructed, vaguely familiar buildings.

The way came off the vessel altogether. Genghis sank to the ground, pulling *Neptune* down with him.

Everything seemed to stop.

Richard sat up straight, allowing his forearms to relax at last, surprised to see that they and the screen above them were smeared and spattered with blood.

'What were you saying?' he asked Robin, his voice rasping.

'I have no idea,' she answered. 'Are you all right? You look as though you've gone several rounds with Mike Tyson.'

'I'm fine,' he answered. 'I'm not so sure about you, though. You look as though I've just taken up wife beating. And, I have to say, not before time . . .'

Robin opened her mouth to answer that, but before she could do so, Captain Chang's voice came over the intercom. 'Come up here,' she said. 'Come up here and look at this.'

Richard and Robin pulled themselves up on to the command bridge moments later and stood, as awed as the rest by what they could see. Captain Chang stood with her father on one side and Lieutenant Ping on the other, staring out through the clearview. Everything ahead of them was water. Up from the slowly heaving surface of the flood rose the spires of Pudong and Shanghai, standing tall and sturdy. Surviving. Already, the first of the boats designated to come in over the Shi and begin Operation Dynamo were arriving.

They had heard nothing from the Mayor, but Richard was certain of two things: the plan for the relief of Shanghai was already under way, and somewhere there was a computer screen showing that the Bailianjing river pump and all of its ancillary systems were back on line.

He put his arm round Robin and walked her to the starboard bridge-wing so that they could look away towards the ocean and see the little ships coming in. But halfway there he stopped and stared, open mouthed. The whole stern section of the corvette was berthed in a great haven of steel. A wide grey harbour that seemed to tower like friendly cliffs put there on purpose to keep them safe.

Poseidon had come to rest safely and securely between the wide-spread, welcoming steel wings of the United States' Bald Eagle pavilion from the 2010 Shanghai World Expo.

THIRTY-EIGHT
Flight

L ess than a week later, Richard and Robin were seated safely and comfortably aboard the JAL flight from Nagasaki via Tokyo to London. Their faces were still a little battered-looking, but not enough to turn heads at the airport or raise eyebrows at passport control.

They could have used a range of transport options to a number of cities in China, but the international relief system was really beginning to kick in now, so much of Chinese airspace – and most of Chinese airports – were busy. And, to be fair, Nagasaki was not too far for *Poseidon* to go. She was no longer needed for relief work in Shanghai, and she was en-route for England now that Heritage Mariner had definitely completed the purchase agreement for both her and the robot submarine *Neptune* that she carried.

They had left the river pilot and his wife Mei-Feng together with their quiet parents in Shanghai, both now, like their daughter, honoured members of the Invisible Power Triad. As, indeed, they had left Lieutenant Ping and his little command. Captain Chang and her crew had taken *Poseidon* to Nagasaki, but there they had handed over to captain Fujimoto and his men. En route they had held a short service for their departed comrades Steady Xin and Straightline Jiang, together with the comrades ill-advised enough to follow them aboard *Marilyn* – though their bodies were actually waiting formal autopsy aboard the *Luyang*, still wedged in the ruins of the Custom House halfway up the Bund. And, given the state of his command, it was hardly surprising that Commodore Shan was currently suspended from duty, getting ready to face a board of enquiry, with Political Officer Leung at his side.

As Richard and Robin were soaring up towards their stopover at Muharrraq International on Bahrain Island, so Chang and her remaining men were flying back to the recently reopened Pudong. And, for the captain at least, suspected Robin, wedding bells.

Robin leaned over, looking out through the window, half imagining that she could see the Shanghai Shi, which must lie somewhere beneath them now. The week since the flood had been one of frenetic activity. Only the restoration of the pumping system to full capacity had saved downtown Shanghai, and there were stories emerging of near miracles of survival there. Some of them so wonderful as to put the story of Daniel and Wen-Qi's rescue by Mayor Hong himself into the shade. But of all the happy outcomes of the dreadful incident, that had been Robin's favourite. For she had always held, deep within her heart, a little flame for Daniel Huuk. And, she suspected, always would. Though she rather suspected he had another woman in his life now: his daughter Wen-Qi.

During the last seven days, Daniel and Mayor Hong had performed miracles of rescue, organization and reconstruction. Aided, it must be said, by the committee in Tiannenman Square, who had managed to organize support for the Shi, while getting impressive amounts of aid to all quarters of their earthquake-stricken and flooded heartland. Mayor Jaa in Nanjing had come in for a great deal of praise. As had the manager of the Tongling Non-Ferrous Mining complex. As had a naval Lieutenant called Tan, who had pulled things together in the flooded ruins of Zhenjiang.

A helicopter pilot called Quing had been awarded the Mayor of Shanghai's special commendation for his work pulling people off the roofs of flooded buildings downtown. The papers worldwide were full of it. As were the news channels and, increasingly, the Internet feeds. And the international community had rallied round in the face of the simple enormity of what had happened.

In amongst everything else, Daniel had managed to settle Wen-Qi close to him and to see her every day. To tuck her in each night. While he and Mayor Hong had even managed to arrange for the battered Genghis to be rescued from the Expo site of the Americas, and he was to take his rightful place in Shanghai's most prestigious museum, his story encompassing almost legendary history and the much more imme-diate past.

Robin leaned over the other way, looking towards Richard. He had picked up a laptop – not a hard task in Japan – and had been busy on it ever since they took off, much relieved to learn that the Internet was now back up and running. He had mumbled something about 'busi-ness', before he immersed himself. But she knew for a fact that there was more to what he was doing than simply clearing out his electronic in-tray at Heritage Mariner. He was wearing earphones for a start. Never a good sign in her experience – for it usually meant he wanted to avoid questions as to what precisely he was up to. At last, she tapped him on the shoulder.

He pulled off his earphones and she was just able to hear the distant strains of Max Bruch's underrated 3rd Symphony. So he was into his Spotify account at least, she thought. 'What's that?' she asked.

A little shamefacedly, he turned the screen towards her. And there was a picture of *Marilyn*. Bright Ferrari-red, long and lean, and breathtaking.

'FOR SALE' she read, '*CIGARETTE 39 Top Gun Unlimited*. Contact MRL Ltd, Southampton, England . . .'

'All right, it's nearly your birthday,' she said indulgently. 'We can look into it sometime in the next month or so . . .'

But his face had folded into that slightly anxious expression she knew so well, like a schoolboy caught while deeply involved in some murky mischief.

'Actually,' he said, 'I've just emailed them. We're taking her out for a test run to the Isle of Wight and back on Saturday afternoon . . .'

Acknowledgements

Red River begins where *River of Ghosts* stopped. Literally. In Richard and Robin's world there are mere moments between the end of one and the beginning of the next. It is a very different book, however, with a range of new characters joining the ones familiar from the earlier story. It is obviously a sequel, therefore, but I designed it with great care to ensure that it stands alone. There is no need to have read the earlier story to understand – and hopefully enjoy – this one.

By the same token, although I was able to use a good deal of the research I did for *River of Ghosts*, a new story required new information. And, as it is a narrative on an entirely larger scale, that information also needed to be greater in every respect.

I was able to transfer basic – irreplaceable – texts such as the Lonely Planet Guides to China and Shanghai from one project to the next. Though, as ever, I have taken one or two unavoidable liberties with the detailed descriptions they offer to the Yangtze River Basin at the Three Gorges and downstream, at Nanjing and Shanghai itself.

As ever with a new project, I first turned to Kelvin Hughes. Their chart and pilot sections have never let me down in the thirty years of our association and they did not do so this time. Though I must admit that I was simply astonished when they were able to add to the charts they had already supplied. To the China Sea approaches to Shanghai and the mouth of the Yangtze they sent an additional range of charts that took me more than halfway up the river – far beyond Nanjing itself.

Readers familiar with my work and my research methods will not be surprised to learn that I next turned to the Internet. Google supplied almost all my needs here. I simply cannot speak too highly of Google Earth in this context. I literally traced the length of the Yangtze from the Three Gorges Dam at Yichang through a thousand miles to Shanghai and the sea. I was able to overlay maps with terrain and supplement both with on-the-spot photographs. To a resolution of twenty metres to the inch. I know more about the hotels beside the Three Gorges Dam, about the dock facilities in Nanjing and about the Huangpu River in Shanghai than I ever thought possible!

Shanghai itself, with Expo 2010 in full swing, was a treasure-trove of details – everything from the responsibilities of the Mayor's office to the design of the American pavilion.

I must admit in closing, however, that I played fast and loose with the University of Nottingham's China Institute Discussion Paper 44: *Scenario Analysis Technology for River Basin flood risk management in the Taihu Basin: A Chinauk scientific cooperation project*, by Gemma Harvey, Edward Evans, Colin Thorne and Xiaotao Cheng, dated February 2009. Which gave me details of the current situation of – and the immediate plans for – the flood drainage system for the entire Shanghai Shi, and the ideas I needed for the climax. I rearranged the Shanghai flood drainage system described in this fascinating document to suit my purposes. Hopefully, neither their analysis nor my peculiar spin on it will ever be tested in fact rather than in fiction.

Peter Tonkin, Tunbridge Wells, June 2010.

MDE - 9|11|10
RGD - 13.10.14
Sk - 07/4/21